'Look what you've driven me †
wanted. You destroyed my life
you know it's true. You led me on, pretenᵤₑₐ ᵢ__ ⌄
You played your game. Now I've beaten you at your own
game.'

She lay still on the ground, blood trickling from the
side of her head. Her body would be washed away by the
sea, never found, no trace, gone.

The seagulls wheeled above, a menace of grey feathers
and beaks, making frenzied dives at the limp body that
lay beneath the wooden pier. Her hair stuck to her face,
her eyes were closed, one boot half-on, clinging to her
foot as if she had tried to stay upright, one lost in the
struggle. Her knees were grazed and caked in dried
blood from the sharp shells that had scraped against her.
Her face was a porcelain white, sand particles smudged
against it. Her body was cold and marble-white. She lay
motionless, alone, cold.

GIRL
ON THE
BEACH

J. V. PHAURE

Photography by J.V. Phaure

Cover Design by Robin Freeman
www.robinfreemandesign.com

ISBN 9781913663018

Typeset, Printed and Bound in Great Britain by
Biddles Books Limited, King's Lynn, Norfolk

2020

Dedication

To those people who shared this journey with me

Acknowledgements

This novel couldn't have been written without the support and encouragement of so many people.

I was inspired to write it because a cherished friend told me not to stop but to write another book, when life seemed a little hazy.

There have been many tears and laughs whilst writing this novel and learning how control and fear can present in many different ways.

To those who inspired me to write this novel...

How strength is a part of every person and with the right people around you, life becomes brighter.

There are so many people I want to thank but my list could go on longer than this novel. Whether you want your name here or not you're going to get it.

Matt for being you and making me smile and just being there for those calming moments. The tunes you always sent, although "it's so my generation!"

Andrew for all your police information and telling me "that really being in custody doesn't last for two weeks!!!" I wasn't going to get away with that even in fiction!!!

My siblings and parents and family for listening to me constantly. So needed for me, I love you!

'The Girls' who have had my back and kept me upbeat with ridiculous Whatsapp messages "umm times up guys."

Robin for coming back into my life and designing my cover and believing in me and making my dream become a front cover and a real picture.

Sarah "you gotta love a light" for reading my novel without letting the world know. Gosh that must have been hard!!! And being every bit the right person to read my novel in secrecy. Your words of support meant the world to me.

Finally, my gorgeous girl Tor, my agent, my dearest friend, who read my novel and said "I cried real tears." For having my back, believing in me and sharing copious amounts of Vodka and Tonics in London! You are every bit how Jo Segal should be. I love you!

There are so many more people who have made my dream come true, thank you from the bottom of my heart.

The Epigraph

"Keep writing. Keep doing it and doing it. Even when it's so hurtful to think about writing."

Heather Armstrong

Chapter One

The waves slowly washed onto the shore. A small wooden fishing boat tilted to one side. It looked forlorn and broken; it had seen better days at sea. Huge cranes stood like giant giraffes of steel on the far pier lifting containers onto the waiting ships.

A girl sat on a stone step that led down to the beach, her hair tied back loosely in a ponytail, the wind blowing wisps of her hair into her face. She wrapped her scarf a little more tightly around her neck, clutching a warm peppermint tea. As she sat and scribbled over a clean white page of her notebook the sky above turned grey and the halyards clinked in the cold, whistling wind.

A girl's shoe lay on the beach. She wondered how the shoe had got there. Where was the other one? Where was the person who had been wearing them? What had happened?

Lucy, a writer from London, had moved to the coast for a quieter life, an uncomplicated life, narrowly escaping a huge white wedding that she'd almost been roller-coastered into. Life was simple now. It was just her, nobody else to complicate her day. Each day she sat on the beach with her notebook and pen. There was something comforting about the beach: although an industrious port town, it had the familiarity of London about it. The huge cranes that loomed over the dark sea reminded her of Battersea and the Thames. It wasn't like any other seaside town; it wasn't quaint, it was raw and urban

1

and had an international train line to a waiting ferry for the Hook of Holland. Not quite Eurostar, but there aren't many small seaside towns that offer destination Europe.

She watched a young mother playing with her small child, who was picking up slimy green seaweed and throwing it into the sea, leaving particles of it clinging to his chubby hands. An old fisherman tended to the forlorn boat, emptying out buckets of sea and rainwater. He'd be doing that again the next day, she thought. As she looked up from her notebook, a young guy rode past on an old red racer bike, whistling to the tunes that played into his ears. He seemed content, she thought. Carefree. It's funny how in a few moments of sitting on the beach Lucy could get a small glimpse into another person's life and begin to make a picture in her mind: she could make up stories about the people she saw. She wondered what these people would do after playing on the beach, emptying out water from an old fishing boat, cycling.

Lucy wrote ever more fervently and watched the guy cycle into the distance, his hoodie flying behind him in the wind. Where was he going? she wondered. What did he do? An old collie dog came sniffing around her, its owner a few paces back. He looked a little dishevelled, maybe homeless, she thought, clutching a rope for a lead. He smiled as he wandered past. He seemed harmless enough, just a little raggedy.

The air began to get colder and she could feel it bite at her nose. She'd spent most of the day at the beach. As the light began to dwindle, she packed her satchel and made her way back to her classic Mini. Pulling her seatbelt around her, she turned on the engine. The heaters blew air noisily at her, giving an almost suffocating instant heat. That was the problem with old cars. They were either hot or cold; there was no in between. Driving along the parade she could see the huge wind farms in the distance and the low lighthouse near the shore. The sea churned and tossed around it. Her tummy rumbled, at home her fridge was pretty bare. She drove past a line of beach huts, the flashing of the fish and chip shop's neon sign caught her eye. Fish and chips, she thought.

The wrapped newspaper parcel sat on the front seat of her Mini, the smell of vinegar wafting around the car. She pulled up to her terraced cottage and grabbed her satchel and fish and chips. Pushing open her door, she turned on the hall light and closed the door. She dropped her keys on the table in the hall and picked up the post. Nothing hugely important, she thought as she looked through it. Nothing for her, at least, but a mound of junk mail and some letters for the previous owners. Slipping past the boxes in the hall, she made her way into the kitchen. It was small but cosy. She'd managed to find and unpack her kettle, which sat alone with a box of peppermint tea next to it. She'd moved in with very few belongings of her own but she knew she could make this her home. Her refuge.

She sat at the table and unwrapped her supper. Not bothering with a plate, she poured a glass of wine and began to read what she had written that day, licking her fingers after each mouthful.

She liked what she had written: it was a love story with a twist. She'd written several short stories in London for magazines and had five bestselling novels under her belt. She'd been lucky enough to keep the same literary agent since her early writing days, and she was now a trusted, loyal friend. Today had been a good day. She had watched so many people and the sea had let her forget her past, her tormented memories. She had needed that.

Today had thrown her back into the world she loved – writing. She was never happier than when she watched life unfold in front of her. Her imagination let go, to run wild. She'd made the right move, she thought, sitting with her notebook. Definitely the right choice. She smiled to herself.

She could forget her past and concentrate on the present. A new life, a new chapter, with no more dramas and no more fear. She already felt a sense of belonging in her new home.

The kitchen clock ticked in the silence. It was nine o'clock and she still had boxes to unpack. Tomorrow, she thought, drawing the flowery curtains that the previous owner had left. They weren't her style but she was grateful for the privacy they gave her. Once she had settled in, she would begin to replace the tired furnishings that had been left, but for the moment they were fine. She threw her unfinished supper in the bin, turned off the light and locked the front door before making her way up to bed. Her mobile, which she clutched, pinged in three messages. She sat on the edge of the bed in the dim light and opened them.

Lucy, for fuck's sake will you talk to me?

You owe me that at least.

I want to see you. Where are you? I'll find you.

She dropped the mobile on the floor, her legs shaking, her fists clenched. Another message came through. She picked up the phone, scared to look. She opened it hesitantly and checked the message.

Hey, Lucy, haven't seen you lately. Let's do coffee. Come over. Rachel x

She climbed into bed reaching over for her book, leaving the phone on the bedside table. Snuggling down under the covers, she turned the pages until her eyes began to close and the words danced on the page. She turned out the light. *He'd never find her. Never.* She let the night steal her away.

Chapter Two

The dawn came, and along with it the musical chorus of birds. A new day, new possibilities, fresh pages yet to be written. Lucy was woken by leaves brushing against her bedroom window. She wasn't used to the dawn chorus; she was used to hearing the hydraulics of the low-flying planes over her London flat, or the rumbling of the Tube line beneath her. The sound of the birds was loud and unfamiliar, the brushing of the leaves against her window calming and pleasant. She looked at her phone. Seven thirty-four. A few days ago, she would have been bustling around her flat, throwing on her clothes, grabbing her satchel and racing for the Victoria line, grabbing a peppermint tea from Costa on her way.

Today was different. Today there was no Tube to catch, no chance to watch the people on the escalator as she passed them like robots on a conveyor belt: a second of eye contact as she passed a stranger, wondering who they were, where they were going, what their life was like. Each person was like a picture in her head to write about. She sat up in bed and read her new messages: another from Rachel, her old neighbour, asking if she'd be at Joe's Brasserie for Richard's thirtieth on Saturday, a message from her literary agent Jo saying she hoped the move had gone smoothly, and another message from Charlie, the man she'd escaped from. She read them all and replied to Jo.

She fell back against her pillows and covered her head with her duvet. Ugh, the boxes still stood in the hallway, waiting. She had to unpack first, then she would reward herself with the beach and her notebook and write until she was content with the words on each page. She climbed out of bed and made her way across the landing to the bathroom. It was compact and tired-looking, with blue and white Victorian-style tiles around the basin and bath. The paint on the walls was peeling. The basin was chipped and had a blue stain beneath the cold tap, which dripped.

The bath needed a good scrubbing and the vinyl floor had seen better days, peeling slightly away from the skirting board. She brushed her teeth and cleansed her face. Before emptying any boxes, she needed to buy cleaning products. She googled the postcode of her local supermarket. Thank goodness for 4G, she thought, and sat-nav. She'd got no Wi-Fi yet and needed to install a landline too, jobs that had to be done over the next few days, but until then 4G worked. The supermarket was a ten-minute drive away.

As she drove home, she noticed a post office on the corner opposite the Hungry Hound pub, a Victorian police station with a blue lamp outside, a small train station and an idyllic church, with a woman decorating the arched gateway with flowers. Somebody was getting married. She thought she might feel a pang of envy, but she didn't. Instead, an overwhelming sense of relief engulfed her.

Back home, she rattled the key in the lock. At first it jammed then finally gave way. She entered, passing the cardboard boxes stacked in the hall. On them was scrawled in black felt-tip: 'kitchen', 'sitting room', 'bathroom' and 'Lucy's books and writing'. Black bin bags had labels marking clothes and bedding. She'd unpack the boxes later. First she needed to scrub the house from top to bottom. The cupboard under the stairs harboured an old-fashioned hoover with a cloth bag. She'd never seen a hoover like it before. When she switched it on, a billow of dust blew up from the bag and she coughed, waving the dust away from her face. It worked, she thought, but she wasn't sure how she'd empty it.

Struggling upstairs with the mop and bucket and various chemical products, she set to on the bathroom, which looked like it hadn't been cleaned for years. She scrubbed the bath and basin and mopped the floor at least three times. As she wiped down the walls the paint peeled off, leaving patchy gaps. She didn't know the first thing about painting, and decided she would need to find a professional decorator. She scrubbed at every stain, brushing her hair away from her face. Finally, she thought, it's done. She stood back and looked at the bathroom. It will have to do, she thought. It was clean, at least.

Next, the room to the left of the bathroom. She hadn't been in there since she'd viewed the house four months ago. She opened the door with trepidation, not knowing what she might find inside. Her mind began to play tricks on her. She turned away from the room and slumped to the ground, burying her head in her arms.

***

'You wore that dress, what for? Who for? Get in, you filthy whore.' He pushed her into the room. It was dark and cold. She sat in the corner, her nose running, her dress ripped at the front, her lipstick smudged. She swayed backwards and forwards, hugging her knees. When would this stop? Why was he doing this? Her wrists were sore from where he had gripped her. Nobody knew – why could nobody see? She heard the key in the lock. His mobile rang.

'Ollie? Sure, sounds great. Lucy, yeah, she's fab, but she's out with the girls tonight. Come over – we could play poker or go out for a drink. See you soon.'

Slowly Lucy's eyes adjusted to the dark as she cowered in the corner of the room. She heard the front door close. He'd gone out.

***

Lucy lifted her head from her knees and looked at the door. She knew nothing would be in there. It wasn't the room in her old flat, but for some reason she was still frightened. Frightened to open a closed door. What was behind it? *Who* was behind it?

Come on, Lucy, she said to herself. You're thirty years old, there can't be anything in there. He isn't here. Pull yourself together. It's only a room. He's not here, he can't hurt you. It's your house.

Taking a deep breath, she pushed the door open. An umbrella fell to the floor in front of her, and she jumped and screamed. *It's just an umbrella. Calm down.* She pushed the door open further and took another step forward. There's nothing there. Go in, she told herself. She didn't dare go beyond the door. There was something holding her back: his voice in the back of her head, laughing as she fell to the ground in the dark room. Come on, Lucy, she said over and over again. It was only a room. You've escaped. This is not the same room. Don't be scared now. As she took another step, the floorboards creaked.

She stopped and stared at the room. She wasn't expecting what she could see. She stood silently for what felt like an age but was probably just a few minutes. The room was small and dusty. A cobweb trailed across a bureau in the corner, a wicker wastepaper basket held a few crumpled notes, a small cabinet was full of novels, all by the same author. On the bureau was a typewriter, a pile of paper, a dried-up bottle of Parker ink, and what looked like a leather-bound journal. A bundle of letters, tied with ribbon, lay in one of the cubby holes of the bureau.

The room smelt musty and damp in the autumn sunlight that beamed through the window. Floral curtains were tucked behind the curtain hooks. A thick layer of dust covered everything and a lamp above the bureau harboured fine webs that glistened in the sunlight. Lucy had remembered it as being dark and cluttered with boxes and paraphernalia. She couldn't see the furniture behind the stacked boxes. It was clearly used as a storage room. Why had the previous owners left the bureau, cabinet and chair? They weren't on her inventory. She looked more closely. The author's name was Margaret Arthur. Lucy hadn't heard of her.

Leaving the door open, she went back downstairs to retrieve the hoover, dusters, polish and window cleaner. The hoover weighed a ton and smelt stale. As she wiped the dust from the typewriter, each key gave a click. The keys were cumbersome and slow and so high up, unlike her sleek MacBook Air. She opened the window and let in some fresh air. From here she could see her front garden and the path that led to her front door, a bent, twisted rose bush to one side.

Her car was parked on the road outside her gate. She tried to shake the curtains outside the open window. The familiar smell of a cigarette hung in the air. She looked down the street. The street was empty, apart from a few parked cars. Maybe it was her mind playing tricks on her, but it smelt so real. It smelt like his cigarettes. The fresh air made little difference to the curtains. She didn't have a washing machine either, so if they were to be cleaned it would have to be by hand. Unhooking the hooks, she threw the curtains on the floor to be washed. She polished and dusted the bureau, wiped down the silk lampshade then hoovered the carpet from corner to corner. The room looked more charming now: it was in need of a lick of paint, but there was something appealing and romantic about it. It would be the perfect writing room, she thought.

When she had finished, she left the windows open and closed the door behind her. The sound of it shutting frightened her; she didn't like the idea of a closed room. She opened the door again.

Her bedroom was stark; only the bed had been left, along with a bedside table and curtains. The seller, a Mrs Richardson, had asked if she wanted them and Lucy gladly accepted; she didn't have her own bed, but had ordered a new mattress. It took no time to dust the room and hoover under and around the bed. She unhooked the curtains, plumped up the pillows and opened the windows to let in the fresh air. The air was fresh; she was sure she'd imagined the cigarette smell. Done, she thought, looking at her watch: ten fifty-six. She climbed down the stairs carrying the hoover and curtains. Now for the sitting room and kitchen. She would be done by midday and could then start to unpack. As she walked into the kitchen, the letter box clattered and a few letters dropped through onto the mat. Most of them junk mail, but a couple were addressed to Mrs J. Richardson, the previous owner. She scribbled 'unknown at this address' on the letters and left them on the table to post them later.

The kitchen was the final room to clean. She wiped down the wooden table and spindle-style chairs. The fridge next to the sink had already been cleaned. She wiped down the opaque ribbed glass of the pantry doors with disinfectant, then opened them to clean the shelves. She cleaned all the worktops before filling the sink to soak the curtains. Soapy bubbles popped as she submerged the small curtains under the water. Wringing them out, she hung them on the radiator to dry. They smelt of lilac and looked a hundred times better.

The house had been cleaned from top to bottom and the smell of bleach was heavy in the air. Now for the boxes. Lucy had arrived with no furniture other than a leather beanbag she had had since university. It had travelled with her wherever she lived. It would take her no time at all to empty the boxes, flat-pack them and put them out for recycling – when was recycling and bin day? Another thing she needed to find out. As she unpacked each box, the house began to fill with her belongings and the house Lucy had moved into became a home once more, awaiting a new life: her life.

The last room she tackled was the room that had filled her with fear. She carried the box marked 'Lucy's books and writing' upstairs, banging into the banister as she went. Balancing the box on one knee, she pushed the door open, this time with no fear. This was her room, her safe space, where her thoughts could run wild and where she could be herself, not live in fear, repulsion. Not a room for a STUPID Lucy, BAD Lucy, DIRTY Lucy. She pushed the door open further with her foot and carefully placed the box on the floor. Ripping the masking tape from the seal, she emptied it. She took her laptop from its cushion of newspaper and bubble wrap and placed it on the bureau next to the typewriter. The laptop made the typewriter appear archaic and obsolete. Lucy liked it, and left it there. She had left the papers and journal where she had found them, only moving them to dust. She opened the cabinet and added five books to the collection. These were all by the same author too, only she knew this author – very well. Lucy Carter.

The sound of her stomach rumbling reminded her that she hadn't eaten since her fish and chips supper. Leaving the box almost empty, she scooped up the typewriter, letters and journal and put them in an empty box. She would take them with her when she went to the supermarket. Closing all the windows, she locked the front door behind her and left to do a food shop, placing the box of belongings on the front seat of her Mini.

She whizzed around the supermarket and bought all the necessary provisions to last a few days. She bought more than she would normally have done in London as she no longer had late-opening shops on her doorstep. Outside the police station, she pulled the car up and leant over to take the box, then walked up the path to a blue door, which she pushed open. She looked around before putting the box on the counter.

'Hello, how can I help you?' said a friendly face from behind the desk.

'Hello,' she said. 'My name is Lucy Carter and I've just moved into a house I've bought down the road. I found these items in the house and I'm not sure what to do with them. The estate agent said they had no forwarding address for the previous owners.'

The police officer opened the box and looked inside. Lucy watched him intently. He looked to be in his early thirties. She hadn't expected such a young officer in a village station.

'Right, what do we have here? A typewriter, a notebook – nothing much, really. Well, if they've left them behind, they couldn't have been important,' he said. 'You can keep them – the property is yours and the belongings are now yours too.'

'Really?' she said.

'Really. It's up to you what you do with them. You could chuck them or sell the old typewriter on eBay – your choice, but they're yours. I hope you settle in and enjoy living in Wrabness.'

Right, that seems pretty straightforward, she thought. If the police officer figures they're mine now, who am I to argue?

Lucy closed the box and left the police station. Driving home, she wondered about the previous owner and the village she had moved to. She knew very little about it. But she could afford the cottage, the village was by the sea, and there was a direct train to London Liverpool Street if she needed a London hit or to see Jo. It ticked all the boxes for her and gave her everything she needed.

She leant against the cottage door to open it. Again, she thought she could smell cigarette smoke. She turned sharply to look around, but nobody was there. The road was silent. Why did she keep smelling it? Why wouldn't it leave her mind? She hurriedly pushed the key into the lock, it jammed finally giving way. She needed to get it fixed. She went in and closed the door behind her. Across the road a lone figure walked through the churchyard, slinking between the gravestones to a car parked on the road at the other side of the churchyard. He lit a cigarette and let down the car window before driving off.

Carrying her shopping and box back into her new home, she breathed in the fresh, clean smell. She dumped the shopping on the kitchen table and unpacked it. Making a ham sandwich, she took it, along with the box, upstairs to the room with the typewriter. She placed the notes back in the cubby hole, the leather-bound journal on the bureau, and the typewriter next to her laptop. New and old, she thought. Pulling up the curved wooden chair, she sat at the typewriter. Taking a piece of paper, she twisted the dial to feed it through the roller. She typed her name, the inky black ribbon jumped up to be pounded.

Lucy Carter lives here xx.

As she approached the end of the row, there was a ping. She pushed the roller back and it made a whirring sound. She smiled at what she'd written and the romantic sound of the typewriter. Taking a bite of her sandwich, she typed some more. She looked at her watch: two twenty-eight. She still had time to sit on the beach and write. She ran down the stairs, loving the feel of the smooth banister under her hand. She loved the old typewriter too. Why on earth would anybody want to throw it in the bin? She'd keep it.

The drive down to the beach was growing more familiar each time. She sat on the stone step where she'd sat the day before and opened her satchel. Taking out her notebook, she opened it and took out the journal and bundle of letters. She undid the ribbon from the letters then unfolded the first letter. The paper felt soft. The black ink had faded over time. As she brushed her fingers across the faded ink, she began to read:

4 September 1939

My darling Peggy,

I am here in the trenches; the sound of the bombs landing is frightening. The trenches are wet and cold, and I am full of fear. As I write this, I know you will be helping at the village hall with the soldiers who are being enlisted. Please, my darling, excuse me if I don't write much. Today I don't know what to think and I miss you – God knows I need you. I love you, my sweetheart – know I am writing this with all the love in my heart. Please give all my love to everybody at home and tell them I am OK.

God bless you, darling Peggy,
With love
Jim

Lucy sat on the stone step, bent over the letter. She felt the hair on her neck stand on end and tears welled in her eyes. She brushed over the words with her fingers as she read, and began to picture the story of Peggy and Jim. Peggy must have died in the house she now lived in. The love Jim had for her and his fear of being in the trenches were clear. Lucy thought of her own comfortable life and how she had run away from a man she was afraid of, a future she didn't want. And here she was, reading a love letter. The future was all Jim and

Peggy had wanted. Did he return from the war? Did they live happily ever after?

She brushed away a tear that trickled down her cheek, then carefully folded the letter, placed it back into the bundle and tied it carefully. She stared out to sea and let her mind wander. As she watched the waves ebb and flow, the familiar figure of the man with the bucket walked along the shore, again emptying his boat of water. This time, he pushed it further out into the water so it no longer sat on the sand but bobbed in the water. He waded out with it. She watched him climb in and start the engine, a billow of smoke puffed out. She watched him until he became a small dot in the distance. Brushing her hair from her face, she looked to her right. The guy she had seen yesterday on the bike rode up and passed her. He had strawberry-blond hair and was wearing the same navy blue fleece hoodie she'd seen him in before. Whistling to the tunes he was listening to as he rode past, he smiled at her. Brushing her hair back again, she smiled back then turned to her notebook and began to write. Words filled the page, falling onto it like snow falls from the sky and covers the grass like a white blanket.

She liked this spot on the beach. It gave her the space she needed. She hadn't spoken to anybody in days, except the young policeman. Lucy stared out at the shipping cranes that dominated the horizon, her phone pinged. It was Charlie. She picked up her phone and read the message.

Talk to me, you owe me that.

She closed the message and put her phone away. Why wouldn't he leave her alone? she thought. She didn't want to talk to him. Everything that needed to be said had been written in her letter the day she'd left. He had lifted his hand to her, filled with rage, and had frightened her, hurt her. He filled her with a fear she never wanted to feel again. There was nothing more to say. She'd finally left, leaving him enough money to cover her share of any bills. The flat was his and she'd only taken what was hers. She'd asked for nothing financially, even though she'd contributed to the flat. She didn't care; she just wanted her life back, to be free of the man who had hurt her, abused her, controlled her, frightened her.

She sat contemplating life play out in front of her. She'd felt trapped by him, like the sea gets trapped in a rock pool. But like a small rock or pebble she was able to throw her past out to sea and let it splash into the water leaving behind only a ripple dispelling the memory.

Chapter Three

Tuesday 12ᵗʰ November

Lucy's phone danced across the kitchen table. She ran down the stairs. Too late. She'd missed the call. She rang her voicemail.

Hi Lucy, it's Jo. Just wanted to catch up and see how life in the country is treating you. Give me a call, we need to talk about your book. I want to see your new pad too and catch up with my best friend. Love you lots.

Second message: *Lucy, it's me. Talk to me, for God's sake!*

Third message: *Talk to me. You owe me that. I was angry – you made me angry. I shouldn't have—*

Lucy turned the message off. She couldn't hear his voice. His words – they were lies, and the sound of his voice made her skin crawl. She felt dirty again.

Lucy rang Jo.

'Lucy, hi! How are you, gorgeous?'

'I'm good, Jo, settling into my new life.' She smiled thinking about her days on the beach. 'How are you?' She flicked on the kettle.

'Oh, you know me, racing around like a bat out of hell. Time doesn't seem to stop and let me breathe.'

'Sounds like you need to live where I am,' Lucy said, pouring hot water over her peppermint tea bag.

17

'I read your manuscript, by the way,' Jo replied.

'You did? What did you think?' she asked, holding her breath. This was her sixth novel. It had taken almost eight months to write and when she wrote the last line, she had felt a deep sense of satisfaction. A warmth with the characters, a warmth and understanding with the mother of a lost child she had so candidly talked to in her research, for Lucy to be able to write, the true depths of despair and love for a child and mother. Such a heart-wrenching real-life story in a fictional capacity.

'I love it!' Jo replied. 'I just love it. It made me cry – it's emotionally empowering and yet such a simple story. It left me with goosebumps.'

'You really liked it? Really?' Lucy squealed. This novel had taken everything out of Lucy; she'd dug deeper than she'd ever dug in writing a novel. She knew she'd written her best novel yet, and one that would capture the hearts of readers.

'Yep, can we talk about it? I can come to you. I need a break from this rat race anyway and I'd love to see your new home – and of course I need to see my bestie. I'm missing you.'

'Sure, Jo, when were you thinking?' Lucy had nothing in the diary other than her daily trips to the beach.

'Right, today's Tuesday, I've got a few things to clear here so how about Thursday 14th November? Does that work?'

'Sounds perfect,' Lucy replied, jotting it down on her calendar. There were no other appointments on it other than the plumber. She'd never had a calendar so clear of dates, and it felt freeing.

'Great, buzz me your address and I will train it down – I assume there is a train.' She laughed.

'Um, yeah, Jo, I don't live in the Outer Hebrides, you know. See you Thursday. I'm so looking forward to it.' She ended the call and scooped the tea bag from her mug. The water had cooled enough for her to drink it.

As the sun began to set, Lucy's courtyard garden began to lose the light. She loved her new home, she thought. She took her tea into the sitting room and lit a fire. A stash of logs had been left at the house and she had bought kindling from the gateway of a nearby house. She hadn't yet worked out the heating properly, but she'd found a plumber to fix the dripping tap in the bathroom, plumb in her newly purchased washing machine and sort out the flush on the loo – it was an old-fashioned chain pull which never liked to go back up. Hopefully he'd also sort the thermostat for the heating, but he wasn't coming until Friday. So until then the fire would warm the house.

She sat on her newly purchased sofa. That along with a mattress were her immediate buys when she'd moved in. She decided she'd make do with the other furniture and bed; she'd grown to like them. She liked the simplicity of her home. She sat with her legs curled up under her, she picked up the bundle of letters to Peggy. Untying the ribbon, she took out another letter.

1 April 1941

My darling Peggy,

I'm writing hoping this letter will reach you in time. I'm being transferred, I think to Dieppe, but I'm not sure. How is my dream girl tonight? Fine, I hope. I can see your face so clearly in my mind, and your sweet-smelling auburn hair. If I lost that scent my mind would go mad with the rancid smell of blood in the trenches. I am in good health, my love. The bombs have stopped falling and the night is silent: there's a silver moon in the clear sky and the air is cold. You are constantly in my mind; we are inseparable. I must leave you now, my darling, as the light is dwindling, but I will write soon. That is a promise. Goodnight, my sweetest heart.

Much love, Jim

So, Peggy had auburn hair, she thought. She jotted a few notes in her notebook. She read the letter again and could almost hear the voices of the two lovers torn apart by a world war. As she read the last line, she sat and stared at the letter. It was so beautiful, full of the unknown but the only known was the overpowering love of two people.

She heard her mobile ping. The sound scared her. It was too late for Jo to text.

What the fuck have you done? This is my life.

You can't just leave, you fucking bitch. I'll get you.

She closed the messages. Leave me alone, she said in her head. Just leave me alone. You'll never find me, you'll never find me. Her peppermint tea was now tepid. Finishing the last drop, she took the cup back into the kitchen and began to wash the few dishes in the sink. Draining the dirty water and leaving the plates and mugs on the drainer, she double-checked the back door was locked, switched off the kitchen light, locked the front door and made her way upstairs.

Today had been a good writing day. Jo was happy with her manuscript – that was the best news she could have had. Undressing and folding her clothes on the chair, she climbed into bed the side lamp shedding enough light to read. She tried to forget the messages from Charlie, but his face kept appearing in her head, his messages playing on her mind. The only way she would get rid of him completely would be to change her number, but she'd had it for years – and why should she? Why couldn't he accept it was over? She wasn't going to change her mind. He'd made her change her mind so many times before, said he would change, apologised. For a few days things would be fine and then he would start again, tormenting her, making her feel worthless, scaring her, making her life hell on earth, making her feel like she was going mad. She'd been too scared to react, to shout back, to scream: 'You're vile, I hate you.' Those words never came, the feelings suppressed. Who would have believed her? Everybody liked Charlie, the golden boy, the City boy.

As she reached the end of her chapter, she bookmarked her page and placed it on the table. She changed her mobile to silent and checked the time: ten o'clock exactly. Turning out the light, she snuggled under the duvet and closed her eyes.

Chapter Four

A knock at the door woke Lucy. She climbed out of bed and wrapped her bath robe around her before sleepily making her way down the stairs. She pulled back the aubergine velvet curtain that was over the front door, blocking out draughts. She'd had a peep hole inserted in the door a few days after she moved in. She peered through it. There was a DPD van outside and a chap at the door with a parcel. Unlatching the lock, she opened the door.

'Parcel for you, love,' he said, scanning the parcel.

She signed for it, closed the door and took the parcel to the kitchen. The kitchen clock read five past nine. She'd slept longer than she'd normally sleep. It must be the sea air, she thought.

She flicked the kettle on, and popped two slices of granary bread in the toaster. She stood and stared at the package. She hadn't ordered anything, and nobody knew her new address, other than Jo and her solicitor. She hadn't disclosed it to Rachel, her neighbour; she hadn't even told Rachel she was leaving. She wasn't on Facebook and hadn't shared any pictures of her new home. Jo hadn't mentioned sending her a parcel.

The toast popped up and she jumped. She buttered it and spread a thin layer of marmite onto the slices, then sat at the table. A message banner dropped down on her phone.

Hi Lucy, I'll be on the 9.56 from Liverpool Street. I arrive in Wrabness at 11.02. Shall I grab a black cab?

Lucy messaged back: *I'll pick you up. There's no such thing as black cabs down here, lol. I'll be in my Mini. See you soon, can't wait! Xx*

She felt happier hearing from Jo, knowing she would see her soon. She was even more ecstatic that Jo had liked her manuscript. Charlie's messages had unnerved her; smelling the cigarettes had felt like somebody was there with her but she hadn't seen anyone. The unopened parcel unsettled her, and she decided to wait until Jo arrived before she opened it.

She had a little under two hours and her fridge needed to be replenished. She needed to hoover then dash to the shop. She'd be back in time to pick Jo up from the station. She raced upstairs, brushed her teeth, tied her hair in a quick ponytail, threw on leggings, trainers and a jumper, ran down the stairs, grabbed her satchel and keys, locked the front door behind her and started up the car.

Lucy drove to the supermarket, parked the car, grabbed a basket and whizzed down each aisle. Olives, ham, olive oil, chicken, mince, salad, rice, spaghetti, bread, butter, wine – a very important buy, slimline tonic, gin, vodka – an even more important buy, lemons, limes, onions … had she forgotten anything? Yes, chocolate and coffee. Jo wasn't a peppermint tea drinker. After using the self-checkout, she walked quickly back to the car. Engine on, home, unpack shopping, hoover – done in less than forty-five minutes. Record time, even for her. That's what she didn't miss about London: life was fast-paced but you could never get to a supermarket in five minutes. The traffic was unbearable most of the time, and she didn't miss it one bit. She gave the bathroom a quick clean and made her bed. Ten fifty – perfect. She got back into the car and drove to the station at a sensible speed. She watched as the London train pulled up to Platform 1.

The train doors swished open and a throng of passengers got off. She scanned the platform for Jo. There she was, still the same. She looked as cool as a cucumber in oversized Jackie Onassis-style sunglasses, the deepest of red lipsticks on her full lips. Her sleek dark bobbed hair was cut to her jaw line, with a blocked fringe. She wore black skinny jeans to show her off her slim legs and a roll-neck jumper. To finish her edgy style, she wore black biker-style boots and a black denim jacket was slung over her shoulder.

Lucy waved at her as she got closer. Jo beamed.

Lucy hugged her tightly. 'So good to see you, Jo!' she exclaimed. It was a hug that only two friends could ever feel the goodness from: deep, embracing.

'You too, Lucy,' she said, taking a step back and holding Lucy's shoulders. 'You're looking good – in fact, you're looking great. Country life suits you!'

As the two walked up the platform they chattered away until they reached the car.

'So, this is Wrabness?' Jo said. 'It's quaint. I can see why you've moved here – you'll have to show me around. You seem happy – happier than I've seen you in a long time.' She smiled at Lucy and squeezed her knee as Lucy pulled up outside her house.

'I am – and here is home.' Jo unlatched the gate and pulled her suitcase through. Its wheels click-clacked on the path.

Lucy unlocked the door and led the way in. 'Leave your case there, hun, I'll sort it in a mo. Come through, come through.'

They stood in the kitchen. 'Fancy a brew?' Lucy asked, flicking the kettle on and grabbing two mugs.

'Love a coffee, I'm absolutely parched. I didn't have time to grab one from the station,' Jo said, pulling out a chair.

As Lucy poured the coffee the letterbox clattered. She jumped at the unexpected noise.

Jo peered down the hall. 'It's probably junk mail,' she said, looking at Lucy.

'D'you think?'

'I'll go and see.' Jo disappeared for a few seconds and came back with a pizza flyer. 'Yep, your local pizza menu. Are you OK, Lucy? You seem a touch on edge.'

'Not really,' Lucy began. 'Is it too early for wine?'

'It's just gone midday, but let's drink these first.' Jo laughed.

'Let's go and sit in the sitting room. It's more comfortable and warmer than in here – the heating is a bit temperamental. I've got a plumber coming tomorrow so hopefully it will be sorted.' Lucy led Jo through to the sitting room and began to light the fire. She'd become quite a pro at lighting it and it actually staying alight.

They sat on the sofa and Jo asked, 'So what's eating you? You don't seem yourself.'

'I don't know. I just don't think I'm alone here. I keep hearing him – you know, his voice taunting me, the smell of his cigarettes. I feel like it's real, like it's never going to go. Sometimes I sleep well, sometimes I wake in the night,' Lucy stared into her mug of tea and a tear fell down her cheek. 'I feel like sometimes I'm going mad, losing my mind. The room upstairs, the door was closed, and all I could see was the dark room in his flat – you know. I didn't even know what that room looked like; it was in our apartment but I never saw it in the light.'

'I know, Luce. You told me. But why do you think he's here?' Jo shifted position, kicked off her biker boots and tucked her feet underneath the cushion.

'He's been texting me,' she replied. 'He left me voicemails the other day, then God knows how many texts saying he'd find me. He's angry I've left him.'

'Shit, Lucy, that's scary. Did you reply?' Jo asked, putting down her mug. 'Have you told anybody else?'

'No, just you. He can't know where I am. I haven't even told our neighbour, Rachel, that I've moved. I haven't been on Facebook for months.'

'Fuck, Lucy. Rachel couldn't have found out, could she?' There was a nervousness in Jo's voice.

'I don't think so, but you know Charlie and what he was like. If he has told her I've left, he might ask her to find out where I am. I don't know.' Lucy tried to blink back tears as she said it. She just wanted to forget her time with Charlie, be free and live her life without being under his control.

'Lucy, Charlie wouldn't have told Rachel you'd left. He wouldn't admit to that, being rejected. Is there anything else? Why don't you block him?' Jo asked, moving closer to Lucy and taking the tea from her. 'Is there anything else?'

'If I block him, then what if he has found me?' Lucy's voice was agitated. 'This morning I was woken by a DPD driver with a parcel.'

'Right, and what was it?'

'I don't know. I haven't opened the box,' she replied. 'I don't want to.'

'Do you want me to?' Jo asked.

'Can you?' Lucy replied. She felt safer doing it with Jo. It had played on her mind all morning.

'OK, where is it?' Jo asked, getting up from the sofa and straightening her jeans. 'Is it the one in the kitchen?'

'Yes,' Lucy said, looking so frightened that even Jo didn't know how to make her feel safe.

'I'll be right back, we can do it together, be strong kiddo.' Jo disappeared into the kitchen. Lucy watched the fire lick around the log, which was charred and black. The flames danced and curled around the log and sparks flew. It was so warm, so welcoming. Each glowing ember leaped and twirled in a fiery dance.

'Here,' Jo said, breaking Lucy's trance, 'are you ready?'

'Yep, I guess. Can you open it?'

Jo peeled back the Sellotape from the seal and prised the two flaps to open it. Inside was a small box with a beautiful hand-tied bow. Pink tissue paper lined the box. Jo took the paper out, and the gift.

'Shall I open it?' she asked.

Lucy nodded.

Jo undid the bow, then opened the box.

'What is it?' Lucy asked.

'A Dior scarlet lipstick,' Jo said, taking the lipstick out and passing it to Lucy. 'Why a lipstick? Why Dior? You don't wear Dior.'

'Dior – he took me there when we went to Paris when we first met. He bought me a lipstick, it was this colour and a silk scarf. Why's he doing this, Jo? How does he know where I am?'

'I don't know, Lucy, but I think we need to go to the police. There's something not right. Are you sure nobody else knows where you are? He's playing mind games – he has to know where you are.'

'Nobody knows. How has he found me?'

'Are you sure nobody else knows where you live? The solicitor, maybe?'

'The solicitor doesn't know Charlie – you're the only person who knows.'

'Well, I haven't told him. In fact, he hasn't even been in touch with me to ask. There has to be another explanation,' Jo said, placing the box on the floor.

'How long are you staying?' Lucy asked, her voice trembling.

'I can stay for the weekend if you like, but I have meetings next week with Giles at HarperCollins to talk about your novel so I really need to get the train back on Sunday evening. Shall I stay until then? I've packed enough stuff. Get me – organised or what?'

'Will you?' Lucy replied. She felt a little happier knowing she wouldn't be on her own, and she had missed Jo.

'Sure. Now, let's leave this box in the kitchen and why don't you show me around? I'd love to see the beach where you write, and we can talk manuscripts.'

'Sounds perfect,' Lucy said. 'Let me grab the keys and we can head out now.'

She left the box in the kitchen, grabbed her bag, double-locked the front door and drove down to the beach with Jo.

As they drove, Jo chatted about London and what was going on in the world of publishing. Her chatter took Lucy's mind off the lipstick.

As they approached Harwich, they passed buoys, shipyards and an RNLI museum. Lucy parked by a red buoy that was cemented to the ground. They walked past the sailing club, turning left for the beach and the step Lucy had chosen as her writing spot. The cranes blocked the skyline, the colossal shipping containers sat squarely on the water. Lucy thought it was incredible that such monstrous vessels didn't sink with their weight.

They sat on the stone step and looked out to sea.

'I can see why you like it here. It's quite industrious and urban,' Jo said, opening her bag and taking out Lucy's manuscript.

'So, did you really like it?' Lucy asked, turning towards Jo.

'I loved it. There are a few bits I've edited but I haven't changed much. I like the title – it totally works. *Hold my Hand* will be a bestseller. Man, what a tear-jerker. It's more than just a beach read; it has so much depth. I love it, and Giles at HarperCollins will love it too. Have you thought about how you'd like the cover to look?'

'I have. I want it to be simple, with the mother holding out her hand and the child reaching out, but from behind them. Do you like that idea?' Lucy said, tucking her hair behind her ears.

'Oh, I do. That sounds perfect. I'll get on the case with that. You're flying, Lucy, you really are – your dreams are coming true.' Jo put her arm around Lucy's shoulder and pulled her in for a confirming 'you've done it' squeeze.

As the two friends sat on the step chatting about life, the guy on the bike rode past. Lucy glanced at him as he neared them. He caught her eye and smiled again. She smiled back and looked at Jo.

'He's cute,' Jo said. 'Who is he?'

'No idea, but he always seems to cycle past when I'm here, and he smiled at me last time too,' Lucy said, following him with her eyes.

'I think you need to explore a little and find out. He was definitely cute – plus two smiles. Nobody smiles at each other these days, we just ignore people.'

'How do I get to know him? He's on a bike.' She laughed.

'No idea, Luce, you're the one with the big imagination. I'm sure you'll figure something out or you could play the game.'

'Ha ha – the game! It's been a while since we've done that!' Lucy said, nudging Jo's arm.

'Right, I'm starving, and we need a drink to celebrate. Come on, my treat. Where shall we go?' Jo said, jumping up and brushing the sand from her jeans.

'There is a restaurant around the corner called The Pier. It looks nice – and guess what it overlooks?'

'The pier, by any chance?' Jo laughed and linked arms with Lucy. Together they walked through Old Harwich. It was a treasure trove of antique shops and art galleries. A red ship on the pier was decorated with bunting and memorabilia with a sign across it reading 'The Ship that Rocked'.

They entered The Pier and went upstairs to the restaurant. It overlooked the pier, as promised and the inside had a London cool about it. They were the only people dining. They ordered fresh lobster and a bottle of Sauvignon Blanc. Lunch was a success. The view out across the harbour was amazing, the sky the lightest of blues dappled with clouds that gently passed through, borne by the wind. It was quiet, the silence only interrupted by a noisy car or motorbike. There was no frenetic honking cabs or impatient drivers, no buskers on the streets. Lucy loved the peace.

'Blimey, it's four o'clock already!' Jo said. 'Shall we get back to your place, Lucy, before I buy another bottle of wine that I'll have to drink all by myself?'

'Sure, let's,' Lucy said, screwing up her napkin into a ball on the table.

Jo paid the bill and the two ambled back to the car, taking a slightly different route but ending up by the RNLI museum. Driving home, the sun had gone down and the sky was beginning to turn a dusky grey, with the sun slowly falling in the west. Lucy reached the small T-road onto the terrace, a man in a navy hoodie that shielded his face walked down Lucy's garden path, crossed the road and walked quickly away. He ducked through the church yard by the time she'd managed to pull out from the junction and parked the car.

Lucy looked at Jo.

'It's probably nothing, Lucy. Come on.'

Locking the car door, Lucy opened the iron gate and unlocked the front door. Jo was right: wedged in the letterbox was another take-away menu, this time for the local Indian restaurant.

'Well, that's supper sorted,' Jo said. 'I haven't had a curry in ages!' Jo always had a positive outlook on life: she knew Lucy was agitated, but it was only a menu delivery man and he probably had thousands to deliver. It was lucky for them he'd come when he did; neither of them particularly felt like cooking. Now supper was one less thing to worry about. Instead they could open a bottle of wine and do what friends do best: chat.

'Right, first things first,' Jo said. 'That box – I'm going to put it somewhere where you don't need to see it.'

'In the bin,' Lucy said.

'Nope, you need to keep it in case you get another one and we need to show the police,' Jo said, opening a cupboard and grabbing two glasses for the wine Lucy had opened.

'Do you think I will?'

'Who knows? Where shall I put it?'

'In the under-stair cupboard, maybe,' Lucy said, pouring the wine, 'but can you tuck it right at the back, so I don't have to see it every time I get the hoover out?'

'Consider it done.' Jo opened the cupboard door and pushed the box to the back, out of sight.

Lucy pulled the curtain across the window of the back door.

'Have you got a garden?' Jo asked, rustling through her bag for her Marlboro Gold. 'I might pop out and have a quick smoke.'

'Yep, it's quite a sweet little garden. It's pretty basic out there. There's a tiny lawn – I've no idea if there's a lawnmower, though.'

Jo opened the back door. 'Fancy one?' she asked, taking two out of the packet.

'I think I might, actually. I can't remember the last time I had a cigarette – probably with you. You're such a bad influence.'

As they stood outside inhaling the cigarettes and blowing smoky plumes into the cold air, the moon lit the sky and the stars glinted like diamonds. The autumnal smell of bonfires and leaves filled the air. An owl hooted overhead and a bat darted past.

'You can tell we're not in London, can't you?' Jo said, staring up into the sky. 'You can see the stars and the sky is dark.'

'I know – that was the first thing I noticed when I moved here, the sheer darkness. The other thing is the birds – man, they are noisy. I don't need to set my alarm; they wake me every morning.'

Stubbing out their cigarettes and discarding them into a plant pot, they went inside, closing the door and darkness behind them.

'Shall we go into the sitting room? Maybe order a curry later?' Jo said, taking her glass and the wine bottle. Lucy placed her glass on the table and knelt by the fire to clear the ash. Screwing up an old newspaper and laying kindling on top and a fresh log, she lit the paper from the bottom. The flames caught the paper. She placed the fireguard in front of the fire then drew the curtains and lit a candle, which flickered in its jar, its scent of black pomegranate filling the air, stealing away the smell of the fire.

The girls snuggled into the cushions, their feet tucked under them as they drank the velvety red wine. The fire crackled and its warmth made the sitting room perfectly cosy. As Jo took a sip from her glass, she turned to Lucy.

'Do you want to talk about Charlie? I'm here for you if you do – you know that, don't you.'

'I'm just scared, Jo, scared he's found me, scared of what will happen,' Lucy said, looking straight into her eyes. 'He scares me. Why won't he just leave me alone? Why can't I just have happiness again?'

'If he sends any more messages, you need to report it. The police will protect you; you can't live in fear. He controlled you in London, but you're not there now and he's out of your life, thank God. We just need to make sure it stays that way.'

'I'll call the police tomorrow – at least make a report,' Lucy said, feeling happier that Jo was there. Jo knew Charlie – and what he was capable of. She'd seen him whisper in Lucy's ear in a way that was controlling, and pull her towards him when they were in public, squeeze her wrists too hard. She knew he liked to play mind games. She'd seen how his face would change as some exchange was passed and then smile and greet, sickening to watch, clever, menacing. She knew exactly how he could manipulate a situation and make himself the victim. She knew Lucy had finally done the right thing to leave him and run, but she had to be able to stop running and living in fear. She had to regain her own identity again and be the girl she was before she met Charlie. He'd tried to change her, broken her mind, broken her spirit, changed her. It would take time, but it would happen, then Lucy would feel as free as a bird again.

She gave Lucy a reassuring hug. 'Good idea. I'll come with you.' Taking her shoulders and looking into her eyes, Jo asked, 'So, your new novel? Any ideas?'

'Well, actually, yes,' Lucy said. 'I'm not sure how I am going to start it yet – I've got a shitload of research to do.'

'Ooh, I'm intrigued. Tell me more! Do you have a title yet?' Jo asked. She was in awe of Lucy's imagination: she just seemed to write bestseller after bestseller.

'I need to look into the Second World War,' Lucy continued.

'How come?'

'Well, when I moved in here, I did a super clean out, bleached the house from top to bottom. The second room upstairs, where I can write in winter, had a bureau and typewriter left behind and a cabinet full of novels, all by the same author. I took them to the police station, but they said I could keep them as I now own the house and they're legally my property.'

'Awesome, good find,' Jo said leaning forward and topping up their glasses.

'In the cubby hole of the bureau was this bundle of letters. I've been reading them. They're so beautiful – love letters from a soldier called Jim to his darling Peggy. Each letter I've read has made me cry. They're so moving.'

'So, you're writing a wartime love story?'

'I guess. The title I'm using so far is *Letters to My Love*,' Lucy said, smiling with contentment. She always loved it when a new novel unfolded in her head.

'It sounds emotional, Luce. I can't wait to read it.' Jo clinked her glass with Lucy's.

'I'm so taken by the letters – do you want to read one?' she asked.

'Sure thing.'

Lucy jumped up from the sofa. When she reached the sitting room door, she turned. 'Shall we get a curry?' She was hungry and the wine was filling her head with dizziness.

'Sounds fab. I'll order, you grab the letters,' Jo said.

Lucy appeared a lot more relaxed now; chatting about her novel had obviously taken her mind away from what was scaring her.

Lucy went upstairs to her writing room to retrieve the letters and journal. While she was gone, Jo ordered their curry. As Jo put the menu down on the table, a message pinged up on Lucy's phone.

It was from Charlie.

Lucy, talk to me, you fucking whore, you're making me mad now!

'For fuck's sake,' Jo muttered. 'Just when Lucy's feeling more settled. What to do? Delete the message, or keep it as more proof that Charlie's texting her?'

She pushed the phone away and placed it face-down on the table. Lucy came back down the stairs and sat back down on the sofa, holding the bundle of letters. As she passed a letter to Jo, her phone lit up. Lucy picked up her phone and opened the message. When she saw who it was from, she turned ashen and her hand began to shake.

'Show me,' Jo said.

'It's him again,' Lucy said, passing Jo the phone.

'Bloody hell, Lucy, you need to report him. He's a nutter. We'll go straight down to the police station first thing tomorrow and let them see everything. You can press charges. Tell them about your relationship – tell them everything, tell them about the room. Nobody does that to somebody they love. He just wanted to control you. Turn your phone off now and leave it off until the morning, otherwise you're just going to freak yourself out, seriously. He can't touch you. I'm here. Once the police are involved; you will feel safer. I promise you, nothing is going to happen. I won't let anything happen to you. He's just playing mind games, it's what he does.'

She pulled Lucy towards her and hugged her as tightly as she could. Lucy cried, shaking with fear.

'Lucy, listen to me.' Jo cupped her face. 'This is going to end, this *is* going to end.' She pulled Lucy back in, holding her tightly, rocking her as if she were a small child. Jo let her hold go when there was a knock on the door. They jumped.

'It will be the curry,' Jo said. 'I'll go.'

Lucy gave her money for the curry. Jo peered through the spy hole. 'It's the curry. Go and grab plates, Luce.'

She opened the door to the delivery man. 'Thank goodness you delivered a menu today,' Jo said. 'My friend has just moved in and we don't know the area.'

'What menu delivery? We post menus on Mondays only,' he said, handing her the brown paper bag and walking back down the path.

Before Jo closed the door, she looked around. It was difficult to make anything out in the pitch black, but she couldn't see anybody else out. She closed the door and double-locked it, pulling the curtain across, then turned to see Lucy carrying plates and cutlery. She said nothing to Lucy about the menu. The guy in the hoodie hadn't been working for the restaurant – so what had he been doing? Jo went to join Lucy.

Outside, smoke curled from the half-open window of a silver Jaguar that was parked a couple of houses down, out of view of Lucy's house. As the man threw the cigarette out onto the road, he wrapped a silk scarf around his hands. He'd watched the door open and had seen it wasn't Lucy. He recognised Jo. He'd wait. Untwisting the scarf from his hands and placing it beside him. He switched on the engine and drove past slowly, watching the two girls in the sitting room as he drove past. Not until he had passed the house did the driver turn on the headlights. He drove away from the house without a sound, stealing off in the night, undetected.

Chapter Five

'Oh my God.' Jo rolled over in bed, burrowing her head under the pillow. Lucy turned over and laughed.

'Is it the birds?'

'Bloody hell, Lucy, they're making an absolute racket. Seriously, how do you sleep with their din?' Jo threw the duvet over her head and tried to muffle out the noise of the morning chorus. 'What the fuck?' she said from under the duvet, her voice muffled.

'I've got used to it now,' Lucy said, laughing at Jo. 'Fancy a coffee?' She climbed out of bed.

'Sure, I'm awake now. Bloody birds! What time is it, anyway?'

'Just gone eight,' Lucy said, glancing at her watch. She left Jo hiding under the pillow and went downstairs, chuckling.

Taking the drinks upstairs, she handed Jo hers. 'Careful, it's hot.'

Jo shuffled up the bed and pulled the pillows up behind her so she could sit upright. Taking the coffee in two hands, she took a sip.

'How are you feeling today?' she asked tentatively.

'I'm OK, Jo. I haven't cried like I did last night before. I think I needed to, but you're right, I do need to report all this to the police. I can't handle it any more,' Lucy said. She'd had a real heart-to-heart with Jo the night before and had really needed a good cry: so many emotions had been pent up inside her and needed to come out.

Jo and Lucy sat in bed chatting until they were disturbed by the brass knocker on the front door. Jo looked at her phone. Nine thirty.

'Are you expecting anybody?' she asked.

'Oh shit, yes, the plumber.' The girls scrambled out of bed, threw on their clothes, brushed their teeth, and bolted down the stairs. Lucy saw, through the peep hole, a white van outside with 'Jim Brown Boilers and Plumbing' emblazoned on its side. She opened the door and let the plumber in, then explained the situation and showed him the heating system in the cupboard next to the bathroom and the dripping tap in the bathroom. She left him to work and went back to the kitchen, where Jo was making toast and coffee.

'How long do you think he'll be?' Jo asked.

'Not long. He's already fixed the dripping tap.' Lucy cupped her hands around her mug, feeling the heat permeate through her.

As they finished their breakfast and cleared up the sitting room, the plumber reappeared downstairs.

'That's all sorted,' he said. 'The thermostat has been set and should come on now with the timer, washing machine is plumbed in. The bathroom tap just needed a new valve, and I've fitted a new chain and lever on your loo. You shouldn't have any more problems now. Oh, and I'd leave the bathroom window ajar, that'll stop the condensation issue, not open sweetheart, just ajar.'

Lucy paid him and took his card. She would need him again, she was pretty sure of that, and he was friendly and reasonably priced.

They were now free to explore and visit the police station. They grabbed their jackets and bags, locked the front door behind them and drove to the police station.

When they drew up outside the old brick station with the blue front door and a lamp overhanging it, they sat in the car for a few minutes before Jo broke the silence.

'Ready, Lucy?' she asked, taking her hand reassuringly.

'Ready as I'll ever be,' Lucy replied. They got out of the car and made their way up the path to the station. The door was heavy to open but at least it opened. Inside, they rang the small brass bell on the front desk and waited. There were no mugshots of wanted criminals on the walls; in fact, the walls were almost bare apart from a poster advertising a festival nearby, a sheet listing emergency numbers and the names of the police officers on duty, PC Willis and PC Mackenzie. Just as they were about to ring the bell for a second time, a police officer emerged.

'Can I help you?' he asked. It was a different police officer to the one Lucy had met when she took the box of belongings to the station. His badge said 'PC Mackenzie'.

Lucy froze. So many words wanted to come out of her mouth: about the barrage of messages, the voicemails, the parcel delivered by the DPD driver, the tormented life she had lived in London with Charlie, but nothing came out.

Jo looked at her and stepped in. 'Yes, we'd like to make a report,' she said with conviction, taking Lucy's hand.

'A report? What type of report?' he asked, leaning forward and picking up a pen.

'My friend would like to report unwanted calls and texts and threatening voicemails,' Jo continued. As she rattled off the number of texts that Lucy had received, and the days and times they had been sent, the police officer looked at Lucy and smiled. He was young too.

'One moment,' he said, looking at Jo.

She stopped.

'Are you Lucy?' he asked, looking at Lucy, who had stood silently while Jo spoke.

She looked at him. His face was kind with a softness about it, his hair dark and cut boyishly short, his eyes blue.

'Yes, I'm Lucy,' she said, her eyes filled with an open space of nothingness. Suddenly she felt that her voice was being heard and that somebody cared about her: somebody who didn't know her, yet who wanted to hear her story – her real story, not the make-believe stories she wrote for the world to read, but her story, one that she didn't want to have, one that she didn't want to tell, one that was more like a horror movie than a love story.

'How long has this been going on?' he asked, turning down the radio on his walkie-talkie when it crackled.

'About a month or so,' she replied. Her hands were clammy; she could feel a knot in her stomach and sweat prickle on her upper lip. 'They just don't stop. I just want it to end.' Her eyes began to well up and she felt the sting of tears. Hold them back, Lucy, she told herself. Be strong, hold the tears back.

'Do you have your phone?' the officer asked. 'Can I see the messages?'

Lucy unlocked her phone and gave it to the policeman. He listened intently to the voicemails and then scrolled through the bombardment of messages.

'These are not pleasant, but you've done the right thing by coming here today. Can you both come into the incident room so I can fill the report in properly?'

Lucy and Jo followed the officer into the room where they sat side by side, a table that held a computer screen and keyboard between them and the officer.

'I have to let you know there is a camera in this room which is recording – but only images, not voice recording,' he said, opening up the computer. Lucy looked up into the corner of the room and saw the red light flashing. She stared into it. Who was watching them?

'What's your full name, Lucy?'

'Lucy Carter,' she said, sitting on her hands.

'And your address?'

'Three Lambourne Terrace,' she replied.

As he took down her information and logged it on the computer, he made notes on the screen and added screenshots of all the messages. 'So, you have a choice. You can either press charges for harassment or we can log it so there is a record of your complaint. But I have to advise you it could go to court.'

'I don't want him arrested,' she said. 'I just want it to stop. I just want him to leave me alone and stop scaring me.'

'Well, maybe a call from the police will be enough, then. Would you like me to call him?'

'Yes, please,' she replied.

'Leave it with me, we'll sort this for you.' He smiled reassuringly.

Lucy gave the officer Charlie's name, number and address, and thanked him for his help. As they left Jo turned. 'Will you contact us when you have spoken to Charlie?'

'Yes, I will.'

'Do I need to do anything else?' Lucy asked.

'No. You can block him if you like – that might help. I don't think you're in any danger. He's just being a menace and hopefully a call will be enough to deter him.'

'Right.' She took her phone back from him. 'Thank you.'

As they left the station, Jo turned to her and took her arm. 'Feel happier now?'

'Yes, I do. I didn't think I would, but I do.'

'Right what's the plan, Batman?' Jo asked. 'Shall we go and explore the beach?'

'Yes, let's,' Lucy said, switching on the engine and heading for the beach. As Lucy took the A120 to Harwich, a silver Jaguar veered off right towards Bromley. Lucy parked outside the quaint RNLI museum.

'Shall we walk along the parade? See where it leads?' Lucy said as she stretched over to the back seat to grab her satchel. 'Wherever we end up, we can have lunch.'

'Perfect plan,' Jo said, undoing her seat belt. 'A mystery tour and lunch – although I might have to bail if it's a greasy spoon.'

The friends meandered along the parade. The houses that ran along the other side of the road formed an impressive Georgian terrace, typically seaside-looking, every other one showing a bed and breakfast or hotel sign. They had magnificent views of the sea. Some of the detached houses stood, looking important and grand about them, three storeys high with ensigns wafting in the wind, showing they had once belonged to somebody who worked at sea in the higher ranks. Lucy saw the wooden lighthouse and a sign that read 'Welcome to Dovercourt'. She knew there was a fish and chip shop and café at the end of the road.

A wind farm in the distance stood deep in the sea, whirling its huge blades through the air. Nearer the shore, three windsurfers were taking advantage of the blustery winds. A string of brightly coloured beach huts stood like multi-coloured centurions along the front, and the water in the sailing pond shivered in the breeze.

'Fish and chips?' Lucy said, spying the green sign ahead.

'Why not?' Jo replied.

As they walked back along the parade they munched on their chips, their fingers salty and greasy. There was something lovely about eating chips as they walked along, straight out of the paper. The chips warmed their stomachs as the wind picked up. Finally, they reached the sign that read 'Old Harwich'. They had walked from the boundary of one town to another. While they had walked, the sky had turned from a pale blue to a dark grey. The windsurfers still flipped in freestyle moves over the waves. Grey billowing clouds filled the sky and drops of rain began to fall. The temperature dipped as the clouds rolled in. Lucy and Jo speeded up. Neither of them had an umbrella, and the weather had turned from sunshine to cold and grey within seconds. As they discarded their chip paper in the bin, a guy on a bike rode towards them. It was the guy Lucy had seen before. As they moved to one side to let him pass, he caught Lucy's eye.

'Thanks.' He smiled and rode past. Lucy turned around to see where he was heading. As she did, he looked back too. Shit, she thought, he'd seen her look.

He smiled to himself as he rode past the beach huts. Cute girl, he thought.

As they neared the museum a fork of lightning ricocheted across the sky and thunder rumbled. The heavens opened, pelting Lucy and Jo with rain like shards of glass and soaking them through. They ran the last few yards to the car and fell into it, drenched.

'Blimey, where did that come from?' Jo said, pushing her hair off her face and wiping her wet hands on her jeans.

The sky hung over them like a black cloak; the cranes were barely visible, and the sea churned and tossed in the wind and rain.

'Did you notice that guy on the bike?' Jo said, staring out of the window while the windscreen wipers raced.

'Which guy?' Lucy asked, trying to demist the steamed-up windows.

'The cute guy we clocked the other day – the one you turned around and looked at today, once he'd cycled past us,' Jo said, smiling at Lucy, 'I saw you clock him. I notice everything Lucy Carter.'

'Oh him, yeah, he is quite cute, isn't he? Maybe I'll get to find out who he is when I've got to know the area better. He's obviously a local.'

'I definitely think you should. Right, home James! I'm cold and wet and need to get out of these wet jeans.' Jo laughed.

Lucy drove out of Harwich and down the A120, her windscreen wipers still going ten to the dozen. The rain hammered down on the Mini as it sped along. Lucy pulled up outside her house and the two of them made a mad dash for the front door, splashing through the puddles that had formed on the pathway. They stood in the hallway, soaked to the skin,

'I might take a shower, if that's OK,' Jo said. 'I need to warm up and sort my hair out.'

'Sure, no worries. There are towels in the airing cupboard by the bathroom door. Grab one from there,' Lucy said, putting the kettle on.

Jo disappeared upstairs. Lucy could hear the boiler kick in as the shower went on. The house was warm too – the plumber had clearly done his job. It felt cosy. Lucy hung her jacket on the radiator to dry out and got mugs out of the cupboard.

Lucy heard the bathroom door open and the hairdryer buzzing from the bedroom. She poked her head around the bedroom door.

'I'm going to have a quick shower if you're finished in the bathroom. There's a coffee on the side for you in the kitchen.'

Lucy climbed into the bath and turned the shower on. She let the warmth of the water drench her and pummel her back. As she lathered her hair, she felt content. She'd reported Charlie. She didn't want him arrested; she just wanted to be left alone. Life could only get better now, she thought, rinsing the suds from her hair. She closed her eyes and the guy on the bike came into her thoughts. He was cute, she thought. She always seemed to see him when she was at the beach – maybe next time she'd make her smile bigger, so he'd stop and chat, or maybe she wouldn't. She turned off the shower and wrapped a towel around her. Unlocking the bathroom door, she piled her wet clothes at the top of the stairs for washing and went into the bedroom to dry her hair and change. Jo had already gone downstairs. She threw on black leggings and a polo-neck then, scooping up her washing, she went downstairs. Jo was sitting in the kitchen, drinking her coffee. Lucy bundled her clothes into the washing machine and closed the door. The day was turning to evening and the dark clouds were washed away by the darkening sky. Six o'clock. Lucy tipped the rest of her tea down the drain and took two glasses from the cupboard.

'Fancy a glass of something?' she said, placing the glasses on the side and retrieving the corkscrew from the drawer.

'Don't mind if I do,' Jo said.

'Red or white?'

'I think I'll go red. It feels like the nights are drawing in – winter is well on its way,' Jo said.

Lucy poured two glasses of red. 'To new beginnings,' she said, clinking her glass with Jo's. 'Fancy spag bol for supper?'

'Sounds awesome, Luce. Shall I put some tunes on?' While Jo sorted the music, Lucy busied herself peeling and chopping onions and crushing cloves of garlic before scooping them into the pan with a generous slug of olive oil. The smell of onions and garlic sautéing gently in the olive oil was divine. She opened the fridge and took out the fresh mince, adding it to the pan. The smell wafted around the kitchen. She added a tin of tomatoes and a carton of passata. Lucy left the bolognaise gently simmering before adding spaghetti to a boiling pan of water.

'I might have a quick ciggie while supper cooks. Fancy one?' Jo said, taking the packet of Marlboro Gold from her bag and opening the kitchen door. A moth flew in, attracted by the kitchen light, and flitted and darted around the bulb, every so often bashing its wings on the light.

They blew the smoke into the air, watching the resident bat dart around the shed.

'Looks like you have company,' Jo said as the bat flew away into night. 'It's lovely here, Lucy. I definitely think you've made the right choice. I mean, it's not London but it's a perfect spot for you and writing – and you're only an hour away on the train.'

They stubbed out their cigarettes in the plant pot and went back inside to be greeted by the aroma of an Italian feast. Supper was ready, and the two of them were famished. Lucy drained the spaghetti and spooned a mound on to each plate before piling on a generous dollop of bolognaise. They enjoyed every morsel and had a bottle of red wine with supper. Afterwards, they went back outside for an after-dinner cigarette, totally satisfied by their meal. As Jo stubbed out her cigarette, a faint clatter echoed around the garden. It sounded like a metal dustbin lid falling or being hit.

Lucy looked at Jo. 'Did you hear that?'

'It's probably a cat on the prowl,' Jo said. Moments later, they heard footsteps moving hastily away. They looked at each other, both thinking the same thought: it wasn't a cat, it was a person.

'Quick, get inside, Lucy,' Jo said in a hushed voice. 'Lock the door and bolt it.'

With the door bolted and locked, they stood in the kitchen, too scared to move an inch. The house was quiet: the music had stopped, and the only sound was the clock ticking in the kitchen.

'It was him, wasn't it?' Lucy said, her voice shaking.

'Go into the sitting room and don't move from there. Here, take your phone.' Jo darted upstairs. Lucy could hear her footsteps on the landing, and doors opening and closing. Jo looked out of the window that overlooked the front garden and street below. She couldn't make out anything other than the shadow of the trees looming over the road. Lucy's garden gate was open and swinging on its hinge. Drawing the curtain, she went back downstairs to the sitting room, checking that the front door was locked. Lucy was rocking on the sofa, her face white, clutching her phone.

'What was it?' Lucy said, her voice panicked and shaking. 'Did you see anything?'

'I couldn't see anything,' Jo said calmly. 'Nothing at all.' As she spoke, the silhouette of a man walked across the road and opened the door of a silver car. The door shut with a cushioned sound. He opened the glove box and put a white silk scarf in it. The voyeur drove off into the night. Slowly he passed several houses then accelerated, not turning his lights on until he had reached the level crossing. The lights were bright, dazzling a fox that ran across its path.

Lucy and Jo sat together, frightened by the noise and the footsteps. They didn't see the silver Jaguar slink away.

'Do we call the police?' Lucy asked.

'I don't think so. Let's go to bed. We can clear up tomorrow. I couldn't see anything outside, and we're just overthinking what it could have been,' Jo said, trying to inject a little sense of calm. Double-locking the door and leaving the lights on downstairs, they went upstairs. They climbed into bed and lay there until they heard nothing at all outside other than a passing owl calling for its mate. As they succumbed to tiredness, they fell asleep, wondering if somebody was still outside, watching them.

***

Lucy had been in a relationship with Charlie for three years and everybody had thought he was the perfect man. On paper, they were the perfect match, but behind closed doors he was different: he was controlling and frightened her. She'd wanted to leave him so many times, before but didn't know how to. Where would she go? He'd find her if she stayed in London; they shared the same friends. But her grandfather had died the year before and left her some money in his will – it was as if he was guiding her, helping her, protecting her. He had never liked Charlie much. The money he left was enough for Lucy to put a deposit down on a house outside London. She knew this was her only chance to escape. Lucy was too scared to use her laptop to scour Rightmove for houses. Instead, when Charlie left for work in the morning she would go to the cyber café on the high street in Putney and scroll through houses.

One Wednesday morning in June, just as she was beginning to give up hope of escaping, the perfect house came up: a terraced cottage in Wrabness in need of modernising, on the market for £175,000. She googled Wrabness and Essex. She'd never been to Essex before but had simply searched an eighty-mile radius of her home in London; that was an hour on the train or a little longer in the car. She wasted no time in setting up an appointment with the local estate agent and got the train to Wrabness. It was an hour and three minutes door to door – perfect, she thought. The train was quiet, almost empty. Lucy sank into her table seat and opened her laptop. There were only three pictures on Rightmove of her house: the front of the house, a red door in a row of terraced cottages; a sitting room with a floral sofa and chair; and a kitchen with a kitchen table covered in a lace tablecloth. The front garden looked as if somebody had tried to tidy it up. The rooms looked old and forgotten, but what were pictures? Just a memory of what it was.

The train jerked and shunted a little as it left Liverpool Street. Lucy looked out of the window. She'd never seen this side of London by train and yet the buildings were so familiar to her: the Shard, Canary Wharf, HSBC, Deutsche Bank, the Olympic Stadium with its shops and restaurants and cable car. She watched the houses in the East End of London finally disappear and the landscape turn from urban sprawl to farmland. It felt alien to her to see such a landscape; she was used to terraced housing, busy roads, sirens, people, noise. The countryside rolled by like waves crashing onto a beach. Not a house in sight; the odd farm scattered between a patchwork of fields. The skies were open and unblocked by high-rise buildings. Tractors tootled busily across fields, horses nuzzled together, cows grazed. Lucy put her earphones in and set her mobile on the table. The beeping sound of the doors woke her. She must have dozed off. She sat up, startled, wondering if she'd slept through her stop. She had no idea where she was. A few people got on to the train and found their spaces. A lady sat opposite Lucy and smiled at her.

'Er, excuse me, what station is this?' Lucy asked.

'Chelmsford,' the woman replied, taking the *Daily Mail* from her bag.

'Oh, thank you,' Lucy replied, placing her earphones back into her ears.

As the train approached Manningtree station, Lucy stared out at the empty platform. The woman with the *Daily Mail* had got off at Colchester and Lucy was alone again in the carriage. As the train slowed to a stop, Lucy saw a boarded-up waiting room. It reminded her of her school days and the station she got out at when she was in senior school. Her stomach fluttered with nerves and excitement. She tucked her phone into her bag and made her way to the door. At the station entrance, she looked for the taxi rank and walked over to the first cab in the row.

'Are you booked?' she asked the driver.

'Nope, love, where do you want to go to?'

'Um, Wrabness. Lambourne Terrace – number three?' she said.

'No problem, love, in you get.' The cab driver looked in his rear-view mirror. 'Not from around here, then?' He adjusted the meter and set off.

'No, I'm from London,' she said, wriggling in her seat as she tried to do up the seat belt.

'You visiting friends?' he asked.

'No, I've come to look at a house, actually,' she said, catching his eye in the mirror.

'Nice part of the world. Clive Owen lives in Wrabness, although I've never caught sight of him. Big white modern-looking house behind electric gates.' He smiled. 'Who knows? You might get lucky and see him one day.'

'Maybe,' she said. 'I need to like the house first.' She hoped with every inch of her body the house would be right and that she would like it. She wouldn't mind bumping into Clive Owen either, although he had to be at least fifty-something now. She took in the view of the vast sandy shore with sailing boats littering it and absolutely no water at all. Odd, she thought. It hadn't even dawned on her that it was an estuary and the tide was out. A road sign read 'Welcome to Manningtree'. A collection of bikers stood eating burgers and drinking coffee at a burger van, beside a gaggle of swans and a sign saying 'slow, ducks crossing'. The road was winding and fast. She began to feel queasy as the taxi took each bend. The only passing traffic was motorbikes, their engines roaring.

'A bikers' paradise, this road.' The taxi driver laughed. 'They love this open stretch. There have been a few nasty crashes here, though, just people driving too fast.'

'God, that's awful,' Lucy said. She tried to take in her surroundings, but her phone pinged. It was Charlie.

Want to meet for lunch?

She read the message and replied hastily.

I can't. I have a meeting with Jo. Don't wait up, I'll be at work late.

She'd lied – her first ever lie to him about her whereabouts, but Jo knew what she was doing. If he did call her, she would cover for her. How many more lies would she have to tell? She wasn't a good liar and she was thankful this lie was by text. He couldn't hear her voice or see her fidget or twiddle her hair. But lying was her only way out; she had no choice. Tucking her phone back into her bag, the taxi pulled up outside number three Lambourne Terrace.

'Here's your address – number three, you said?' the cab driver said. 'That'll be sixteen pounds, please.' Lucy paid the cab driver and got out of the cab, taking his business card so she could book a return journey.

'Good luck with the viewing, love. Hope it's what you want. Call me if you need a lift to the station, the name's Dave.' He winked and indicated to pull out. She stood on the pavement alone, watching the cab disappear. As she waited for the agent to arrive she walked down the road: there were fields and, just beyond, the most amazing view of sailing boats on a huge expanse of water. She wasn't sure what river it was, but it was breath-taking.

A silver Audi pulled up and a young man got out carrying a bundle of keys and papers.

'Is it Lucy?' he said stretching out his arm to shake her hand. 'I'm Jack Williams from Parker and Lovell.'

'Yes, hi,' she replied, shaking his hand. 'I'm Lucy Carter, pleased to meet you.'

He was a little taller than her, dressed in a snappy charcoal-grey suit, light blue shirt and brown shoes. His hair was gelled and flicked, and he had a Joey Essex-style smile with dazzling teeth. Sharp, she thought, but not her type.

'Shall we go in?' He beckoned to her and led her up the bedraggled, unkempt pathway to the cottage.

'I'm afraid the garden needs some work,' he said. 'The property has been left empty for some time.'

'That's fine,' she said, brushing past an overhanging rose bush. 'How long has it been empty?'

'About two years. The owners inherited it and decided to sell, but I'm not sure if they ever lived here, to be honest.'

He opened the front door to a heap of junk mail and letters. He picked them up and left them on the hall table. The house smelt musty and damp. Jack guided Lucy around each room, she felt drawn to the cottage. It had a kitchen and sitting room downstairs and upstairs were a bathroom and two other rooms, one a bedroom and the other full of boxes and furniture.

The back garden was compact, with a small lawn and a rickety shed in one corner. It was overgrown with brambles and nettles and had a patio with enough space to fit a table for two by the kitchen door.

'I guess it's hard to see the potential when it's been left unlived in for so long,' Jack said.

'Hmm, maybe, but I like it, I like it a lot. Has the house had much interest?' she asked as she opened the under-stairs cupboard and peered in.

'This is the part of my spiel where I say yes and that it's an incredibly popular property, but to be honest, I can't. Yours is the first viewing in months. I don't know why, either. I think they'd accept an offer – they simply want to get shot of the property.'

Lucy didn't really care why nobody else had shown any interest in it. That was perfect – it meant she could go ahead and buy it with no challenges.

She wasted no time in putting in an offer that was £15,000 below the asking price. It did need work and a very good clean, but it was perfect for her and she loved its views of fields and the smell of the sea, just a stone's throw away.

Her offer was accepted with no quibbles. The vendor, as the agent had suggested, really wanted shot of the property.

Three months later, Lucy was the proud owner of number three Lambourne Terrace. She told nobody about her purchase except Jo, and had all correspondence from the solicitor sent to Jo's home address.

As the weeks passed, Lucy carried on as normal in London, saying nothing to Charlie. She met Jo to discuss her novel, and Jo would give her any correspondence from the solicitor. On the thirteenth of October, Lucy's life changed forever: she opened the letter from Stebbings Solicitors. As she read the first line; a tear trickled down her face.

'What's up, Luce?' Jo looked worried. Was the news bad? Had everything fallen through?

'I've done it, Jo! We've completed and the keys are at the solicitor's office. It's mine!' Lucy turned to Jo. 'It's mine.'

The two hugged. Lucy felt a wash of relief come over her in Jo's tight embrace. She'd finally be free.

On Monday, fifteenth of October, Lucy sat in the kitchen cupping her peppermint tea. It stung when the heat touched her lip. She tried to not show the pain. She watched him as he moved around the flat, collecting his wallet, his phone, his jacket. She sat in silence. He came over, the smell of aftershave heavy on his neck. He kissed her head and she flinched.

'I'll see you later,' he said, leaving her in the kitchen. She waited until the door had shut and she heard the main front door close. She walked to the window and watched him walk down the road as if nothing had happened – carefree, normal. She felt sick, knowing he had forced himself on her that morning, split her lip, raped her. Her eyes, bloodshot and swollen, still stung from the tears she had cried in the shower. Her lip was split from where he had punched her. She had bruising on her knees where he'd dragged her across the wooden floor and, if she'd shown her upper legs, she had bruising there from where he had forced himself on her. She hurriedly boxed and bagged her things, her hands shaking as she wrote on each box, and she tried to wrap precious items – her laptop, photos of her grandfather. Quickly, she carried everything downstairs to her Mini.

Her hand shook, she took a clean sheet of writing paper and penned her letter.

15th October

Charlie,

It is hard to put into words all that you did to me. This letter is a vain attempt to master the chaos in my mind. Sometimes I wish you could go through the pain you put me through, but really, I know in my heart that there is no way I'd want another soul to go through it.

I've held onto this pain for so many years because I genuinely believed that some day it would stop. I always believed you were something more than you appeared to be. But you only took advantage of my naivety, until you broke me into a million tiny pieces. You thought you were powerful because you played the attacker? You thought I was weak because I played the victim? But now I see you for who you are. How you crushed me until I couldn't breathe. "If you hadn't made me so angry, I wouldn't have hit you, locked you in a room," you'd say. After a time, I started to believe the fault was mine.

But today, I choose to stop blaming myself. There is nothing I did for you to hurt me with your fists, your words. I am not the names you called me. I am me. I am hope. I am dreams. I will be long-gone from your life and it will be too late to tell me you are sorry, sorry is just a word, meaningless to you. Today I want to be free.

Lucy

She left the note on the table, with no forwarding address and posted the keys back through the door.

She went to turn away from the flat's door, she jumped. Someone was there, she felt their presence behind her. She gasped. He'd come back, he'd forgotten something. She stood, her face against the door, her blood running cold, her breath held.

'Lucy?'

She closed her eyes.

'Rachel, hi,' she said nervously, worried she'd been seen packing the car, relief that it wasn't him.

'What have you done to your lip?' Rachel asked with concern, raising her hand to touch Lucy's face.

Lucy backed away. 'I tripped on the stairs yesterday. Silly, right? Thank goodness for alcohol – numbed the pain,' she lied.

'Right,' Rachel said, looking unsure. 'I wondered if you'd like a coffee? Are you free now?'

'I'm kind of in a hurry, Rach – deadline with a novel.'

'How about a quick one? It's just...' Rachel persisted.

'It's just what?' Lucy asked. What did Rachel want?

'Well, I heard you crying last night and Charlie shouting, I know it's none of my business, but are you guys OK?'

'Oh, it was nothing, really, you know how it is.' Lucy swallowed.

'But you were crying,' Rachel said, taking Lucy's hand.

'Yep, wedding stress. I'm sad that my grandfather won't be there to give me away. Really, I have to go now. Please don't worry, everything's fine.'

She left Rachel on the landing of the flats. Rachel didn't believe everything was fine. She didn't believe any of it.

As Lucy switched on the engine, she felt the nerves bubbling up. She'd done it, she'd finally escaped – now she just needed to drive away. She sat in the traffic on New Kings Road, turning off at Parsons Green to collect the new house keys from the solicitor. The drive out of London seemed to take an age but finally she was on the A12 heading for north Essex.

Chapter Six

Saturday, 16th November

As the sun rose in the sky, Lucy and Jo slept through not stirring from the morning chorus. It was only when Jo's phone buzzed that they began to stir.

'Did you sleep OK?' Jo asked, turning to face Lucy.

'Yes, when I finally closed my mind off. Did you?'

'Yep, considering. Let's not think about it too much today – it was probably just somebody going for a walk with their dog or a drunk from the local. Shall we head to the beach maybe pop into The Pier whilst we are there? We can work through your manuscript, sort out dates for the book launch, run through some ideas for images for the front cover and the blurb,' Jo said.

Lucy could always count on Jo to be the voice of reason. She had the knack of being able to calm a situation down. She was probably right – it had probably been a dog out last night, dashing for something it had seen in the hedge.

They'd slept in. It was already ten o'clock. The night before had shaken them both up. It may have been nothing at all, but neither of them thought that.

They climbed out of bed and made their way downstairs. Lucy turned each light switch off; they'd left the house lit up like Blackpool illuminations the night before, too scared to be in the dark.

The kettle bubbled away while the bread toasted. When it finally popped up and the kettle clicked off, the two sat together munching warm buttered toast and a mug of peppermint tea and coffee. Leaving their plates in the sink, Lucy went into the sitting room and opened the curtains. The sun beamed through the windows and the rays of light that shone into the sitting room lit up particles of dust that floated and danced in the light. Jo was already in the bathroom brushing her teeth and having a quick shower. When she emerged from the bathroom, clad in a towel, she smiled at Lucy. 'You OK, kiddo?' she said.

'Yep, I'm going to jump in the shower too, then I'm ready to rock.'

Jo took a clean pair of skinny jeans from her case and a black ribbed jumper, brushed her sleek dark hair and applied her make-up. While she waited for Lucy to change, she went downstairs and washed up after breakfast, double-checked the back door was locked, and opened the velvet curtain at the front door. It was a gorgeous autumnal morning without a cloud in the sky.

As she read through her emails on her phone, Lucy bounded down the stairs.

'Right, shall we go?' she said, taking her jacket from the radiator. It was toasty warm.

Leaving the house locked up they drove to the beach, with Jo clutching Lucy's manuscript. Lucy parked the Mini in the usual spot and headed down to the beach steps. She threw a picnic rug on the cold stone step, and they sat and looked out at the now familiar landscape of the Maersk containers and cranes. As Jo pulled out the manuscript, the breeze picked up and blew the envelope out of her hands. Lucy jumped up and grabbed it before it headed into the murky sea water. The waves rippled onto the beach and the pebbles clattered quietly as they washed back out to sea. An elderly-looking dog sniffed along the beach, its owner ambling behind, limping slightly. Lucy sat back down next to Jo and wrapped her scarf more tightly around her neck.

'So, front cover,' Jo said. 'Any thoughts?'

'I still like my idea of the mother's hand reaching out to her child as the main image, but maybe with a dark grey backdrop,' Lucy said. She'd decided on the front cover when she'd written the story in her head a year ago.

'Perfect. If I get the ball rolling on Monday with Giles, we could get it out and launched by June. This is going to be such a hit, Lucy, I can feel it in my bones. I think you might even get another television drama out of it. The Beeb loves your work.'

If Jo was right and it was another hit, it would push Lucy right up in the Nielsen chart of bestsellers.

'So, *Hold my Hand* by Lucy Carter, grey front and back cover, an image of the mother and daughter's hands – it will look fab, I can see it now. I'll get us booked into the Savoy for the book launch. This will fly off the shelves, I have no doubt.' Jo handed Lucy the manuscript, ran down the beach and did a cartwheel. Lucy sat on the step, bent over with laughter.

'Come on, Lucy, come and cartwheel!' Jo shouted up the beach. Lucy tucked the manuscript back into the envelope and popped it into her satchel, buckling it closed and placing her jacket on top to shield it from prying eyes.

'I'm coming,' she squealed, racing down the beach. Throwing her hands onto the sand she cartwheeled, one, two, three times. The two friends lost all their inhibitions and played like children. As they pulled their clothing back into place, they saw the guy on the bike. He stopped at the beach wall and rested his leg on it, balancing himself as he watched Lucy and Jo. As they walked back up the beach, laughing and giggling and falling into each other, Lucy brushed her hair from her face and tightened her ponytail. She saw him watching.

She blushed slightly and glanced at Jo. 'We have a spectator.'

Jo looked up and saw the guy on the bike, smiling.

'Oh bugger. Do you think he saw us? Shit!'

'I think he did,' Lucy said. 'Let's pretend we haven't noticed. Act normally.'

The girls went back to the step. As they sat back down, the guy took his foot off the wall and pedalled past them, smiling at them.

'Great day for cartwheeling on the beach,' he said and rode off, smiling to himself.

'He saw us, then – shit, how embarrassing,' Lucy said.

'Oh well, he spoke to us too,' Jo said. 'A chink of the ice has been broken, I guess, and he's right – it is a good day for a cartwheel. Although I've got a bit of a head rush. I'm not sure I could do it again. I think the last time I cartwheeled was when I was about twelve.'

'Shall we get something to eat, maybe at the wine bar around the corner?' Lucy said, her stomach reminding her it was lunchtime.

Scooping up the rug and folding it, they walked back to the car and popped the rug in the boot. The wine bar was a short walk from the car, not even a hundred yards. They walked along the main pier. The harbour was busy with boats coming and going. The wine bar looked like it had stood still in time. It was nothing like a trendy London wine bar; the dark wooden floor was etched with wood worm and stains from spilt drinks. The walls were adorned with paintings of the sea and a portrait of Samuel Pepys; the bar was a dark wood and covered in towelling beer mats. An old leather sofa sat against a wall, with dark wooden chairs and tables. It wasn't quite the kind of wine bar Lucy and Jo were used to. The barmaid was bottle-blonde with fuchsia-pink lipstick that matched the ruffled blouse she wore.

'Hello ladies, what can I get you?' she asked in a broad Essex accent, smiling at them and resting her hands on the beer pumps.

'Are you serving food?' Lucy asked, searching the bar for a menu.

'I am.' She handed them a menu each. 'The specials are sea bass which has been caught locally and a homemade locally caught crab pâté. Can I get you some drinks while you decide?'

'I'll have a gin and slimline tonic, with a slice of lime if you've got it,' Lucy said.

'Me too,' Jo chirped in.

'Lemon, I'm afraid, will that do?' She filled the slim glasses with ice. 'Gordon's or Beefeater?'

This definitely is a wine bar from prehistoric times, Lucy thought. Gordon's or Beefeater gin, not even a sniff of rhubarb-infused gin.

'Um, Gordon's,' they said in unison.

As she pressed the glasses to the optic, Jo and Lucy perused the menu.

'I think I'll go for the crab pâté,' Lucy said, placing the menu back down on the bar.

'Me too,' Jo said. Taking their drinks, they sat on the Chesterfield sofa, which made a squidgy crackling sound as they sank into it.

Clinking their glasses together, they took a sip of their drinks.

'Here's to your local wine bar.' Jo smiled. The barmaid disappeared into the kitchen with their orders, leaving them alone.

'Do you think it's always so quiet?' Lucy whispered. She wasn't sure why she was whispering, as the bar was empty, but at the same time, she didn't want to be heard either.

'I guess it's lunchtime in this sleepy fishing town,' Jo said. 'Maybe it gets busier in the evening – why don't we see? We could come back down tonight, it's Saturday night after all. Why don't we book a cab and have some fun?' She chuckled. 'Phone a cab now, let's sort it.'

Lucy dialled the number of the local cab company and booked a cab for an eight o'clock pick-up from her home and an eleven o'clock collection from Harwich pier. She didn't know the name of the wine bar, but they'd find it and could easily walk back to the pier when it closed. As she ended the call, the lady in the fuchsia blouse appeared at their table with a generous portion of crab pâté and a basket of brown toast. As Jo and Lucy tucked into their lunch, they chatted about the next novel Lucy was writing and the love letters she had come across and still hadn't finished reading.

After spending the best part of two hours in the wine bar, they were ready to leave. As they were about to head out of the door, Lucy turned around. 'Oh, by the way,' she said, 'what's this wine bar called?'

'Samuel Pepys, my love, the oldest wine bar in Harwich,' she replied, smiling.

'Great, thank you. It's been lovely, and the crab pâté was to die for.'

The door swished shut behind them and Lucy and Jo headed back to the car. 'Should have known it was called Samuel Pepys.' Lucy laughed. 'There was a socking great painting of him on the wall. We must have seemed like a couple of complete fuckwits from London.'

They parked the car outside Lucy's house and went in.

'Well, today has been fun,' Jo said as she collapsed onto the sofa, 'and tonight will be great too. We could hitch up with a fisherman.' She laughed.

It was already six o'clock. The cab was arriving in two hours, which gave them enough time to shower, get ready and have a drink. It had been ages since Lucy and Jo had gone out together in London and really let their hair down. They took it in turns to shower and dry their hair. A heap of clothes cluttered the bed until they had picked out their favourite outfits: Lucy opted for a black leather mini skirt, fitted black polo-neck and stiletto-heeled ankle boots. Jo wore tight black trousers, strappy gun-metal-coloured heels and a sheer black top that showed the contours of her body, and a pretty black lace bra. They looked sleek and super-cool with a London edge. They waited downstairs with large gin and tonics until the cab pulled up. Lucy locked the front door behind them and closed the gate. It was the same taxi driver Lucy had met when she first arrived at Manningtree station. He smiled at her as she opened the door and climbed into the taxi.

'Where to?' he asked.

'Samuel Pepys in Harwich,' Lucy said with confidence.

'Right you are. Out for the night, girls?' he asked, looking in his rear-view mirror.

'We certainly are,' Jo said, 'Do you know the pub?'

'Samuel Pepys? Yes, I know it,' he replied. When they arrived, he stopped the meter. 'That'll be eleven pounds exactly.'

They paid and got out of the cab.

'Samuel Pepys, here we come,' said Jo. 'Let's go and have some fun, Lucy Luce.'

The wine bar was definitely different to how it had been on their lunchtime visit. The bar had a row of young men drinking at it and in the far corner was a live band. As they walked through the double doors, men turned to look at them. Lucy and Jo felt a little uncomfortable but they were in now, they'd been noticed, and there was no way of turning back. They made their way to the bar, still with the men watching them as if they'd never seen two girls before. As they reached the bar, the men moved aside for them, smiling.

The lady in the pink blouse was still on duty, this time with the help of a younger barmaid, wearing jeans and T-shirt, her hair tied up in a high ponytail.

'Ah, you two are back.' She smiled. 'Two gins, or something different?'

'Two double gin and tonics this time,' Jo said. She paid for the drinks. As they were about to move away from the bar, Lucy turned quickly and knocked into a man who was standing right behind her, spilling her drink. She was about to say sorry but, as she looked up, she recognised him. It was the guy from the beach she kept seeing on his bike.

'I'm so sorry,' she said, feeling herself blush. She was hoping he hadn't recognised her as the crazy cartwheeling girl. He stood there smiling at her. Every inch of him was heart-lurchingly gorgeous. He had a knock-out smile that showed a line of straight white teeth, and wore a cool T-shirt, jeans that hung off his hips, and Vans-style trainers. Had he recognised her?

she wondered. She definitely looked different at night – and a little less windswept. He stood there, still smiling. She wanted to say, 'excuse me, can I get past?', but she also wanted to stare at him for longer. She felt a nudge in her back as Jo jabbed her to keep moving, 'Sorry again,' she said and sidled past him. He followed her with his eyes and saw where she went to sit. He was with the crowd of men at the bar, a mixed-age group from perhaps mid-twenties to early forties. He was chatting to a guy in a baseball cap and with dark hair, leaning against the bar drinking a bottle of Budweiser.

As Jo placed her bag on the free table they'd found, she glanced around the people in the bar. 'That bloke you bumped into? That's the guy on the bike, isn't it? He looks good tonight – and his mate in the baseball cap is cute too. We might get to meet them properly.' Jo laughed.

As the live band kicked off with George Michael's 'Faith', the volume of chatter in the bar escalated. Lucy and Jo laughed together. The gin was going down remarkably swiftly – perhaps a little too swiftly. It was soon Lucy's turn to go to the bar.

'Same again?' she said, swivelling off the high stool and adjusting her skirt before making her way to the bar. All eyes were on her as she made her way to the bar, already feeling a little unstable on her heels. The thought of having to try and navigate her way through on her own filled her with dread. She hated that part of buying drinks; it made her feel awkward. Or did she feel like that because of Charlie? She had always been made to feel she was deliberately tempting other men whenever she went out with him. Her hands were clammy. She adjusted her skirt again, pressing her hands against it to dry them a touch. She felt the need to turn and look at Jo for reassurance.

'Ben, move out the way and let this pretty young lady through,' one of the guys said. Lucy looked at the man who had asked Ben to move. His hair was short, dark, he had a slight beard and kind eyes. He smiled at her and held his arm out, as if ushering her safely to the bar. When she turned to walk away from the bar, the guy on the bike caught her eye again. 'Sorry, I'm still in your way,' he said, smiling the smile that she thought was deliriously gorgeous.

'Oh, it's fine,' she said, smiling and trying not to spill either of the glasses this time around.

***

He looked at her face, trying to figure her out. Who was she? he thought. He'd seen her so many times in the last month, yet he'd never seen her before. She seemed familiar and yet she was a complete stranger. He wanted to get to know her: he definitely wanted to find out who she was and why she sat on the beach in the autumn and winter every day. She was pretty hot and tonight had an edgy coolness about her. He let her past again, kicked himself for not saying hello properly or introducing himself. Instead his gaze followed her back to where she was sitting with her friend. As she sat down, the guy with the baseball cap turned around from the bar and looked at Lucy and Jo. Jo caught his eye and smiled. He smiled back then turned away.

'I think we have some interest from the guys at the bar,' Jo said, shielding her mouth with her glass.

'Do we?' Lucy said, searching her bag for her lip gloss. There was only one guy who had caught her attention; the guy on the bike. She wasn't interested in any of the other guys. There was something about him she liked, even though she didn't know him.

'Don't look now, but they're coming over,' Jo said, taking a sip from her glass.

Lucy tucked her lip gloss back in her bag and took rather a large mouthful of gin. Dutch courage, she thought.

The guys took seats at the high table close to the band.

'False alarm,' Jo said, and laughed, shaking her hair and almost falling off the high stool.

'You're such a muppet, Jo.' Lucy giggled. 'I'm kind of relieved they didn't come over. It's fun only being here with you. It's been so long since I've been able to let my hair down and not be worried about the consequences at home. I feel so much more relaxed. And if it wasn't for you having my back, it would never have happened.'

'I'll drink to that,' Jo said, clinking her glass with Lucy's. 'I'm a brilliant friend, although I could do with a man's touch once in a while. Man, I've missed it.' She laughed tipsily. As the band played on, Jo and Lucy drank and laughed, forgetting about the guys at the high table. But the guys hadn't forgotten them; their attention was on Jo and Lucy, the guy in the baseball cap checking out Jo and the guy on the bike keeping a watchful gaze on Lucy.

Lucy let her head rest on the table.

'Jo, I feel a bit tipsy,' she said and laughed.

'Me too. Our taxi should be here soon anyway. Let's get out of here,' Jo said. As the two girls wobbled off their stools and straightened up before making for the door, the guys at the high table near them glanced over. Lucy adjusted her skirt and tried to keep her bag from falling off her shoulder. She must have tried four or five times before giving up and holding it instead. There was a comical loveliness about them; they had simply laughed and chatted all evening and let the alcohol take them to an enjoyable oblivion. They left the bar, trying to pull the double doors open and failing miserably until they realised that pushing would be easier. Lucy doubled over in a drunken laugh when she realised that she was incapable of doing anything properly. They'd probably drunk their body weight in gin and tonic that night. The guys watched as the girls toppled out of the bar. As they rolled out onto the pavement, they were struck by the cold night air. The astringent smell of the sea almost had the same effect as smelling salts. They stood on the pavement, gently swaying back and forth.

'Do you think anybody saw us leaving?' Lucy asked, realising that they had taken an age trying to master the door, that could only ever have been push or pull.

'Um, I think we had an audience, yep,' Jo said, 'but who cares? Tonight is tonight and tomorrow is another day.'

'Did you see the guys at the table?' Lucy asked.

'The cute ones? Yeah, I saw them and they probably saw us. They didn't take their eyes of us for most of the night – didn't you notice?' Jo said. 'It was pretty obvious they were interested in what they saw. They were playing it cool, I'd say.'

'Played it too cool, though, didn't they? They didn't talk to us and I'm not likely to come here on my own when you leave,' Lucy said, dismayed that she hadn't got to know them.

'Well, we can come down tomorrow night, if you like,' Jo said, holding her knee up to balance her bag on it as she rummaged for her Marlboro Gold and a lighter, before Dave's taxi arrived to scoop them up and take them home.

'Ha, found them,' Jo said, waving the cigarettes jubilantly at Lucy. 'Why is it you put them in the same place you always put them and then when you go to take one they've moved, like they're having their own little party inside my bag? It's the same with my lipstick. It's never where I put it, it's always had a rejig in my bag. Fancy a smoky Jo ciggie?' she said, smiling and handing the packet to Lucy.

'You're leaving tomorrow, aren't you Jo? It's Sunday,' Lucy questioned, taking a cigarette from Jo and sparking up. She felt a sudden head rush and wobbled in her heels. As she inhaled, she leant against the wine bar's wall and placed a foot up on the wall, looking like a cool, moody model on a night shoot.

'Yeah, I know, but I could get an early train on Monday as long as I'm back in London for my meeting at 11.30am. I can go straight to Browns after that for brunch, which works perfectly. I'll leave my case at reception – that won't be a problem. Shall I stay until then? Does that work for you?' she asked, blowing smoke into the cool night air.

'That sounds perfect, Jo, thank you.' Lucy stubbed out her cigarette on the ground. The door of the wine bar swung open and the laughter and deep voices of the guys from the bar rolled out onto the street. Lucy looked up. It was the guy on the bike, his arm around his friend wearing the baseball cap.

'Come on, boys,' came the slurred voice of the bearded guy. 'Mr Wings closes in twenty minutes. My belly feels like it hasn't been fed for a week!'

'Yeah, alright, Pete, we're coming. Is there any time when you don't think about food?' asked the guy in the baseball cap.

The bright lights of a silver estate car with 'Dave's Taxis' advertised along the door pulled up outside the wine bar, narrowly missing the kerb. Jo walked up to the taxi and bent down to the open window, checking it was their booked cab.

She turned to Lucy. 'Come on, Lucy, it's our cab, let's go.'

Lucy pushed herself off the wall and walked towards the taxi, trying to walk in a straighter line than she had managed to walk out of the wine bar.

'Night, Lucy,' came a voice. Lucy turned and looked at the men. She had no idea which one had spoken. She glanced at all of them briefly then got into the taxi and closed the door. She said nothing. She didn't want to acknowledge them knowing her name. She didn't know them – and what if they were like *him*, like Charlie?

The diesel engine of the taxi turned over and Dave's light on the roof shone a neon white in the darkness, leaving the men behind.

'Cute girls,' said the guy in the baseball cap, turning to walk down the dimly lit street towards the pier.

'Nice bum, the one in the mini skirt,' replied the guy on the bike. 'In fact, more than nice. I wonder who they are?' He walked a few steps behind the bearded guy, who was making a beeline for Mr Wings.

'Rob, Ben, I'll catch you lads tomorrow. I've sunk too many beers tonight. I need some food. Mr Wings does the meanest chicken chow mein this side of town. A man has to look after himself.' He laughed while patting his stomach. 'See you at the harbour at midday, night boys.'

The two guys took a left down an alley, their shadows disappearing from sight as the streetlights turned off.

***

Jo and Lucy snuggled under the duvet to warm up.

'One of them knows my name,' Lucy said, breaking the cosy silence.

'What do you mean, one of them knows your name? One of who?' Jo asked, shuffling up the bed and turned to face Lucy.

'One of those guys – he said "night, Lucy" as I walked over to the taxi. He knew my name. How did he know my name?'

'Which one knew your name?' Jo asked, switching on the bedside lamp.

'I don't know which one, but one of them said it. How do they know my name, Jo?'

'He probably heard me saying your name when I said it was our taxi, you plum. Just a bit of drunken bravado, no doubt. Shame we don't know which one it was. Are you ready to sleep now?' she said, shifting her pillow back and leaning over to turn the light out.

As the moon shone high in the sky, the wind blew through the branches of the tree outside the bedroom window. The smaller branches had a splattering of burnt orange and brown leaves, which clung on until a gust of wind caught them and blew them to the ground. The branches tapped and swished lightly on the window, in a melodic way, and the girls fell asleep to the dulcet tones of the wintery night.

Chapter Seven

Sunday, 17th November

In London, the phone rang on the bedside table, the screen showing *'Caller Unknown'*. A hand crawled out from under the pillow and picked up the phone.

'Hello?'

'Is that Charlie Wainwright?' the voice on the line said.

'Yes.'

'This is PC Mackenzie from Essex Police,' said the caller.

'Right,' Charlie replied, still half asleep.

'We've had a complaint from a Miss Carter regarding nuisance calls and unwanted messages.'

Charlie sat bolt upright in bed. 'Hang on a second, who is this?' He was pissed off that somebody had had the nerve to wake him on a Sunday morning and pretend to be the police from Essex.

'As I said, it's PC Mackenzie and I am calling regarding a complaint we have received from Miss Carter. Please do not contact Miss Carter again by phone, email or social media. She doesn't want to hear from you again.'

'Right, wait a minute … Miss Carter – Lucy – is my fiancée and you have no right to tell me what I can or can't do. Who the fuck do you think you are?' His voice was raised and his anger rising.

'Mr Wainwright, please refrain from using that type of language with me. As I have said, I am PC Mackenzie from Essex Police. I am telling you that you are not to contact Miss Carter again. She doesn't want to have any contact with you. If you don't listen to this advice, you will be arrested.' PC Mackenzie changed his tone, adding a level of authority. 'She has reported your calls. You are not permitted to make contact with Miss Carter, and failure to comply will result in immediate arrest. Miss Carter does not want you arrested; she has asked us to stop you from contacting her.'

'She is my fucking fiancée, for fuck's sake! What the fuck? We have a wedding to plan – how the fuck am I supposed to plan a wedding and honeymoon without speaking to her, the fucking bitch?'

'I hate to be the one to break the news to you, Mr Wainwright, but I think you might find the wedding is off. As I said, if you contact her again, you will be arrested. I hope I have made myself clear. Goodbye.' PC Mackenzie walked away from the phone. 'Bloody hell, Wills, that was one angry guy. I reckon if I'd knocked at his door, he would have lamped me.' He logged the date and time of the call he had made.

'I could hear his voice from here, Mackie. I don't think you've heard the last of him. Something tells me he's not going to walk away quietly. What are you going to tell Lucy?'

'That I don't know. I'll make a house call and have a chat with her, try and work out what to say on my drive over there. Either way, I think we're still going to have a pretty scared girl on our hands. She's a pretty thing too – what an idiot he was to lose her. Are you OK to man the station while I drive over? I shouldn't be long – half an hour max, I reckon.'

'Sure, no worries. Good luck, mate!'

PC Mackenzie took the squad keys and laptop and drove down the quiet road, taking a left into the main village then right into Lambourne Terrace. He pulled up outside number three and waited for a few minutes before he took his file and made his way up Lucy's pathway.

He knocked loudly on the door and turned his walkie-talkie down before the door was answered.

'Miss Carter, could we have a chat?' he asked, scanning the street before he was invited in and the door closed. The net curtain of the terrace cottage opposite twitched. Neighbourhood Watch at its best, he thought: Gladys Pope ready to catch the latest village gossip. No doubt she would be on the phone letting the villagers know the police were at number three.

'Can I get you a tea or coffee? I'm afraid I only have peppermint tea,' Lucy said, showing him into the sitting room.

'A coffee would be great – milk, no sugar. Thanks.'

Lucy left PC Mackenzie alone in the sitting room.

'Fancy a coffee, Jo? The police are here – well, PC Mackenzie at least. He's sitting in the sitting room,' Lucy said, standing on her tiptoes showing her midriff as she stretched to reach mugs from the back of the cupboard.

'Oh, I thought I heard the door. Want me to sit with you?' Jo asked, looking up from typing an email to Giles at HarperCollins.

'Yeah, could you? D'you mind?'

'No worries. Let me finish this email to Giles and I'll help bring the drinks through. Mackenzie – is that the one we made the report to?'

Lucy stirred the coffees until all the granules had disappeared and the milk swirled around the top of the mugs, then discarded her teabag in the bin.

'Yep, it is. Right, come on, let's go through. Can you grab your mug, Jo?'

Lucy placed the coffee on the table and sat on the edge of the armchair, her arms crossed. Jo sat on the bean bag and PC Mackenzie sat alone on the sofa.

'So, I phoned Charlie,' he began. 'Not an easy call.'

'Why, what do you mean?' Lucy asked, leaning forward in her chair and searching his face.

'Let's just say he wasn't very receptive. He was angry.'

'So what did he say? Was he threatening?' Jo took a slurp of her coffee.

'He swore a lot, he called you a fucking bitch and said I had no fucking right to tell him what to do. He said you were his fiancée. Is that true?' he continued.

Jo looked at Lucy. 'Tell him everything, Lucy, you have to tell him everything.'

'What do you need to tell me?' PC Mackenzie asked. 'If it will shed some light on his anger and his reasons for harassing you, we may be able to deal with this. But to be honest, it doesn't sound like my call fazed him. It just made him angrier, and I can't see that changing.' PC Mackenzie took out his laptop. 'I will take anything you say down as a statement. If you can tell us anything else relevant, then we can get the Met involved, but at the moment all you've told us about is nuisance calls and messages. We can't arrest him for that, unless you want to press charges, unless there is something else. Something more serious.'

Lucy stared into space, wishing she was anywhere else, wishing she'd never gone to the wine bar on Fulham Road three years ago. If she'd gone somewhere else, she would never have met him. If she hadn't played the game she wouldn't be sitting here with a policeman asking her awkward questions. The game she and Jo would play when they were in their early twenties, carefree. Placing a bet as to how they could get a guy to buy them a drink. A ridiculous game but always timed, a ten second rule. She played it that night in a bar, Charlie their target. She won, but did she?

'It's not just the messages,' she stammered. 'I received a parcel when I first moved in. From him.'

'Do you still have it?' PC Mackenzie asked.

'Yes. I didn't open it until Jo arrived, I was too frightened to,' she continued.

'Why were you frightened of a parcel?' PC Mackenzie asked.

Lucy's eyes glazed over. PC Mackenzie recognised the look on her face: the glazing over that only comes when the fear inside a victim's body is ripping them to pieces, shattering their confidence and their ability to speak up and tell somebody what's happening.

'Nobody knows I'm here except Jo. I bought the house with money my grandfather had left me. I found the house on Rightmove at an internet café in Putney, so he couldn't trace my history on my laptop. All my solicitor's letters were sent to Jo and she's the only person who knows this address. I haven't told a soul. I left him in October with a letter saying I was leaving, and it was over. I posted my keys to our flat back through the door and left. Rachel, my neighbour, saw me that day, but I lied to her, said I couldn't talk, that I had a deadline to meet. I got in the car and drove, I just fucking drove. I kept driving until I couldn't see London any more, until I didn't recognise the roads, I just kept driving, I just kept driving, do you hear me? I kept going until I...' Her head fell into her hands and she cried, rocking backwards and forwards like an inconsolable child.

'Lucy, take your time, it's alright,' PC Mackenzie said. Jo put her arms around Lucy and cradled her. 'You said you received a parcel. What was in it?'

'A scarlet Dior lipstick in a box stuffed with pink tissue paper. It was from him. I know it was, and he knows where I am. He's here, he's here, I know he is, he's watching me.' She looked up momentarily, her eyes bloodshot and her face streaked with tears. Her nose ran, and she wiped it on her sleeve, leaving a silvery smear like the trail of a slug.

'Lucy, the parcel, do you still have it?' PC Mackenzie asked.

Lucy stared into the fire. She liked lighting the fire: she watched the flames jump and dance around the logs, sparks flying like fireflies on a balmy summer's evening. Now it was dead, grey ashes. She tried to remember the flames, she tried to remember life before him, she tried to find a place in her soul that was happy. But it didn't exist; it was broken, she was broken. She felt as grey and black as the hearth.

'Lucy?' PC Mackenzie's voice broke her trance.

'Yes,' she said, still staring into the hearth. 'I need to go to the loo.' She got up and walked up the stairs, one step at a time as if every stair was an unachievable climb. She stood in the bathroom and stared at herself in the mirror, stared at her bloodshot eyes and tear-streaked face, the reflection of a damaged girl. Running the cold water until it was icy cold, she gripped the basin so hard that her nails dug into the porcelain. She doused her face with cold water and stared again into the mirror. What had he done to her? Sighing, she left the bathroom and went back downstairs, where Jo and PC Mackenzie waited for her.

'Sorry,' she said, 'I needed to take a moment. It's under the stairs in the cupboard. Jo put it there so I didn't have to see it or be reminded of it.' Her face felt cooler, thanks to the cold water, and her thoughts were more collected.

'Jo, could I ask you to get it?' he asked, leaning forward.

'Sure,' Jo said, getting up and leaving the room.

'Lucy, is there anything else you need to tell me? I know this is difficult and I can see you are distressed but I need to know everything. Everything you can tell us will help us and we can pursue this.'

As Lucy was about to answer, PC Willis radioed in on the walkie-talkie.

'Sorry, one moment. Don't be alarmed but I'm going to ask PC Willis to come over. Is that OK?'

'Yes, that's fine,' she said, her face blank, her eyes wide.

'Bravo November Five, are you receiving? Over.'

The radio crackled and buzzed until the response came through,

'Bravo November Five receiving, over.'

'Can you attend number three Lambourne Terrace? Over.'

'Received, I'm on my way, over.'

Moments later, there was a knock at the door. Jo jumped up from the bean bag. 'I'll get it.'

'You've got a good friend there, Lucy,' PC Mackenzie said, smiling at Lucy. His face told her that he could be trusted.

The net curtain opposite twitched again. 'There's something going on at number three, Stanley,' Gladys called from her place at the window. 'Both police con-stu-ba-buls are there. I knew there was something fishy about that 'ouse and it being empty for so long. A young girl answered the door – different girl I saw moving in, Stan, are you listening to me? Turn the telly off, would you?'

Gladys Pope lived at number eight Lambourne Terrace. She was something of a busybody: she knew the ins and outs of everybody's business in the village and she made it her job to find out any gossip first. Her curtain regularly twitched and Stan, her husband, who had put up with her busybody ways for years, would sit in his chair, the football on, trying not to become involved in her need to spy on everyone in the village. She was a large woman who liked to think she was the matriarch of the village. She had beady, penetrating eyes in a face that was leathery and wrinkled, and wiry iron-grey hair cut short with a blue rinse though it. She worked as a cleaner in the post office.

'Come away from the window, would you, woman? Leave the poor girl alone, you've no idea what's going on,' Stan grumbled from his chair and turned the football up even louder.

'Well, nobody calls both police out unless it's something serious. Maybe there's been a murder. You mark my words, there'll be something in the *Gazette* tomorrow,' she said, heaving herself away from the window and tucking the curtain back into place.

Lucy could hear voices in the hallway then Jo ushered PC Willis into the sitting room. As Jo closed the front door, she spotted the curtain opposite move quickly back into position. Neighbourhood Watch, she thought. Welcome to village life. She closed the front door.

'Coffee with milk and sugar, did you say?' she said. She left the sitting room and went through to the kitchen to make coffee. While the kettle boiled, she closed the kitchen door and dialled a number on her mobile.

'Giles, hi, it's Jo. Apologies for calling on a Sunday, but something has cropped up and I'm going to have to cancel our meeting tomorrow. Can I call you and rearrange when I'm back in town?'

'Sure, no worries. Everything OK?'

'Yep, everything's fine. I'm just out of town for a few days, probably until the end of the week. I'll call you when I'm back.'

Jo left her phone on the table and took the four drinks into the sitting room. She placed them on the table and took the empty mugs back into the kitchen.

'Lucy, this is my colleague PC Willis.'

'I know, I recognise him,' Lucy said, 'I met him when I first moved in.' She cupped her mug in her hands.

'Did you?' PC Mackenzie replied hesitantly.

'Yeah, when I moved in the previous owner had left some belongings in the house, a typewriter and notes. I took them down to the station to hand them in and your colleague told me I could keep them.'

'Ah yes, I remember. I thought you looked familiar,' PC Willis interjected. 'You brought in the old typewriter. Did you throw it away?'

'No, I kept them. I'm a writer and the typewriter is special. Somebody used that to write with before computers. I couldn't throw it away. It's in my writing room now along with the notes, which turned out to be wartime love letters...' Talking about the typewriter and notes seemed to calm Lucy.

'Quite a find,' replied PC Mackenzie, taking a mouthful of coffee. 'Does it work?' He asked Lucy, interested in her find.

'Yes, it does. It's a bit heavy going compared to my laptop but it works.' She said.

'Well, that's good. Now, are you able to tell us some more about Charlie?' PC Mackenzie asked. Lucy hesitated, her eyes went back to the fire again. She swallowed and took a deep breath.

'Take your time. There's no rush and we can always continue another day if it gets too much for you,' PC Willis said.

'Yes, I'm OK. I'm sorry, I didn't mean to swear or cry. It's just….' She looked at the policemen. They were young yet they had a calming presence. She felt they could sense her fear and unease. She wondered if they would understand how she felt, what Charlie was like.

'So, the box, the gift? Do you remember the date it arrived?'

She nodded. 'Yes, I moved in on Monday the fifteenth of October and the parcel arrived on Wednesday the fourteenth of November by DPD at about 9am. I remember it being early morning because it woke me. I wasn't expecting anything in the post or even by courier, not yet at any rate. All the mail that has been coming here has been for Mrs Richardson – that's who I bought the house from,' she said, swivelling in her chair to look at Jo. 'All of my legal letters were sent to Jo's address in London and I had no mail coming here. I still don't. Not yet anyway, I do most things online.'

PC Willis scanned over the parcel. It had come from London, but he was unable to make out the postal drop off point as the DPD driver had stamped across it.

'Did you sign for it?' PC Mackenzie asked. If they could get a little more on this, they might be closer to finding where the parcel had started its journey and who the sender was.

'Yes, on one of those hand-held devices.'

'I know what you mean. Would you be able to give a description of the driver? We might be able to locate his depot.'

'I vaguely remember him – tallish, dark hair, Eastern European accent, I think, but that's about it. That could be any courier, really.'

'Yes, it could, but that's not to say it won't help. Is there anything else?' PC Mackenzie typed on his laptop.

'Tell them about the room, Lucy,' Jo said, clasping Lucy's hand.

'What room?'

'In London,' Lucy said, 'there was a room in the apartment we had. When I moved in, it was locked. I thought it was a study, private. I didn't think anything of it. When I asked Charlie about it, he said it had to be locked because it contained sensitive material and he couldn't risk it being stolen.'

'Like what?'

'Charlie works in the City, in equities or something. I don't really understand it. He used to say the room was locked because he kept things in there that related to his clients and equities. I don't know, I just believed him.'

'Right,' Mackenzie said typing Lucy's words onto the screen.

'And then once when we went out, I did something wrong. He was angry with me because I talked to another guy, a friend of mine. When we got home, he unlocked the door. There were no lights in the room, it was just a dark room. He threw me on the floor and hit me, told me I was bad, a slut, that I would stay there until I had learned my lesson.' She sobbed into her hands.

'How long were you locked in the room for?' PC Mackenzie asked.

'I don't know, maybe a couple of hours,' Lucy said, reliving it in her mind.

'How often did this happen?' PC Mackenzie asked.

'Weekly, monthly, and then less often,' she said, her gaze fixed on the fire.

'Did he do anything else? Did he assault you?'

Lucy looked away. If he saw her eyes, he would know.

'No,' she lied.

'Is there anything else you'd like to tell us?'

'The bins,' Jo interrupted. 'Sorry, but it might be something.'

'What about the bins?' PC Willis asked, leaning forward in his seat.

'Well, on Friday night, we had been at the beach all day,' Jo said, looking at Lucy as if to say 'don't worry, I'll tell this part'.

'What beach were you at?' PC Mackenzie asked.

'Harwich,' Jo replied.

'So what happened at the beach?' PC Mackenzie asked.

'Well, Lucy and I went to the beach on Friday. We were cartwheeling on the sand, I don't know – being frivolous, carefree. We noticed some guy smile and watch us. We've seen him a few times now, cycling past us, always in the same spot.'

'Some guy? Did you talk to him? You said you'd seen him a few times,' PC Mackenzie said.

'Nope, he commented on our cartwheels – he said something like "it's a good day for a cartwheel" then smiled and cycled off. Why?'

'Just wondered. Got a description of him?' Mackenzie asked, looking at Jo.

'Umm, medium height I guess. He was on a red racer, wearing a navy fleece hoodie. Strawberry-blond hair, nice smile, slightly weather-beaten, tanned face, regular build. But we saw him in the bar too with his friends, just a guy we'd seen about, I don't think there's anything bad about him.'

'OK. So, the bins – why did you mention the bins?'

'When we got back from the beach, we had supper – we ate at nine-ish. We drank a bottle of wine between us and then had a cigarette in the garden. It was dark but I don't know the exact time – about ten-ish, I suppose. We were chatting and then there was a clatter of a bin lid – Lucy's got one of those metal bins, you know the ones I mean. Anyway, the clatter came from the front of the house. I thought it was a prowling cat, knocking the lid, but then we heard footsteps walking away fast. It was no cat. We came inside, pretty scared, bolted the kitchen door. I went upstairs and looked out of the landing window, which overlooks the road. I couldn't see anything. It was pitch black and the streetlamps weren't on. That's it, really. I couldn't see anything, but the garden gate was open and I remember closing it when we came in.'

'Might have been a late drinker from the pub?' PC Willis said.

'Maybe. But that's not all,' Jo said.

'What do you mean?' PC Mackenzie asked.

Lucy looked agitated. She didn't remember anything else happening, yet Jo knew something else.

'Well, there was another time we'd been out to the beach and when we came home, there was a guy in a hoodie leaving the house. He crossed the road and had walked away by the time we had parked. I spotted him at the T-junction,' Jo said.

'Can you describe him?' Mackenzie asked.

'Not really. He was wearing a dark hoodie, scruffy cheap trainers, but his face was shielded by his hood. It was a snapshot of a second to see his clothes, but his trainers were cheap looking. We thought it was a guy delivering menus, as there was a take-away menu on the mat.'

'Right, sounds plausible,' PC Willis said.

'Well, maybe. We ordered a curry that night from the menu and when I said to the delivery guy that the menu delivery had been well timed, he said they only post menus on Mondays,' Jo said.

'It was him, wasn't it? You think it's him, don't you? The footsteps, the take-away menu – do you think it's Charlie?' Lucy stammered, clasping her hands.

'It's difficult to say at this point. Like PC Willis said, it could have been a drinker from the pub staggering home. The menu delivery sounds a bit suspicious, but your description sounds like it could be anybody. Cheap trainers that's what we have?'

'I guess and Charlie isn't a trainer type of guy, or cheap. But what about the Dior lipstick? That has to be from Charlie. He knows the address,' Jo said.

'I will speak to my sergeant and see what information we can get on Charlie from the Met whether he has previous allegations and also try and locate the DPD courier. What isn't good is what you've told us about your relationship – that's domestic violence. I know it's hard, but please try not to worry. You are in safe hands now. If Charlie contacts you, phone the police immediately. I've written everything down that you told me. If you could read it, I will print it off for it to be signed at the bottom, it will act as your formal statement. You'll need to come to the station when you can to do that. I will leave you our mobile numbers – all calls to them are monitored. Do you have something to write the crime reference on?'

Lucy opened notebook on her mobile and typed in the crime reference number.

The two policemen got up from the sofa. Lucy took the crime reference number from PC Mackenzie, showed them to the front door and thanked them for their time. She closed the door behind her and stood with her back to it for a few seconds, taking deep breaths.

'I need a cigarette,' she said.

As the policemen made their way down the path, number eight's bright yellow door swung open.

'Any bother?' called Gladys Pope, her hands on her hips, wearing a tatty apron and holding a duster.

'Ah, Mrs Pope, good morning,' PC Mackenzie called back.

'Mackie, I'll see you back at the station. I think you've got this covered,' Willis said, winking and patting PC Mackenzie on the back.

'I'll take this for the team, Wills. It's your round when we finish work. See you back at the station – and can you grab me a prawn and mayo sandwich from Molly's café on your way? I'm famished,' Mackie replied.

'Any bother at the 'ouse? Is the new girl all right?' she said again. She was like a dog with a bone when she wanted information.

'No, nothing for you to worry about, Mrs Pope.' PC Mackenzie said.

'Well, you wanna be 'aving a word with drivers who drive up and down 'ere with no lights on and speed through the village – 'e almost took me and my Barry out on our evening walk the other night. 'e could have knocked us both over,' she said.

'Will do, Mrs Pope,' Mackenzie said, ducking his head to get into the squad car.

'It's a small village road – flash silver car, racing through, no lights. That was Friday evening and I dare say it was the same car I saw t'other evening.'

'Friday evening?' Mackenzie got back out of the car. 'Did you say Friday evening?'

'Yes. I was walking my Barry for 'is last whoopsie of the evening. When I was about to cross by the Black Horse pub, 'e sped past me like a bat out of hell. No lights on – I almost got knocked down by 'im. 'e was going like the clappers, in a 'urry. When 'e got to the level crossing, 'is lights went on.'

'Silver, you say? What time was Barry's walk, Mrs Pope?' Mackenzie stood and took in Gladys Pope. She was a battleship of a woman, coarse in her manner, but she knew everybody's business – and if she didn't, then she'd find it out.

'Like I said, it was a flash car, silver. Probably a BMW or Mercedes, might even 'ave been a Jaguar. It went too fast for me to see. You make sure you sort it out or I'll be 'aving a word with your sergeant. D'you 'ear? It almost killed me and my Barry.'

'Thank you for that information, Mrs Pope. We will keep a look-out for the car. You've been most helpful. Have a good day.'

'Always glad to 'elp to keep the community safe, that's what we want. About ten thirty, that was the time, Barry's last whoopsie.' She turned to go back into her cottage. 'I told them about that flash car, Stanley, d'you 'ear me? The one who nearly took me and Barry out,' she hollered as she passed Stanley, snoring in front of the telly.

PC Mackenzie got back into his car, opened his laptop and scanned his notes. He added: *Gladys Pope, number eight Lambourne Terrace, eye-witness to flash car driving at speed Friday*

16th November 2018, approx. 10.30pm. Same car seen on other night too.

As he took the short drive back to the station, he mulled over the morning's events. He felt sickened by what Lucy had told him, but what played on his mind was Gladys Pope. Her need to be the eyes and ears of the community had made her a possible eye-witness.

Chapter Eight

'Prawn and mayo sandwich on the desk for you, Mackie,' Wills called from the compact kitchen in the station. 'I'm putting the kettle on – d'you want a cuppa?'

'Yep, that would be great, thanks,' Mackie replied, sitting at his desk, opening the white paper bag and taking out the neatly folded sandwiches. Mayo oozed out of the sides and onto the paper. He pressed the sandwich down, making it more manageable to eat. As he did, he thought about the morning and about Lucy. This could all escalate into a mess, he thought. Lucy had gone through an ordeal that no woman should go through.

'Cuppa for you – looks like you could do with something stronger, mate. Maybe we should shut up shop and head to the pub for an afternoon beer.' Wills put the mug down on the table and sat down, swivelling his chair around, putting his feet up on the counter and lounging back in the chair. Nobody would come in over lunchtime, and seldom did anyone come into the station on a Sunday anyway. The pub seemed like a perfect option.

'Penny for them,' he said. 'It's Lucy, innit, mate?' He took a mammoth bite of his BLT and wiped mayo from his lips. 'What d'you think – has her ex found her?'

'I don't know. The bins,' he said, 'that could be something or nothing.' He pushed his sandwich to one side. 'The menu delivery guy and the room in London – Jesus Christ, she must have been terrified.' He opened up the laptop again, and read Gladys Pope's words. He tapped his pen on the desk.

'How did you get on with Gladys Pope? You know what she's like – bloody old battle-axe, she's got her finger in all the pies.'

'Yeah, I know she's the curtain-twitcher of the year, but she said she saw a flash car speed through the village late on Friday evening, about the same time as the girls heard the bin lid. But the girls made no mention of a car, a silver one. It's not stacking up. Who around here has a flash car? Nobody. And it's not like this is a cut-through for anywhere. There's something in it, there has to be, but I don't know what?'

'Right, OK, so a flash car was seen driving fast in the village? So what? What have we got to go on? It could be anybody's car, come on.' Wills finished his sandwich, rolled the paper into a ball and lobbed it into the bin. 'Bull's-eye!'

'Yep, you're right, but why was it speeding and why no headlights until it was out of sight? Gladys said he drove with no headlights until the level crossing. The level crossing leads to Bromley not London or town? Well, he must have realised he had no lights on – the streetlamps weren't on. Jo said she could see nothing from the landing window because the streetlamps weren't lit. Jo also said she'd closed the gate and it was open – there are too many coincidences here. I might do a bit more investigating and find out what car our Charlie Wainwright drives. And the gift he no doubt sent to her? She fled London because of what he did to her; you wouldn't treat an animal like that.'

Meanwhile, at number three Lucy and Jo sat in the kitchen. 'You didn't mention the gate being open, Jo, or the menu delivery,' Lucy said, opening the fridge and taking out a slab of cheddar.

'I know, I'm sorry. I only just remembered. I remember shutting it because it's such a rusty old latch and I figured the wind would keep swinging it backwards and forwards in the night. I noticed it was open, but didn't think anything of it at the time. And the menu guy – I didn't want to worry you. I'm sorry.'

'Do you think they'll take this seriously, though Jo? I mean, a Dior lipstick – it's not like there was a pig's heart or a dead cat or anything gruesome inside it,' Lucy said, spreading butter on the bread, which tore with each spread of the knife, and lining the cheese up in soldiers along it.

'I think so, they seemed pretty serious. You were locked in a room, he played mind games with you, tormented you mentally. They were trying to find out as much information as they could. Listen, I rang Giles while I was making the coffee and I've postponed seeing him on Monday. In fact, I've taken the week off. You've got me for the week – or at least until you're feeling happier. How does that sound?'

'Are you sure, Jo? I don't want to mess up your week. I mean, this is crazy. You come for the weekend and it spins into a horror weekend.' Lucy cut the sandwiches and slid one in front of Jo. 'Hope you like your sandwiches large and cheese and tomato – I'm all out of anything interesting or exotic!' she said, trying to muster up a cheery face.

'Love a doorstep, and actually I could do with the break. There's nothing in London that can't wait. Giles was cool about meeting later, and as long as I have Wi-Fi I can work from here. I need to use your washing machine, though. I haven't come down with a week's worth of clean clothes.'

'No worries – chuck your stuff in,' Lucy said, shivering. 'I'm freezing. I'll pop the heating on. I feel cold to my bones.' The morning had taken its toll and she felt emotionally drained.

The terraced house was wonderfully cosy and warm when the heating kicked in. There was no need to light a fire any more, but the idea of having one still appealed; it made the sitting room even cosier. The sun had dipped from the sky and a blanket of grey had been thrown over the village. Winter was definitely knocking at the door. The girls were warm and snug inside while the fallen leaves whistled around the ground outside. The rickety picket fence swayed in the wind. Lucy and Jo sat snuggled on the sofa.

'You know those guys in the bar?' Lucy piped up. 'What do you think they do? I mean, it seems pretty quiet around here, what do people do for a living?'

'I dunno, Luce. They looked quite weather-beaten. Maybe we could strike up a conversation with them if we see them in the wine bar again? We could always go out tonight for a drink, see who's about, get to know a few faces. It seems like a nice place and last night was fun – great band too. And then if we like them, at least I'm here for the week so you've got a wingman. Anyway, the one in the baseball cap was pretty cute. Man, I need a man. I feel like I'm going to shrivel up like a prune if I'm not touched soon,' she declared with a mock sigh.

'So, let's go,' Lucy said. 'The one in the baseball cap was cute, definitely your type – let's hope he's single!'

'And you?' Jo asked, nudging her arm. 'I think I know which one caught your eye – the guy on a bike, am I right?'

'Yeah, he seems nice. But I don't know. This whole thing with Charlie has really screwed with my head. I'd hoped moving could give me my life back. It feels like I'll never get back to where I used to be, and going out with any guy seems a world away at the moment.'

'It takes time, Lucy. You spent a long time with Charlie and he treated you like shit. You should have gone to the police in

London, man you should have left him all those times I said get out. One day you'll forget it and it will become a distant memory. Break-ups are crap at the best of times, but what you went through was hell. Give it time, gorgeous, that's all you can do, not every guy is a Charlie.'

***

Lucy had just finished drying her hair and applying the finishing touches to her make-up when there was a knock on the door.

'I'll get it,' Jo said from downstairs. 'Taxi's here – are you ready?'

'Yep, coming. I'm putting my boots on and I'll be there,' Lucy said, sitting on the bed and putting on her stiletto ankle boots. She ran down the stairs and out, locking the door behind her.

The curtains opposite peeled open. 'They're off out again, them two girls.'

'Come away from the window, goddammit! Woman, will you leave that curtain alone?' Stanley mumbled from his armchair.

'Where to, ladies?' the taxi driver asked.

'Um, Samuel Pepys, please,' Jo said.

'Ah, you liked it then. I took you there last night and picked you up – I never forget pretty faces. New faces too – have you just moved in?' He glanced at them in his rear-view mirror. 'It's a nice bar, gets some good bands in. The sailors around here like it too – nice bar, nice crowd.'

'Yes, about a month ago. So d'you know the town well?' Lucy was good at talking to people and finding out about them, asking them stuff that wouldn't interest anybody else. It was her writer's mind: she wanted to glean as much information as she could and turn it into something, make a story with it.

'Yeah, I used to play there myself with a band. They always had a good crowd in and Sheila, the owner, always gave new bands a gig. Have you met Sheila? She's been there since she was eighteen. Her dad ran it before, and she took over when he passed away. She's the eyes and ears of Harwich – doesn't do bar gossip but she knows who's who and what's what. I'm Dave, by the way, the local taxi driver for the village. I haven't picked up a fare from number three in over two years – no, it must almost three.'

'Are you still in a band?' Lucy asked. She felt confident in situations like this, yet put her in a room with a hundred people she didn't know and she'd cling to the wall, hating every minute, wanting to disappear. But Jo thrived on socialising and would throw herself into it, love it all, make herself known, flirt outrageously and never spend a penny at the bar.

'Yeah, I played the drums. Still do some garage drumming now,' he said, turning left onto the A120.

'You're into garage? Wow!' Jo exclaimed.

'No, not urban grunge, I mean I drummed in my garage.' He laughed.

'Right,' Jo said, flicking her hair back from her face and rolling her eyes.

'So what happened? How come you stopped?' Lucy said, narrowing her eyes at Jo.

'We didn't stop, love, we lost our lead vocalist. He actually made it and got signed up to a music producer in London. I'd like to get back into it, we just need a singer. Fancy a job?'

'Er, nope, I can't sing!' She laughed. As they neared Harwich's harbour, Jo fumbled in her bag for her wallet, ready to escape from the taxi.

'Right, well, here you are,' he said, pulling up outside the bar. 'Twelve pounds, please. D'you need a return journey?'

'That would be great, thanks – ten thirty?' Lucy said, shuffling along the seat. 'I'm Lucy, by the way. It's been nice talking to you. Hope you find a singer soon, see you later, Dave.' Lucy slammed the door and caught up with Jo.

The bar was pretty full for a Sunday evening, without any free tables. 'Looks like it's standing room only,' Lucy said. 'Wine or gin? I'll get this round in.' Making her way past the throng of bodies, she sidled up to the bar.

'What can I get you, love?' asked Sheila, with a lipstick grin. 'Two gin and tonics, maybe?'

Sheila was not one to forget a face.

'Er yes, you've got a good memory,' Lucy said, her eyes lighting up. She felt like she belonged here now that Sheila remembered her.

'Well, you've been here a few times now and I never forget a face in my bar. I'm Sheila.'

'Hi Sheila, I'm Lucy. I've just moved down here, so I guess you'll be seeing a bit more of me,' she said, pouring tonic into the glasses.

'Eight forty, please, my love. Moved from far?' Sheila asked, taking ten pounds from Lucy and handing her change.

'London – not a million miles away,' she said.

'Well, welcome to Harwich. You'll meet some friendly people down here – a pretty girl like you, you'll be batting the boys away.' Sheila pushed her ample bosom off the bar and made her way to another customer. 'What can I get you, love, pint of IPA?'

Lucy took her drinks and edged away from the bar. As she turned, she spotted two familiar faces. The men sat at a table close to where Jo was standing, eyeing up the potential for free drinks. She was clearly playing the game.

'Hi Lucy.' A familiar voice came from behind her as she walked past. She smiled, looking a little dazed, like a rabbit caught in the headlights. She wasn't sure who they were at first, and it was only when she said hi that it dawned on her: the men were PC Mackenzie and Willis. Perhaps they looked unfamiliar because they were not in uniform but were casually dressed.

'Oh, um, hi. Sorry, I didn't recognise you at first – you're not in uniform,' she replied, flustered. She could feel herself blush. 'Um, well, hi again and thanks for today.' She quickly headed in the direction of Jo, who was leaning against a wall by a ledge, her hand on her chin, looking cool, tall and slim. Her sleek dark bob swung against her face and her silver hoop earrings jutted through her hair.

'What took you so long?' Jo asked, moving her bag, making enough room for Lucy to put the drinks on the narrow ledge.

'Well, first I got talking to Sheila, the owner. She remembered us from yesterday. She's really friendly. Then, oh my God, I made a complete tit of myself, so embarrassing. Don't look now, but sitting at the table near the door are our friendly policemen. I didn't recognise them at first – well, I did, but they weren't in uniform and I knew their faces but couldn't work out from where. Then I was just like "oh, um, yeah, um, yeah, hi" – so embarrassing! Why can't I be cool like you? I looked like a muppet.'

'Ha ha, that's hysterical. The cool comes after years of experience. But you know what you need to get your edgy self back? Let's play the game again – cool, edgy chicks.' She threw a glance over to the two men, who – out of uniform – were not bad eye candy. 'So what did they say?' Jo asked, taking another sip from her glass.

'Just "hi Lucy", and I got all flustered.'

'Well, let's see if they remember me. Let's say a fiver says I can get them to invite us over for a drink. Shall we play the game like we used to before we got all serious?' Jo said with a teasing smile. She could play the game well. She took her bag and walked across the bar to the loos. She pushed the door of the ladies open and looked at herself in the mirror. She smoothed her hair and brushed her fringe so it lay flat against her forehead. She applied another coat of deep raspberry lipstick and squirted some Prada perfume to her neck then turned side-on to check herself out. She gave herself two minutes before she pulled the door of the ladies open and walked out. As she brushed past the drinkers at the bar, she took on a swagger that told Lucy the game was on. Lucy watched her. She could turn heads when she wanted to. She looked striking. When she walked past the policemen she threw them a sultry look, her eyes narrowed slightly. She counted one, two, three, four – she'd have them on five, she figured, and she did.

'Hi, Jo,' PC Mackenzie said.

'Oh, hey,' she replied and stopped. She leant her hand on the back of PC Willis' chair. 'Off duty?' She knew the answer but she had to engage; there was a fiver at stake. Lucy watched as Jo stood and chatted to the two men. 'So, you drink here too,' she said. 'It's a nice bar – not quite London vibes but it's nice.'

'We do, probably more than we should, but yeah, it's our local. It's a great bar. You're out with Lucy, then?'

She was in – she'd got at least two minutes of conversation under her belt. 'Can I get you a drink?' was the next step and that was coming – give it three seconds.

'Yep, thought we'd give it another whirl tonight. Can't sit in a house like two old ladies all night,' she quipped, playing with her earring. 'It's pretty busy in here – didn't think it would be so packed.'

That was it – she'd laid it out. There were two spare seats at their table and she needed them for the fiver to be hers. *Come on, boys, let's go… take the bait, one, two, thr—*

'Would you like to join us? Can we get you a drink?'

Bingo! She'd done it. Not bad, Jo, not bad … you've still got the touch.

'We have plenty of space here. Please grab Lucy – you guys don't want to be standing all night. This place never empties out, it simply gets fuller and fuller. You'll never get a seat now,' Mackie said, beckoning to Lucy to join them.

Hats off to Jo, Lucy thought. She'd played the game and Lucy was now a fiver down. Lucy took her bag and both drinks and made her way to Jo, who was now sliding past people to reach the seat next to PC Willis.

Lucy stood at the table. 'Here, Jo, take the drinks. I'm just popping to the loo. Back in a minute.'

Standing in front of the mirror, Lucy looked at herself. Her feline eyes shone and her straight, dark hair fell to below her shoulders. She had high cheekbones and dark brown eyes framed by long lashes. They looked even longer thanks to her mascara: they were like the lashes of a camel. Smudging a chocolate-brown lipstick onto her lips, she pulled down her fitted sheer jumper and turned around to check out her rear. Her skinny black jeans gave her bottom a pert, round shape and killer ankle-boot stilettos finished off her gazelle-like legs.

She left the loo and made her way through the customers back to the table. She was beautiful: her face without a blemish, her body a silhouette of black.

Jo watched her as she moved elegantly and sexily across the floor. That was the walk she'd done when she pulled Charlie, the walk she did when they played the game, and now she was doing it again – looking good, without him. Mackenzie looked up and watched her. She was different to the girl he'd sat with that morning; she had swagger, style, confidence and was knock-down gorgeous. She had been seen by another man, a guy in a blue hoodie. Tonight, she had caught the attention of two men. Two men who both had the same idea, yet Lucy didn't know. She sidled past the men on her right, one of them winked at her. She stopped. Gazed at him, felt the breath of Charlie on her, the tight hold on her wrist, the mean whisper in her ear. He wasn't there. She seemed flustered. Come on Lucy, she kept telling herself, let go. Be you. Be the girl you were. Fight this. The noise around slowed, the sounds muffled, the bar slipped into slow motion. She took a deep breath, she came back. She rubbed her wrist.

'Do you mind us joining you?' she said as she slid into the chair and leant forward. Her eyes roamed Mackenzie's face as she waited for his response.

'Not at all. Like I was saying to Jo, you'd be standing all night – and anyway, it would be good to get to know you both. I mean, in a non-working capacity,' he said.

'So, I guess you know our names, are we allowed to know yours? We can't keep referring to you as PC Mackenzie and Willis!' Jo said.

'Yeah, of course. I'm Simon, PC Mackenzie said extending his hand and this is Matt, otherwise known as Wills.'

'Well, Simon and Matt, it's a pleasure meeting you,' Lucy said. Her eyes sparkled when she smiled: they were a deep chocolate brown that locked you in. On the other side of the bar, the guy in the hoodie gazed over as the table of four laughed and joked and more rounds were bought.

'Tell me about your writing,' Matt said as Simon went to the bar to get another round. 'I've never met a writer before. Sounds intriguing.'

Lucy didn't like to talk much about her writing; it was something she kept close to her chest. Jo was the only person she talked to about her writing. As soon as people knew she was a writer, they either wanted Lucy to write them into a book as a character, or go the opposite way and fear Lucy would assassinate their character.' She fidgeted. 'I write fiction – sometimes about love, sometimes grief. It depends on life and where I'm at, and the experiences I've had.'

'Lucy, don't be so modest – she's one of my best authors. Seriously, Lucy, you're an author, not a writer,' Jo butted in. 'She has written five bestsellers – one was made into a BBC series. *Defence*, d'you know it? It aired a couple of years ago as a six-week suspense drama.'

'Yeah, I remember it – that was the court case drama with the lawyer who fell in love with the defence? Bloody hell, that was an amazing drama, totally thrilling. And you wrote it? That's awesome. Do I need to ask for your autograph?'

'Two gin and tonics for you girls, and I thought I'd throw in some peanuts if you're hungry,' Simon said, placing the drinks on the table along with a couple of bags of peanuts. 'What have I missed? Anything good?'

'Only that Lucy is the writer behind that epic drama *Defence*,' Matt piped up.

'Seriously, that was your work?' Simon leant closer in a bid to gain more information. He'd only met her a few times in pretty shitty low situations for her. But he was beginning to fancy her. What was it with her? 'Blimey, you are hard-core. That had me on the edge of my seat, the suspense was amazing.' Raising his beer bottle in the air, he toasted her. 'To our brilliant writer, sorry author, and newcomer to the village, welcome! And of course, welcome to Jo too.' They clinked glasses, took a swig then resumed their chatter. The four new friends sat in the midst of laughter and banter until Sheila's voice resounded around the bar: 'Time at the bar ladies, and gents!'

When the girls climbed into the waiting taxi, Simon and Matt waved them off.

'Good night, girls?' Dave asked, doing a U-turn.

'Yeah, it was a blinder,' Lucy said, feeling tipsy.

As the taxi drove slowly away from the bar, Lucy spotted the guy in the hoodie – he looked into the taxi window then looked away. Lucy turned to catch a glimpse of him, but he veered off left into a mews. He'd been in the bar, she thought. Damn it, he was there drinking, she hadn't seen him. She could have played the game.

The girls paid Dave and walked down the garden path. Jo closed the iron gate behind her. They almost fell through the door, locked it, bolted it and headed upstairs to bed, slightly inebriated.

They lay in bed and chatted about the night until their sentences became vaguer and more incoherent and their eyes slowly closed and gave way to the darkness.

In the dark night, the silver car moved away from the kerb and stole off into the night. Someone was watching them.

Chapter Nine

Lucy and Jo stood on the platform waiting for the nineteen-fifty from Norwich to Liverpool Street. The air bit at their noses as they stood on the brightly lit platform. The waiting room was locked. The station was unmanned at night and had a desolate feel to it; only the automated announcements of arrivals and departures boomed out into the night. The air smelt of bonfires and rotting leaves: the nights were drawing in, the cold days of winter were here to stay.

'It's been an amazing two weeks,' Jo said.

'It's been fabulous – and to think it should have just been a weekend,' Lucy agreed. They'd spent quite a few evenings with Simon and Matt, which had made it even more fun. 'When are you next seeing Matt? You guys are getting on well.'

Jo had exchanged numbers with the guys but had received a few more messages from Matt. There seemed to be a romance of sorts blossoming.

'I don't know – maybe I can come back down in a couple of weeks, we'll see. I'm here for Christmas, don't forget.' Jo said as she checked her bag for her ticket.

'He seems pretty keen,' Lucy said. 'Who would have thought you'd have eyes for a police officer? You'll have to start behaving yourself.' She laughed.

The girls stood back to watch the train pull into the station. The doors whooshed open. Jo swung around to Lucy and gave her a hug that could have lasted a lifetime.

'Stay cool, kiddo. Write lots and don't forget you have Matt and Simon to keep you company and keep an eye on you. Buzz me if you need me – I'm always here and always will be. Hey, you'll be seeing a lot more of me now that I've met Matt...'

Lucy smiled at Jo. 'You like him more than you're letting on, don't you? The game is over.' She knew when Jo wanted something more; she was just too cool to show it.

'Yeah, I do.' She pulled away from Lucy and turned to get on the train, and the doors beeped and slid shut behind her. Lucy watched Jo walk up the aisle to a seat. The train pulled out of the station. Lucy stood alone, watching it disappear into the distance. She shivered in the cold then walked hastily back to her car. On the short drive home along the winding lanes, she thought about the guy in the hoodie. Why did he keep coming into her head when her thoughts were quiet? She pulled up outside her house. As she opened the front door, the smell of the smouldering fire and the two empty wine glasses were the only signs that Jo had been with her. It felt odd without Jo. The house was quiet. The only sounds were the ticking of the kitchen clock and the buzzing of the heating. Lucy slumped onto the sofa with a glass of red wine and let her mind drift back to the last couple of weeks. She'd had an amazing time with Jo, and it had been great to meet the two boys. She felt a tad lost now, she didn't know quite what to do with herself. She switched on the television and flicked through the channels but found nothing she wanted to watch. She pressed the power-off button and went upstairs. She hadn't been in her writing room for well over a week. She drew the chair up to the desk and picked up the bundle of letters. She untied the ribbon and took the third letter out to read.

My darling Peggy

I write from Dieppe where we are stationed. The days are long and hard and cold, so cold. I often think of you to get me through these days of hell. They are hell; I have no other word to describe them.

I received your letter yesterday. I can't tell you how good it was to read your words. I hear your voice in my head, as if you are here with me. I think of you and the warmth we share when we are together, and that helps me survive. I miss you so much. Today we lost three men from overhead fire. I feel their loss. I'm scared and I wish this bloody war would end. I don't want you to be afraid, though. My thoughts can become truly black, but when I think of you and your sweet-smelling hair and your soft white skin and the touch of your lips on mine, I forget where I am for a moment.

I love you and I wish we were together – but until then I will hold you forever in my heart.

Write soon, my love.

I love you, my sweetest heart.

Jim

Lucy touched the letter, she opened her laptop. The story was unfolding in her head and she knew this story was the one she would write. She hadn't written about the war before, and she needed to research wartime England. She took her notebook and scribbled her thoughts onto the page, then the characters' names, the date and the setting. Yorkshire would be a good place. It gave Peggy an element of safety. London and other major cities would have been bombed, but the countryside was a safe haven. She felt there was a warmth in Jim, so decided he should be from the north of England. Peggy's auburn hair made Lucy feel she too had to be a sweet country girl. In her mind the characters, torn apart by war, began to unfold. She took another letter and began to read it. The letters were full of sentiment and desire, a love that only words were keeping them together, letters, the aching feeling of powerlessness against a war, she scribbled more words onto her page until her page became pages and her thoughts meandered and her story began. The story of two lovers kept apart by a bloody war.

She opened Safari on her laptop and googled wartime England. As she read through the links and made notes, her tummy rumbled – a reminder that it was way past supper time. She made her way downstairs to the kitchen, opened the fridge and took out a chunk of cheddar cheese. She felt like something warming and comforting. Cheese on toast, she thought. As the cheese bubbled and melted under the heat of the grill, she topped up her wine then took the simple supper upstairs, double-locking the front door as she passed. Downstairs lay in darkness while the light from her writing room could be seen from outside.

She hadn't looked outside since she had got back from the station. If she had, perhaps she would have seen the car. A silver car … the same car that had driven away at speed last Friday. It was there again. The man inside watched the light in her window, watched the silhouette behind the curtain. The man lit a cigarette and opened the window to let the smoke disperse into the air.

The curtains at number eight stayed shut. There were no voyeurs out except the man in the silver car. He watched the curtain, the cigarette smoke wafting out of the window. Eventually the light went out and the landing light went out. As the road lay in a sheet of blackness, the engine of the car purred. It pulled out from behind Lucy's Mini and drove off slowly. The only sign it had been there was the cigarette, thrown out of the window and landing by the gate of number three.

Then the door of number eight opened and Gladys Pope emerged with Barry for his last walk of the evening. She noticed the car drive off down the road, this time with its lights on, and could see that it was a silver Jaguar. She walked as far as the small recreation ground, and Barry cocked his leg at every opportunity. When she returned, Barry curled up in his basket.

'That flash car was there again,' she said as she hung up her coat, scarf and hat in the hallway. Stanley grunted.

'Looked like one of those Jaguars,' she said. 'Not in such an 'urry tonight, but it seems to spend a lot of time on this road. Nobody around 'ere 'as a Jaguar, do they Stan?'

Stanley snored loudly. Gladys muttered under her breath waddling to the kitchen to make herself some cocoa. She poured the hot milk into her mug and stirred it well, then turned out the light and switched off the booming television.

'Stan get up, you old sod, get yourself to bed. I'm turning in now.'

Stanley lumbered out of his armchair and ambled up the stairs. Gladys took one last look out of the window. There was nothing outside other than darkness. The lights of number three were all out and the gate was closed. Gladys trudged up the stairs, her cocoa in hand. When she got into bed, Stanley was already asleep. She sat in the dim light with her cocoa, took a sip and let out a sigh of satisfaction.

Over the road, the quiet of number three was unaware of either Gladys or the silver car. Lucy slept into the night with the quiet sound of the heating humming through the old pipes.

Chapter Ten

Lucy sat on the beach. She'd come to love her space here in Harwich on the stone step. The day was cold, colder than she'd known it here. The wind howled around her and around the small boats on the foaming waves. They rocked back and forth, clinging to the anchors that held them on the seabed. The choppy sea swished around the boats and waves crashed onto the shore, grasping at the pebbles and shells and whisking them back into the sea with a rattling sound.

She had never seen the sea in such a mood. As she gripped her pen, the tips of her fingers felt numb. She blew on them and shivered. The cold of the stone penetrated her coat and jeans. She wanted to sit on the beach and really feel alone, as the cold air whipped and bit at her face. She wanted to feel how deeply alone she was, how desolate the feeling was; she needed to imagine how the cold could make her lose herself in a feeling of numbness. She wanted to feel how the black clouds that hid the horizon could make her thoughts dark, deep, unwanted. She wanted to feel how Jim would feel: a soldier in a trench, at war, with no warmth, no sunshine, no colours to brighten his day. She wanted to feel the despair and loneliness he might have felt. Now, on the bleak beach she began to feel. She wrote, her hand shaking as the words slowly blended onto the page.

Her nose began to run. She sniffed. Typical, she had no tissues. Would a soldier have a tissue? Would his face be wet from the dank soil? Would he be scared, or would he feel an inner sense of calm? For the first time, she felt lonely, alone. Her body began to ache with cold.

How long she could sit on the stone step and write? How long would a soldier sit in a trench and fight? How long had she been there? How many hours would a soldier have to lie motionless in the wet squalor of the trench, the smell of blood and death all around him?

She stared out into the mass of grey. The foamy peaks of the waves swirled about, the seagulls a frenzy in the air, the dark clouds rolling in. Then the lightning came. It forked across the sky, jagging through the greyish blackness. As she watched, the guy on the bike rode by again. This time he stopped by the wall where she sat and watched the lightning, his face half covered by his jacket. He wore a navy beanie hat, jeans and trainers. She turned and looked at him, her face cold, her nose a shimmering pink, blinking away the coldness of the wind. She turned back to the sea.

'Aren't you cold?' he asked. She looked back at him. She was cold. She was freezing. She felt like she couldn't move from the spot, lifeless and numb.

'Yes,' she said, 'I'm freezing.' She turned back to the sea, ignoring him, then brushed back the hair that clung to her face.

'So why are you sitting here?' he asked.

'I have to,' she said. 'It's important.' What business was it of his where she sat? She turned and took up her pen to write some more.

'Right. I've seen you sitting here a lot,' he said. 'You're always here. It's a good spot but today it's bloody freezing.' He blew on his hands.

'I know.' She gathered her bag and stood up, wriggling some life back into her bottom.

'I'm sorry, I didn't mean for you to leave, it's just...'

He didn't finish his sentence. Lucy had already begun to walk away.

'Wait!' he called. 'I didn't mean to offend you. It's just that I always see you and I wanted to ask...' He stopped.

'What?' she asked.

'I just wanted to ask if you were Lucy,' he said.

'You know my name,' she said.

'Well, I think I do. I wasn't sure,' he said, perplexed by her response.

'You know you do – you shouted my name the other night as I got into the taxi. You shouted bye—' She stopped. She didn't want to say her name, she didn't want him to know her name. He knew it anyway, so why was he asking? She didn't know his.

'That wasn't me,' he said. 'That was Rob, my mate. He was drunk. I'm sorry, we'd had a bit of a night with the band. That was just Rob being Rob.' He looked at her, wondering if he had offended her. 'I'd like to know your name. Is it Lucy?'

She looked out to sea and hitched her satchel further onto her shoulder. Now she stood in front of the guy she had been noticing for weeks, the guy she had smiled at, the guy who had made her feel uneasy at the bar – but a kind of uneasy that she had liked. Why? Because his face was kind and warm and good-looking – but now she had the opportunity to talk to him, she froze and all she wanted was to escape. She turned to walk away.

'Please wait,' he said. 'I'm sorry. Can we start again, maybe over a coffee? You look freezing.'

She wanted him to ask her, yet she couldn't process it. She didn't know how to act any more. What if he was another

Charlie? What if this was a trick? What if he wasn't as lovely as he had looked in the bar and when she had seen him on the bike all those times? What if she had the wrong idea about him? What if she was now the game?

He seemed to sense her unease and climbed off his bike. 'Please, let me start again,' he said. 'I'm Ben and I'd like to buy you a coffee.' He smiled – the smile he'd given her at the bar, the smile that made her want to stay with him and discover who he was. She bit her lip and searched his face.

'OK,' she said, 'a coffee sounds good.'

She walked a little behind him as they made their way to the coffee shop on the corner, turning every so often to look back at the sea, leaving her thoughts about the soldier on the beach. He leant his bike against the window of the café and opened the door, beckoning her to go first. She walked in and stood waiting for him. He led her to a table in the corner from where he could see his bike. The table was covered in a red checked tablecloth and in the centre was a bowl of sugar cubes.

'Shall we sit here?' he asked, pulling out a chair for her. 'I'll grab some coffees – you look like you need to defrost.'

Lucy sat down and placed her satchel on the floor. 'Coffee, milk?' he asked.

She nodded. No words came out – why did no words come out? Here she was sitting with a guy she had wondered about, but she was mute. He stood at the counter and the smiling waitress appeared, wiping her hands on her apron.

'Two coffees please, Stacey,' he said.

Lucy felt the sting of pins and needles jutting through her feet. They were so cold, and now the warmth of the café was beginning to thaw them out, bring them back to life.

'That's three pounds please, Ben,' Stacey said, pushing the coffees towards him.

Ben took the coffees and placed one in front of Lucy. She cupped the mug in her hands. 'Thank you.' Its heat seemed to permeate through her hands, and her fingers tingled.

'So, you know my name,' he said, 'and you still haven't said if I'm right about yours.' She looked at him, holding the mug but not drinking from it. 'My name is Lucy.'

'Well, I'm pleased to meet you, Lucy,' he said and smiled that smile again. She looked away, watching the waitress adding mayo to what looked like a bowl of tuna. She watched her for a while, until she turned to look at Ben.

'So,' he said, 'how come you sit on the beach when it's so cold?'

She stirred the coffee, biding her time. 'I'm a writer,' she said. 'I like sitting on the beach. I can be quiet with my thoughts there.' She brushed the hair away from her face and tucked it behind her ear.

'A writer? That's cool. What kind of writer?' He'd never met a writer before and he would never have guessed that would have been her response.

'I write novels, mainly romances.' She began to feel more relaxed, uncrossing her legs and loosening her jacket.

'Have you recently moved here? I've seen you almost every day for the last month or so, and with another girl – your friend, I'm guessing,' he said, fiddling with the bowl of sugar cubes.

'Jo, yes, my best friend and literary agent. She's gone back to London now – she left yesterday,' Lucy said. She was feeling warmer now. She took off her coat and hung it on the back of the chair.

'So, I guess you live nearby? Sorry, I'm being nosy...' He looked at her: it was the look he had given her in the bar when she'd almost spilt her drinks over him. He wanted to get to know her, wanted to know if he would see her again or whether she had just come here to write and would then disappear back up to London. Was she just here for a quiet retreat? He didn't know how writers worked. He hoped it wasn't a retreat and that he would see her again and that she did live nearby.

'Um, I moved here a few months ago,' she continued. 'I bought a house nearby and Jo came to visit me.' She didn't want to tell him her real reason for wanting to move here; she didn't want to tell him she was running away from a man. She wanted to tell him nothing. He didn't need to know.

'Do you miss London? I've never lived there – visited many times, but never had the desire to jump into the big city. I'd be like a fish out of water.'

Lucy smiled at him. 'Yeah, I miss it but I'm beginning to really love here, and I love this beach. It kinda reminds me of London, I don't know why. I guess it's the way the cranes loom over the sea – reminds me a little of the Embankment. I like the quietness here. Although it took a while to get used to not hearing noise – traffic, sirens, aeroplanes, people, the rumble of the Tube. It's so quiet, you can forget yourself. I like that.'

'Yeah, I guess so. Maybe I need to live in London to appreciate the quiet life more. You don't know what you've got until you miss it,' he said. He could feel her letting go a little, relaxing in his presence. He liked the way she bit her lip when she seemed nervous; she did it a lot while she sat cupping her coffee. He watched her face. She squinted when she didn't quite know what he was trying to say, looking at him side-on, she scrunched her nose when she smiled. He was beginning to like her. She intrigued him: she was closed, guarded, but he liked her. He liked the girl he faced, cupping a mug of coffee. He liked the girl on the beach.

'Is your house around here – in Harwich, I mean?'

Should she tell him where she lived or not? She said nothing, and he didn't press for an answer. She didn't want him to know where she lived, so she answered vaguely. 'I bought nearby, yep. You seem to be asking me a lot of questions. What about you? What do you do, other than cycle around here?' she asked, swirling the coffee around her mug with a teaspoon.

'So, you've noticed me?' he joked.

'Well, I guess it's hard not to. I sit here and write. Not many people pass by so I guess you could say I've noticed you.' She liked his manner, she liked the fact that he had teased her a little, and she liked that he had noticed that she had noticed him.

The door swung open, bringing a flurry of leaves into the café. Two burly men walked in. The cold passed over Lucy and Ben like a sheet of ice, and she shuddered.

'Alright, Ben,' one of the men said and smiled at Lucy. 'Not working today?'

'Not today, Pete, it's my day off,' he said, looking more at ease.

'Chose a good day for it – the sea's rough. Fog horn will sound soon, no doubt. There's a big mist coming in.'

Lucy looked at the men then back at Ben. She wanted to ask again what he did, as he hadn't answered, but now there were other people in the café. She tucked her hair behind her ear again, out of habit, then bit her lip and looked at him. Please just answer my question, she thought. He looked at her: her eyes were deep and dark, her nose a perfect shape.

Her phone beeped from her satchel and she leant down to find it. Two messages flashed in.

All ok, gorgeous? :) Jxx

She opened the second message, which was from Rachel.

Hi Lucy. I hope you're OK. I haven't seen you for weeks. Charlie said you're at your grandfather's? But I thought your grandfather had passed away. Please tell me you're OK. Rx

She tucked the phone back in her bag and rummaged for her car keys.

'Right, I have to go,' she said, gathering her jacket and bag.

'So soon? I'd like to see you again,' Ben said. 'I mean, I'd like to chat to you again. Would you like to?'

'Yeah, sure, it's been lovely.' She walked to the door and opened it. 'Thanks for the coffee.'

The door closed behind her. Puzzled, he watched her unlock the Mini across the road and drive away. So, she was called Lucy and she was a writer. That was all he knew about her. He didn't even have her number. What if she never came back to the beach again, or the wine bar? Dammit. How would he see her again without even knowing where she lived?

He slumped in his chair and stared out into the road. Mate, you lost that girl, he said in his head. She didn't even drink any of her coffee. He got up and pushed the chair under the table with a sense of dejection. 'See you tomorrow, Ben. Pretty girl, by the way. Seemed nice,' came a man's voice from the table behind him.

Ben turned and smiled. 'Yep, see you anon.' He opened the café door and took his bike from where it was propped against the window. Nobody would steal such an old bike; it was worthless. As he straddled it and rode away, her face came into his mind. He took the road past The Pier restaurant then turned left into Smuggler's Walk. As he cycled, he heard Pete's voice play in his mind. Nice girl – yeah, don't I know it, he thought, and now she's gone. Bloody hell.

Chapter Eleven

Monday, 17th December

The rain lashed down, pelting the tarmac and bouncing back up until puddles formed on the uneven ground. The rain falling on the steel dustbin in Lucy's front garden sounded like a timpani drum. It made her feel relaxed and in no rush for the ominous clouds to disappear. Lucy sat in her writing room, her phone on the bureau, her laptop open in front of her. She had already typed thirty thousand words of her latest novel – her wartime love story. Lucy opened her phone and reread Rachel's message. Should she tell her? Could she trust her? She closed the message.

She laid the letters out across the bureau, the journal still untouched. Her shoulders relaxed into her writing chair, she picked up Peggy's journal and opened it. The sound of the rain grew heavier and more constant, she had a feeling of certainty that this was the only thing she needed to do for the rest of the day. The raindrops trickled down the windowpane. She watched them for a while as they fell into another, connecting and trickling down to the sill. It brought a sense of calm.

She read the first line of the journal.

Tuesday, 10th January 1941

If you were here at home, I would have to ruffle your hair. My words are limited. This is unusual for me, as normally I fill pages with words. But now, without you, I sit alone and struggle. I sit here wishing you were here. I ache for you. I saw Mrs Jenkins today and she wished you well. I was pleased, knowing that you are in her thoughts. So long as your heart beats, I don't feel as desperate, but my desperation seems misplaced: why do I feel that way when I am safe, and in the warmth, and you are in the trenches, cold, alone and scared? Not alone – I guess you are with your men, but you are not with me. Today, I read your letter and I knew I could do nothing but reply straight away, to keep your spirits high. Today, this war seems endless. I walked on the moors today – it was so peaceful. Nothing seemed to matter when I looked down onto the valley. Tomorrow I shall go to the hills on the other side and, when you return, we will do these simple things together once more.

Damn this war, I want my love home with me. When will this all end, when?

Lucy read through the journal, finally going back to the line 'My words are limited. This is unusual for me, as normally I fill pages with words.' Why did she normally fill pages with words? Was she talking about her journal? Lucy kept a journal of her own and sometimes she wrote a couple of lines about her day, sometimes pages and pages. The other woman's thoughts seemed familiar; Lucy recognised her in some way. Yet Lucy knew nothing about her apart from her name: Peggy. Who was she? Lucy sat and thought about her. She knew she had auburn hair and that she lived in the countryside, but how had these letters come to be here, in Essex? Was this the place she was writing about? Surely not, there were no moors or valleys. Lucy had been struck by the flatness of Essex and the skies were far reaching. Even London appeared to be hillier. Where were the moors and valleys? She thought about what Peggy had written, and thought about the line, the familiar tone...

Was she... Could she be...?

Lucy understood the line with the simplicity that it had been written. She picked up her phone and sent a text.

Hi Simon, wondered if you guys were about for a drink. I need to pick your brains. Let me know if tonight suits? Maybe the wine bar, 7pm? Lucy x

A text pinged straight back.

Sounds great, would love to. See you there at seven. Sx

Lucy wrote as much as she could that afternoon. At six o'clock she closed her laptop and put the journal and letters safely away. She jumped into the shower, and thought only of the journal. She'd forgotten about her coffee with Ben a few days ago; her mind was fixed on one thing: her novel.

She chose black tights, black polo-neck, mini skirt and over-the-knee leather boots and dashed out to the car. As she drove off, the line from the journal kept coming back to her. Who was Peggy? There was more to her than simply wartime love letters and a journal, Lucy knew it. Her journal had captivated Lucy and she hoped Simon or Matt could throw some light onto it. Taking a left turn off the main road, she dipped her headlights as a silver car passed her at highspeed. She looked in the rear-view mirror, nutter she muttered to herself. It was sporty, streamline, she caught sight of the tail-lights as they braked in the distance.

The boys were already in the bar with a couple of beers. Simon got up from his seat.

'What will it be? Wine, gin, something soft?' he asked kissing her on the cheek.

'I'd love a glass of red,' she said, drawing up a chair.

'So, what's up?' he asked, placing a glass of Pinot Noir on the table.

'Well,' she began, 'you know I found those letters and the journal and stuff in the house when I first moved in...'

'Yep,' Matt replied.

'Well, I'm kind of using them to base my next novel on. I need you guys to help me out.' She took a sip from her wine and opened the journal.

'In what way? Sounds intriguing, tell us more,' Matt said.

'I was reading the journal today. It's obviously written by Peggy, whoever she is. And I think she must have lived in the house or is a relative of someone who lived there.' She said opening the journal at the page that had caught her attention. 'You see, she's written that normally she fills her page with words and now she is struggling...'

Simon and Matt looked at her, confused.

'So?' Simon said. 'I don't get it. What are you asking?'

'Well, why has she said that? What does she mean? Nobody would write that except...'

'Except what, Miss Marple?' Matt laughed taking a gulp of beer.

'The only person who would fill a page with words and say they could a fill a page with words would be somebody like me.'

'You mean somebody gorgeous, edgy, perfect, sweet and kind?' Simon smiled and winked and threw Lucy a cheeky look.

She laughed. 'Well, yeah, obviously, bang on, but somebody like me – I mean a writer. That's such a writer's thought. As soon as I read it I thought, she's like me. I could feel she was like a kindred spirit.'

'Right, so what are you asking, then?' Matt chipped in.

'I guess I'm asking who lived in the house before me. What did she do? These must have belonged to her,' Lucy said. 'I need to know the history of my house and find out who it once belonged to for this to make sense. I need to find out more to write her story and fill my page with words. I only have the Richardsons as the previous owners – who owned the house before them? Absolutely nothing comes up before them. All I have is a name Peggy, how many Peggy's in the world are there?'

'Matt, you know the residents better than me, you'll know who lived there,' Simon said. 'I'll get another round in. Lucy, are you driving?'

Lucy nodded.

'Something soft?' Simon asked taking her empty glass.

'So, number three has been empty for at least a couple of years, if not more. It was owned by a lady who really kept herself to herself. Gladys Pope at number eight would be your best bet for the info you're looking for. She's a walking encyclopaedia of village life,' Matt said, taking the fresh pint of lager from Simon.

'Gladys Pope?' Lucy asked. She'd not heard the name before.

'Yeah. She lives opposite you, at number eight. Curtain-twitcher of the century, I'm surprised she hasn't knocked on your door yet.' Matt said.

'She may well have done, but I'm always writing at the beach,' Lucy said, wondering why a curtain-twitcher hadn't introduced herself. Surely she would have made it her business.

'Number three was owned by ... oh God, what was her name? Hang on, it will come to me. She would have been a looker in her day, quite refined ... Margaret ... Margaret, come on, Si, help me out here.'

'ARTHUR!' Simon shouted. 'Margaret Arthur, that was her name.' As he shouted the name, the door opened and three guys walked in. Briefly, Lucy turned to look at them, then looked away.

'Are you sure?' Lucy asked, swirling the ice and soda water in her glass.

'Pretty sure, why?' Matt asked.

'I'll tell you later. Listen, boys, you've been fab, but I'm going to have to go home. I need to check something out,' she said.

Lucy left the bar and walked back to her car, sure the answer lay at home. As she walked down the mews, she sensed somebody behind her. She quickened her pace, holding her keys so they jagged through her knuckles. She crossed the mews. The sound of a tin can scuttled across the pavement. She speeded up. Her heart beat faster. She pushed the keys into the lock, her hand shaking. Behind her, the footsteps stopped.

'Lucy?'

She turned, frightened, holding her breath.

'Sorry – I didn't mean to make you jump.' It was the guy on the bike. 'It's just that when you left the other day, I didn't get...'

She opened the car door.

'Please, wait.'

Her face was as he remembered it: her straight dark hair fell to her shoulders and was tucked behind her ear.

'Can we talk more? I mean, can we get to know each other?'

Part of her wanted to say yes, but she didn't want to complicate her life more than it already was. Why couldn't she trust him? Why was she comparing him to Charlie? He wasn't Charlie, he was Ben, and he deserved a chance.

'Could we at least meet for a drink? Maybe?' His face was kind.

'You scared me,' she said.

'What in the café?' he was confused, 'is that why you left in a hurry, you didn't drink your coffee?'

'No, I mean now, why didn't you call my name,' she said.

'I don't know, it seems kinda obvious now,' he said. Unsure of why she would be so scared or anxious.

She had to let go, this guy liked her. Memories bad memories were stopping her, allowing her to move on, trust again. Lucy opened the car door and went to put her foot in, then opened her bag and took out her journal.

'Right that's it, fine, OK, I get it, it was nice knowing you Lucy,' Ben said, scuffing his foot to walk away.

She tore a page from the back, she scribbled her number. She had to start to trust men again; she couldn't keep running.

'Wait. A drink would be good. Call me.' She got into the car and drove away. Ben watched her go, then tucked the paper into his pocket and went back into the bar, her face in his head, why was she so hesitant with him?

At home, Lucy pushed the front door shut behind her and ran up the stairs. She threw open the door of her writing room and stared at the cabinet and the books lined up on the shelves. The name on each spine was Margaret Arthur.

She knew it; her gut feeling had been right. *Struggling with words on a page when words should come so easily.* The journal, the love letters – they were Margaret's. She opened the cabinet and took out a novel. This house, this room – this was where she should be, among Margaret Arthur's works. Margaret Arthur was Peggy and now Lucy was writing about Peggy's love story. Peggy had lived like Lucy: she had been an author, she had sat in this room and typed on the typewriter. Lucy sifted through the letters until she found the final one.

2nd February 1945

My darling Peggy

I write knowing this wretched war will never end. The days and nights are cold and I miss you, my sweetest love. Many of the men have not returned, and I fear the same fate. I want you to know that I have always loved you and I always will. If I don't return, please remember I love you. You are my world – you keep me sane. When I feel desperate and lost and afraid, I see your face. The nights are cold and I miss the warmth of your embrace.

I fear I will never see you again. All I have is my memories – they keep me in a place where I can be with you. Now, I must leave you. The light is dwindling and the skies are filled with the wretched sounds of bombs.

I see only your face.

Goodnight, my love. My love, my love, my sweetest love,

Jim

Lucy sat in her chair, tears streaming down her face. There were no more letters to his sweet Peggy. The war ended in September, his letter dated February. His final letter of love seven months before there was world peace. That was the last letter to the woman who had kept his mind sane, kept his spirits high.

He had been killed in action.

And here Lucy was, in a world where a man should have protected her, loved her, cared for her, but who had only hurt her, made her insane. She placed the beautiful letters together, then sat and wept.

Chapter Twelve

The white lights on the Christmas tree twinkled and flickered among the pine needles. Mistletoe hung above the fireplace and white baubles shimmered in the fairy lights. An opened bottle of wine sat on the table, along with four glasses. Excited voices outside the front door told Lucy her guests had arrived. The Christmas wreath shook as Lucy threw the door open to see the faces she loved: Jo, Simon and Matt.

'Merry Christmas, my gorgeous!' Jo exclaimed, throwing her arms around Lucy. She'd arrived that day and Matt had picked her up from the station.

'Hi, guys.' Lucy smiled she closed the door behind them. The smell of a beef casserole wafted down the hallway.

'Wow, your tree looks amazing. I can't believe it's only three days until Christmas,' Jo said, piling three gifts under the tree. As Lucy poured a glass of wine for herself and Jo, the boys raided the fridge for beer.

'So, how's it going with Matt?' Lucy asked, handing Jo her glass and nestling into the sofa, with Jo opting for the armchair.

'Really well. I really like him. Wish I could see him more, but yeah it's going OK.'

Lucy held her glass up. 'I'll drink to that,' she exclaimed.

The boys came into the sitting room. Simon plonked himself down on the sofa and Matt slid onto the arm of the chair and stroked Jo's hair as he leant against her.

'So, what are you two girls raising your glasses to?' Simon asked.

'Oh, nothing really, just girls' stuff,' Jo said with a smile.

As chatter and laughter filled the sitting room, on the street outside a silver car sat several doors down, out of sight of number three. A plume of cigarette funnelled out of the open window. The driver had watched Jo and the two guys arrive with bags, overnight bags; he'd recognised her immediately. Jo hadn't noticed the car; she had been too busy chatting to Simon and Matt. The man watched intently as the front door closed behind them. Jealousy swirled inside him and his breathing became deeper. Who was she with? Who were the guys? Which one was she screwing? Who would be touching her body? Bastard! She was his.

His eyes were trained on Lucy's sitting-room window. He saw Lucy get up and refill the wine. She stood at the window and lit some scented candles on the windowsill. Her dark hair shone in the light, she was wearing a sheer black top. She looked stunning, laughing and happy. She didn't see the car outside; the street was dark. He watched her body. The smooth lines of his Lucy. From the passenger seat he picked up a silk scarf – one he'd given her. He pressed it to his nose and smoothed it across his mouth. Her scent was still on it. He twisted it around in his hands, his thoughts dark, menacing, out of control.

He homed in on Lucy. His Lucy. He would have the final word not her. He was in charge not her. He drew hard on his cigarette, almost burning his lips. He wound the window down and flicked the butt across the pavement. He pushed the button on the door and let the window close, keeping it ajar so he could hear the laughter and voices from inside number three, his gaze unwavering. Now and again his grey eyes watched the rear-view mirror when a car came up behind him. He watched until their rear lights were no longer in view.

Then the door of number eight opened and Gladys Pope shuffled out with Barry on a lead, wearing a thick blue coat. His eyes followed her as she crossed the road and walked up the lane towards the cemetery. She peered into number three's window, making no effort to be subtle about it. She walked ahead of the silver car, not noticing it or the driver. He lit another cigarette and let the window down.

As Barry pulled her forward, she took a left down the small lane. It was perfectly safe and was lined by cottages. It was a good spot for Barry to do his last of the evening's whoopsies, as she called them. She took him as far as the cemetery, let him perform, then cleaned up after him. She tied the bag and turned to walk back home. She turned right onto the street and passed number three, staring in through the window again. This time she walked on towards the dog bin a little further down, Barry trotting ahead on his extendable lead. Barry stopped at the silver car. He'd been startled by the movement inside it, and growled and barked. Slowly, the car window closed.

'Barry, be quiet! Stop that noise,' she called. Barry stood at the car and barked again. The man discarded his cigarette, the window went up slowly and he faced away from her. Gladys stared into the car. She could see the outline of a person but no more. She dropped the bag into the bin and crossed the road, then opened the door to number eight and unlatched the lead from Barry's collar. She looked back at the road and the parked car.

'That car is there again – made our Barry bark. Stan, it's that flash car again.'

Stan muttered under his breath while Gladys shuffled into the kitchen to make her cocoa.

The driver let his window down again and watched.

'Did you hear that dog bark?' Lucy said, standing up and walking to the window. She looked both ways along the road. The man in the car saw the face he knew so well, the eyes he'd looked into when his body was on top of hers. Then she drew the curtains and went back to the sofa.

Nobody left the house that night. Instead, Jo slept in Lucy's bed with Matt, Lucy put an air bed on the floor in her writing room and Simon crashed on the sofa.

The man sat and watched as each light went out. He took the silk scarf and wrapped it around his fingers, passing its softness through his hands, drawing it up to his face and inhaling the scent of her. His Lucy. She would only ever be his. If he couldn't have her, nobody would.

The sound of the milk van woke Simon. Lucy came down the stairs in a T-shirt, her feet bare. She unlocked the door and shielded her bleary eyes from the morning light as she bent down to pick up the two pints of milk, eggs and orange juice. Turning, she saw Simon behind her.

She smiled. 'Cuppa?'

'Love one,' he said. 'How do you look so good in the mornings, Lucy Lu? Look at me with my five o'clock shadow, but you look as gorgeous as always.'

She did look gorgeous, with her slim, silky legs on show and her painted toes manicured to perfection. She tossed her hair to one side and smiled again. 'I might look OK, but my head is a bit achey. How much did we drink last night?'

The kitchen table had a medley of wine and beer bottles on it, the dinner dishes piled up with the empty casserole pot on the worktop.

'Enough to let us know about it,' Simon said, clearing the bottles and taking them outside to the recycling bin. He looked down the street to see if anybody was about. There were a few parked cars and a space between a red Ford and a mint-green Volkswagen Beetle. As the bottles clinked and clanked into the bin, the curtain of number eight peeled open.

'That policeman stayed over! I just saw 'im putting the bottles out, Stan. In fact, they probably all stayed over – the car is still there. The flash silver one 'as gone now,' said Gladys, letting the curtain fall back and waddling into the kitchen to tend to the black pudding and bacon that sizzled in a pan. Simon looked up as he placed the bottles in the bin. He caught Gladys peering out and sighed.

He went back in and closed the door. 'Well, no doubt there'll be a bit of gossip running though the village over the next few days,' he said, running his hand through his hair.

'Why? What d'you mean?' Lucy asked, filling a cafétière with hot water. The aroma of fresh coffee infused the kitchen.

'Gladys Pope – she caught me putting the bottles out. Give it a few hours and no doubt it will be bigger news than the *Gazette*'s headlines.'

'Does that bother you?' Lucy asked.

'Nope, not in the slightest. Just thought I'd let you know.'

'Let you know what?' came Matt's voice from the hallway.

'Gladys Pope saw me putting the bottles out. I was just saying to Luce, she'll have that around the village in no time,' Simon said, pouring coffee into his mug and adding milk.

'Is Jo still sleeping?' Lucy asked.

'Nope, she's in the shower,' Matt replied, taking two mugs for him and Jo and pulling out a chair.

'Great night last night. The food was awesome, Lucy,' Matt said as he adjusted his boxer shorts and stretched out his legs.

Lucy cracked six eggs into a bowl and whisked them furiously.

'Um, Lucy, something bothering you? I don't think you could whisk those any harder if you tried,' Matt said, taking a sip from his mug.

'Did you hear that dog bark last night?' she said.

'Yeah, I heard it, why?' Matt asked. Jo appeared in the kitchen and perched on his lap, taking his coffee. 'Oi, cheeky,' he said. She turned and kissed his forehead.

'Just thought it a bit odd,' Lucy said, pouring the eggs into the pan.

'It was probably nothing,' Simon said, watching Lucy scrape the eggs as they caught on the bottom of the pan.

'Maybe, but I've never heard a dog bark around here. It's always so quiet at night. It's normally cats or foxes we hear,' she said, stirring the eggs. Simon took the bacon that was sizzling under the grill and plated up. 'We'll do a check on the car,' he said.

'Car?' Lucy turned. That was the first time a car had been mentioned. 'What car?'

'When I first came to see you. You talked about Charlie and I took a statement. When I left that morning, Gladys Pope stopped me as I got into the car to go back to the station.'

'Right,' Lucy said. 'What did she have to say?'

'She mentioned seeing a car a few times outside – a silver car.'

Lucy froze, the cutlery clutched in her hand, her hands suddenly clammy.

'A silver car? I haven't seen any silver cars. When I leave in the morning, when I come back, there's no other cars than the few that belong to the cottages. What silver car?' She stared at the three of them.

Simon broke the silence. 'She said it was a flash car – a Jaguar.'

There was a crash as Lucy dropped the cutlery, which sprayed across the floor. Her face froze.

Jo turned to Matt. 'Charlie drives a silver Jaguar,' she said, looking at Lucy then at Simon. 'He's here! He knows where Lucy lives, he's found her.'

Simon bent down and picked up the cutlery. Lucy just stood there, fighting back tears. Then there was a piercing howl: the kind of heart-wrenching sound that makes the hair on the back of your neck stand on end.

Jo grabbed her. Lucy clung to Jo as she slid down the side of the cupboard and onto the floor. The noise that came from her was unrecognisable. She was no longer safe. He had found her! She sat on the floor, her knees bent up to her chest, cradled by Jo. Jo looked at the boys and shook her head, her expression telling them to sort it, to escalate it, to fucking arrest the guy and charge him with stalking and whatever other shit they could throw at him.

Simon knelt down by Lucy and took her hands. 'Lucy, look at me,' he said.

Lucy lifted her head and looked at Simon, the mascara smudged around her eyes.

'We will sort this, Lucy. We can have a warrant put out for his arrest. I need more on the car, it may be nothing. Trust me, you are safe here. Nothing will happen to you, do you hear me?' He lifted her from the floor and sat her in a chair. 'We're here. You have made a statement already. He can be arrested just on your statement alone.'

Jo took a chair next to Lucy. 'So do it. Charlie needs to be arrested. Lucy, stop protecting him.'

The mood had changed: last night's joyous Christmas banter had changed to a fear of the unknown. Lucy pushed her food around her plate. She wasn't hungry, she felt sick. She ran upstairs and locked the bathroom door. They could all hear her coughing and hurling into the loo. She flushed the chain, undressed and climbed into the shower. The water was cold but she didn't care. She felt it freeze her body, freeze her pain. She let the icy water wash over her face and body.

Finally, she turned the tap off and climbed out, her body covered in goosebumps. She wrapped herself in the warmth of a towel and opened the door. She sat on the edge of her bed and stared at herself in the mirror. Her eyes were haunted. On autopilot, she dressed, went downstairs and opened the front door. She stood there with it wide open, long enough to be seen, long enough for him to see her. But he didn't see her; he'd gone.

Chapter Thirteen

Saturday, 23rd December

After breakfast, the four friends left the house.

'Let's take my car today,' Simon said. Jo and Lucy climbed into the back. 'We'll go to the police station first – in fact, give me five. I want to see somebody,' Simon said, undoing his seatbelt and walking across the road to number eight, Gladys Pope's house.

'It's that policeman again,' Gladys said.

'Well, answer the door, woman. He's probably come to tell you to leave the damn curtain alone,' Stan snapped. It was the most he'd said to her all morning.

Simon scanned the cars parked outside Lucy's house: there was a space beyond her gate about two cars down, then a brand-new Beetle. The door of number eight opened and Gladys stood there, filling its frame.

'Officer,' she said, 'is everything all right?'

'Do you mind if I come in?' he asked. Matt and the girls watched from the car as Simon wiped his feet on the mat and closed the yellow front door behind him.

'What's he doing?' asked Jo.

'Search me,' Matt replied, although he knew exactly what he was doing. He would be questioning her about last night, about the dog barking, about the car. If anybody had seen anything, Gladys would have. She would be able to give a reliable eye-witness statement.

'Turn that telly off, Stan, we've got company,' Gladys said, pushing his slippered feet off the pouffe.

'I won't take long, Mrs Pope, but I would like to ask you about last night,' Simon said.

'Last night, what about last night? Me and our Stan were 'ere all night,' Gladys said.

'That's great,' he continued. 'Did you notice anything unusual?'

'Unusual? Can't say I did. Me and Stan 'ad our steak and kidney pie in 'ere on our laps and I tended to the church rota and our Stan watched some comedy, then I took Barry out for 'is last evening's whoopsie.'

'Do you remember what time that was, Mrs Pope?' Simon asked.

'It was dead on ten o'clock. I always take 'im out at ten o'clock. I took 'im up the cemetery lane – it's well-lit along there. I walked past number three and then came 'ome.'

'And that was it?' Simon asked.

'Pretty much. We walked up to the doggy poo bin. Barry barked at a car – I think 'e was startled – then we went back indoors. I don't like to 'ear dogs barking at night, so I 'ushed him.'

'Barry barked at a car?' Simon asked. Matt had said he'd heard a dog bark late at night, and Lucy too. 'Barry barking – is that usual for him?'

'Not for Barry. 'e doesn't bark at anything, not even the postman. 'e's a placid old boy. But there was somebody in the car and the smell of cigarette smoke in the air. Whoever it was startled 'im, it did. I couldn't see who was in the car as it was dark, windows were that dark colour, like the Queen 'as you know? 'e was a smoker, though, definitely a smoker.'

'Thank you, Mrs Pope, you've been most helpful,' Simon said. He gestured goodbye to Mr Pope and let himself out. Gladys folded her arms across her mighty bosoms. 'Don't you want to know what kind of car it was? It was that flash silver Jaguar again. It was parked by the Beetle. Had a Fulham sticker on it.' Simon turned back to Gladys. He hadn't been expecting that.

Gladys pushed the door to and went back into the sitting room. 'There's something fishy going on. 'e's out of uniform, comes round on a Saturday morning, asking questions,' she said, gathering up her church rota and plumping up the cushions before sinking into the sofa.

'Everything OK?' Matt said as Simon got back into the car.

'Yep, I just need to go via the station. I won't be long,' Simon said. He looked pointedly at Matt. He pulled out of the space and did a three-point turn. As they drove the couple of miles to the station, Lucy stared out of the window at the fields and scattered cottages they passed. Her head was full of the terrifying realisation that he had found her. Simon parked in the empty bay at the front of the station. 'Wait in the car with Matt, Lucy. I'm just going to call this through to the Met and send them your file.' He closed the car door and walked up to the station. The heating was off in the station and he could see his breath in the air as he walked across the waiting room. He turned on the computer and brought up Lucy's notes. He sat behind the counter and phoned the Met's CID.

'This is PC Mackenzie, Wrabness police station, North Essex Constabulary. I'd like an arrest on an owner of a silver Jaguar, registration number OE63 TBD. It's registered to a Charlie Wainwright, Flat 2, Mansion House, Waldermar Avenue, Fulham,'

'And the postcode?' CID asked.

'SW6 5QJ.'

'That's Sierra Whisky six, five Quebec Juliet,' repeated CID.

'Correct,' replied Mackenzie.

'Why would you like us to arrest him?'

'Harassment, stalking, he needs to be brought in for questioning,' Mackenzie replied. 'Is it possible to carry out a swoop arrest to avoid the suspect disposing of any objects or devices? I'd like the suspect to be held in custody and questioned about alleged stalking, harassment, intimidation and possible domestic abuse, false imprisonment.'

'Do we have a crime reference for this?' the CID officer asked.

'Crime reference two five seven six, dated second of October,' Simon went on. 'The victim is a Miss Lucy Carter of three Lambourne Terrace, Wrabness, Essex.'

'We're on it,' came the response. 'We will contact once the suspect is in custody.'

'I'd like to order a search of the property for anything linked to Miss Lucy Carter. I'd like his phone, laptop and any other devices to be seized, his car to be impounded, and the flat to be searched. We're looking for any evidence of DPD courier accounts, receipts for fuel, and destination entries on his sat-nav in the car or on any other devices,' Simon said. He wasn't going to leave any stone unturned.

'Leave it with us. I'll get my DI to call you,' came the reply.

Simon sighed. Now it was Charlie's turn to feel the force of the law on him; now it was his turn to run scared. Simon closed the computer and took his police mobile with him. He turned out the lights and locked the front door.

'All done?' Matt said as Simon climbed into the car.

'Yep. I called CID. I hope the DI will call me back today. It's done now, Lucy.'

'Good work, Si. He'd better get used to living at Her Majesty's.'

'Her Majesty's?' Lucy said, looking at Simon in the rear-view mirror.

'Prison,' Simon said.

'D'you think it will come to that?' she asked.

'I'd be pretty surprised if it didn't. Harassment alone can put somebody away, but with everything else you've mentioned, this is serious, Lucy. It's now in the hands of the Met.'

Simon reversed out of the station and drove towards Harwich. They had decided to take a boat trip to the idyllic fishing village of Shotley and have lunch at the The Shipwreck. Simon parked the car near the pier and they walked to the boat. Simon wanted to take Lucy to Felixstowe and show her the most amazing old-fashioned bookshop, an Aladdin's cave of books. She needed to be looked after, protected. As they neared the pier, Matt took Jo's hand and held it. She nestled her head into his shoulder,

'I kinda like you lots, Officer Matthew Willis,' she said.

'Ditto,' he said and kissed her forehead.

'Lucy!' came a male voice from behind them. Lucy jumped and stopped dead in her tracks. Jo took her hand.

'Lucy, hi, I'm glad I've seen you. I've been meaning to text you, but I haven't had my phone. I smashed the screen.' It was Ben.

Jo nudged Matt and Simon to carry on walking. She let go of Lucy's hand and walked ahead with the boys. Lucy stood and stared at Ben. She hadn't expected to see him, and she didn't know what to say or do. He hadn't texted her and she'd left it, thinking he simply wasn't interested.

'That's bad luck,' she said finally. 'I'm sorry to hear that.'

'Yeah, it's a bit of a ball-ache. I should get it back in a couple of days with a new screen, but I wanted to ask if I could take you out for a drink,' he said, moving closer to her. She looked into his eyes. They were brown with a hint of green in them. His face was weather-beaten by the sea air and sun, and he was wearing the blue beanie he had worn the day he had bought her a coffee.

'I guess you're busy with your boyfriend, though?' he said, looking at Simon.

'My boyfriend?' Lucy questioned. 'I'm not with anyone.'

'Oh, I figured the guy over there was your boyfriend.'

'Simon? No, he's just a good friend. He lives near me, and Jo, my friend from London, is with her boyfriend Matt.' Lucy felt she needed to be honest although she wasn't entirely sure why.

'Right, well, that makes it easier, and now I feel like a bit of a fool for assuming wrongly. Can I take you out for that drink?'

'I'm kinda busy,' Lucy said, brushing her hair away from her face.

'Right, I'll take that as my cue to not bother you again. You're letting me down gently,' Ben said. 'It was nice meeting you.' He turned to walk away.

'No – wait.' She felt her arm reach out to grab his hand. Now it was her go to feel awkward. He looked at her hand on his and she let go hastily, realising what she had done. 'I mean, not no, I am busy. It's Christmas in a few days and Jo is staying with me, but I would like to go for a drink with you. I figured you didn't want to because you hadn't messaged me, but you couldn't if you didn't have your phone.'

'How about tomorrow then?' he said. 'I could pick you up if you tell me where you live.'

'Tell you where I live?' She seemed nervous.

'Well, I'll need to know, to pick you up?' He looked puzzled.

'You're right. Tomorrow sounds perfect. My address is...' She stopped. 'Will you remember if I tell you? I don't have a pen or paper.' The wind blew her hair across her face, and it caught on her lip gloss. Ben watched her. She was stunning. He decided to memorise the address, the same way he had memorised her face.

'I'll remember it,' he said.

'OK, if you're sure. It's three Lambourne Terrace, Wrabness. You'll see my Mini outside and I have a red front door with a Christmas wreath on it. It's the only door with a wreath on it, in fact.'

'It's a date. I'll pick you up at seven o'clock.' He had an urge to kiss her there and then. What was it about her? Why did she make him feel the way she did?

'I'm going to have to go, Ben. My friends are waiting for me. See you at seven tomorrow.' She turned and walked quickly to the others.

'Guy on the bike?' Jo said, smiling at Lucy.

'He's called Ben and he's taking me out tomorrow. You don't mind, do you? Will you stay close, though?' Lucy seemed a little more at ease. Maybe meeting Ben had been a good thing for her. Now she was friends with Simon and Matt, they were in her life, but she and Simon were nothing but good friends. There was something about Ben she liked, but she didn't know what, because she'd never talked to him. She saw him daily when she sat at the beach. She often thought about him. Now she wanted to know more about him. Whether that was the right thing to do, she didn't know, but at the moment he was in her thoughts. She didn't want to see Charlie in her head. She didn't know why, but Ben was able to make her forget the face of the man who hurt her. But why though, what was it about him? How could a guy have such an impact on her? A guy she hadn't even played the game with. He'd bought her a coffee when she was cold. He stopped at the beach when she cartwheeled and cheekily said 'nice day for a cartwheel.' His smile got her at the first post. There was a simplicity to him, carefree, maybe a little vulnerable. He reminded her of herself, of who she was. Simple, carefree, vulnerable.

The foot ferry pulled up alongside the pier and the four friends embarked. The sea foamed up against the sides of the ferry as it sailed out to Shotley Peninsula.

As the boat sailed across the estuary, Simon's phone rang. He moved away from the other three and walked to the end of the boat, where there were no passengers.

'PC Mackenzie speaking,' he said.

'PC Mackenzie, this is Detective Inspector Phillips from the Met.'

'Afternoon, DI Phillips. I was expecting your call,' Simon replied.

'You've requested an arrest on a suspect by the name of Mr Charlie Wainwright and a search on his property and car,' he said. 'I will be handling this operation. Do you have any evidence that he has been present at, or near, Lucy Carter's address?'

'I do. I have a credible eye-witness who has spotted the car, I believe to be the suspect's on several occasions. Miss Carter has also reported in her statement that she was imprisoned in a dark room in their flat. Domestic violence has been reported. I have also seen the DPD parcel that was sent to Miss Carter. Could we have it sent to forensics for fingerprints? It might not be from him, but it's a bit odd.'

'Any positive sightings of the suspect?' the DI asked.

'None that are confirmed, but a male was seen leaving the residence on Thursday 14th November. Negative on positive face identification, just scruffy trainers and hoodie.'

'And who saw this?' the DI asked.

'A Miss Segal from the car,' Simon replied.

'Right, so domestic violence, false imprisonment, Miss Carter clearly knows the suspect?' the DI asked. 'What was their relationship?'

'Miss Carter was in a relationship with Charlie Wainwright for approximately three years, engaged for one. She left him in October because he was abusive and controlling in their relationship, and moved here.' Simon turned his face away to hide his conversation from the passengers on the ferry.

'Did she report Charlie Wainwright at all in London?' the DI asked.

'No. She made a statement at the police station here,' Simon replied.

'Why not in London?' the DI asked.

'Fear. She left him secretly, without telling him, but he has somehow found her,' Mackenzie said.

'When was the report made in Essex?"

'I believe on the 16th November, I'm off duty so can't give an exact date,' he replied

'So why is it only coming to us now, a month later?' the DI asked perplexed by the delay in reporting to them.

'Again, she was frightened, she didn't want it to go any further. It's taken a lot to get her to do this,' Mackenzie replied.

'Do we know how he's located her?' the DI asked.

'No, we don't know how he located her,' Simon replied.

'So, we have a case of domestic abuse on our hands as well as stalking and harassment– not a nice situation. All too often they are too scared to come forward. Right, I will have the crime bureau phone Miss Carter for any support she may require. How is she?'

'This morning she wasn't great, but she's bearing up now. She has a close friend staying with her over Christmas, but she's frightened,' Simon said.

'Understandably,' the DI replied. 'We will have Mr Wainwright arrested and brought in for questioning and the necessary searches put in place. Could you give me the name and address of your eye-witness?'

'Yes. It's a neighbour, Mrs Gladys Pope, residing at number eight Lambourne Terrace, Wrabness, Essex. She has seen the car on several occasions, last night being the most recent. She has been unable to ID the number plate, but interestingly said it had a Fulham sticker on it,' Simon said.

'Fulham sticker?' the DI sat upright.

'Yeah I wasn't sure if she meant the garage it came from,' Simon said.

'Fulham sticker could be football? Fulham Football Club is down the road. My hunch, it's his permit holder badge for parking, every car in London has one for the Borough they live in, shame we didn't get a letter on the sticker,' DI Phillips replied.

'A letter?' Simon quizzed.

'A letter is for your street or streets surrounding,' the DI replied.

'Right, that makes sense,' Simon replied.

'She will have to be brought into the station to make a statement. In the meantime, we will keep you informed of our progress. I'll be in touch.'

Simon put his phone back in his pocket and joined the others at the side of the boat.

The boat chugged alongside the harbour at Shotley. A crew member jumped alongside and threw a rope around an iron bollard to tie the ferry in place letting down the fenders to protect the boat from bashing against the quayside in the wind. The foot passengers disembarked from one end while the return day-trippers boarded at the other end. Shotley was a quaint fishing village with a marina and lock. Flags hung from the front of a few of the houses and fishing nets lay in most of the front gardens. Plastic buckets and children's crabbing nets lay strewn across the lawns, having been buffeted about by the wind.

'I need to grab some cash,' Jo said as they passed the post office with a sign outside advertising Free Cash Withdrawals. Lucy smiled at the prospect of free cash from an ATM. The sign creaked as it blew in the wind. A bell rang as she walked in. She drew out one hundred pounds and bought a packet of Marlboro Gold before leaving. As they walked along the narrow streets, Jo pulled Lucy in, arms linked.

'So, a date with Ben? That's cool,' she said.

'Yeah,' Lucy said, brushing the hair from her face. 'I didn't think he was interested.' She burrowed her hands deeper into the pockets of her three-quarter-length tailored camel coat.

'How come? You've just said hi to him, haven't you?' Jo said, giving Lucy a quizzical look.

'I had coffee with him the other day,' Lucy said nonchalantly. Jo stopped and looked at Lucy. 'Hang on! What? You didn't tell me about this. Coffee? You don't like coffee! Where, what, when, who, how?'

'The other day I was writing on the beach and it was absolutely freezing. He rode past and stopped. He asked me why I was sitting in the freezing cold and we got talking, and he offered to buy me a coffee to warm me up. That was pretty much it. He asked me for my number, I gave it to him, but he didn't call or text me, so I figured he wasn't interested. I was going to tell you this morning at breakfast but then everything went wrong and I didn't. It seemed pointless. I'd been thinking. If he had called, would I be scared of him like I am of Charlie, or would I give him a chance? D'you know what I mean?'

'I get it. This morning was pretty bad. Fuck, I don't know. If I could make it go away, I would – you know that, don't you? But Matt and Simon know what they're doing. Not every guy is a Charlie – you've had a bad experience but not all men are monsters and control freaks and bullies, they're not. Ben seems genuine and nice, and he's obviously pretty keen. He asked you out even when he thought Simon was your boyfriend. Go for it. Are you nervous about seeing him? Maybe it's time for you to learn to trust again.'

'I don't feel nervous around him. I don't know why, but there's something about him that puts me at ease. I get that flustered kind of feeling but is that because I like him? Who knows? Ask me tomorrow when I'm getting ready. I'll probably be a panicking mess.' She laughed.

As the girls walked on, Jo turned to the boys. 'Is it this pub, Matt?'

'Yep, that's it. Go on in, we'll catch you up.'

The girls left the boys, who slowed their pace. 'Was Gladys Pope a credible eye-witness?' Matt asked.

'Yeah, I think she was. I was kinda hoping she wouldn't be, but she said it was her dog that barked. It was spooked by someone in a car, but she couldn't give a positive ID on the person. The car windows were tinted and it was obviously dark, but as she approached the window closed,' Simon said. 'Then as I walked out of her house she dropped the bombshell.'

'What?' Matt asked.

She said it was the same silver Jaguar she'd seen before. Then she said there was a Fulham sticker on it.'

'Fuck!' Matt said, shaking his head. 'Jo was right – he's found Lucy. No one around Wrabness has a Jaguar. So what did the Met say?'

'The Fulham sticker either means football supporter or safe punt resident permit holder. That was the DI on the phone. I've asked him to carry out a swoop arrest, take Wainwright in for questioning, impound his car and devices and do a house search. The Met wants a statement from Gladys Pope and obviously they'll want to speak with Lucy.'

'What are you going to tell Lucy? She was freaked out this morning. This is going to send her over the edge. You're gonna need to pick the right time, mate,' Matt said, lighting a Marlboro and inhaling hard in the cold air.

'When's a right time for this? There is no right time.' Simon kicked a pebble across the road.

'I know, but you can't keep it from her. You're going to have to tell her. Jesus!' Matt flicked his cigarette across the street and patted Simon on the back. He was a good police officer but an even better friend.

Chapter Fourteen

Saturday, 23rd December

One squad car and a black BMW, blue lights flashing across its radiator grill and a temporary blue light on the roof, sped down Fulham Broadway. Buses, black cabs and cars pulled in to avoid them. How the London traffic, even when gridlocked, had the ability to move and part like the waves of the Red Sea was incredible. Pedestrians looked on as the police cars raced across Munster Road. Sirens pierced the calm of the leafy Fulham streets. The cars turned right into Waldemar Avenue and screeched to a halt, the squad car hemming in a silver Jaguar, registration number OE63 TBD, the undercover black BMW pulling up outside Mansion House. Three officers and a plain-clothes policeman climbed out of the car. Detective Inspector Phillips opened the front door of the black BMW. He was tall with short greying hair and a chiselled jaw. He was cleanly shaven and wore a dark grey suit, black shoes, dark tie and a long navy mac. Hands in his pockets, he perused the area then walked coolly to the front door, police either side of him. He pushed the buzzer for Flat 2. No answer. He pushed it again, holding it down for longer. No answer. From the first-floor window a man had spotted the cars. He stood to one side of the window, waiting. An officer spotted the reflection of the man and he signalled with his hand: suspect inside. DI Phillips pressed another buzzer and the speaker phone crackled.

'Hello?'

'No need to be alarmed. This is Detective Inspector Phillips, Met Police. Could you open the front door? We need access to the building.'

The buzzer sounded. He pushed the heavy door open, signalling the officers to go in, holding two fingers up to show the door and floor number. DI Phillips led the way, Detective Sergeant Murphy by his side, and the officers following. DI Phillips knocked on the door of Flat 2. No answer. He knocked again. Still nothing. He knocked a third time and heard a phone ring. It stopped abruptly.

DI Phillips gave a nod.

'POLICE, STAND BACK!' he shouted.

Two officers bashed open the door and went in ahead. The DI walked around the flat, slowly pushing each door open. One door was locked. His heels clipped on the oak floor. There didn't seem to be anyone in, although there was no way of escaping, other than out of a window onto the street, which would have been a bit of jump. DI Phillips pushed the bathroom door open. Charlie ran past him and down the hall towards the front door. The two officers who had not gone into the apartment blocked the front door. He was trapped.

'Going somewhere in a hurry?' the DI said. His voice carried a hint of an East End accent. Charlie turned around and looked defiantly at him.

'Would have been easier to open the door, Charlie. It is Charlie, isn't it? Costly business, locksmiths in Central London.'

Charlie smirked at him and shooting a look towards his phone, which lay on a table.

'Charlie Wainwright, I am arresting you on suspicion of stalking and harassment. You do not have to say anything, but it may harm your defence if you do not mention when questioned something which you may later rely on in court. Anything you do say may be given in evidence.' DI Phillips moved away. He knew just from looking at Charlie that he was hiding something. As he walked away to the table where Charlie's phone and keys lay, he turned to one of his officers. 'Cuff him and take him to the car. DS Murphy, stay here. Carry out a thorough search, then retrieve Mr Wainwright's car, phone, and all other devices. You know what you're looking for. Make sure you find it – and get the door to that room opened.' DI Phillips spun on his heel.

'Yes, guv.'

The door opposite the flat opened, and a young woman came out, open-mouthed. She went back inside and closed the door then ran to her window and looked out. She knew this had something to do with Lucy, oh my God where was she? She felt totally paralysed, what the hell was happening? Her breath deepened, her hands clapped together quickly in panic. She left the window. Two officers led Charlie down the stairs, DI Phillips following. A small band of residents had already gathered on the street, eager to see what was going on. DI Phillips opened the rear passenger door and ushered Charlie in.

The girl hurried back to Charlie's open flat and went in.

'Can I help you?' DS Murphy asked her.

'Um, this is Charlie and Lucy's flat. I saw you take Charlie away. Is everything OK? Is Lucy OK?' she asked in a nervous way.

'I'm afraid I can't tell you anything,' DS Murphy said, trying to usher her out.

'I live opposite. I'm Lucy's friend. Is she OK?' she said again, sounding concerned. DS Murphy softened his approach. She'd made no mention of Charlie; all her concern was for Lucy.

'Is there anything you'd like to tell me about Lucy and Charlie? What's your name?' he asked.

'Jones. Rachel Jones, I live opposite. I think I might have some information, I don't know,' she said.

'What kind of information?' DS Murphy asked.

'I saw Lucy a while ago. October, it was. Said she was in a hurry, she couldn't talk,' Rachel said, twiddling her shirt cuff. 'She brushed me off.'

'Maybe she didn't have time – is that not plausible?' DS Murphy asked.

'Not for Lucy, she always had time for you. She seemed agitated. But it wasn't just that,' she said.

'Go on,' DS Murphy said, noting Rachel's name and address.

'I heard screams and shouting from their flat the night before she left. I heard her crying, saying "I'm sorry". It didn't seem like a normal argument. The day after, she had a split lip. She said she fell up the stairs but I don't know. She sounded like she was begging Charlie when she cried. He shouted back – he was angry. I heard her scream and a door slam. That's how it sounded. Has he done something to her? Has he hurt her?'

'Miss Jones, how long have you known Charlie?' DS Murphy asked.

'I've known him a while – about seven years or so. We lived in the same apartment block long before Lucy moved in with him. We were good friends,' Rachel said.

'Good friends, you say?' DS Murphy continued.

'Yes, we'd have the odd drink together or coffee, or go out for breakfast on a Sunday morning on Fulham Road. Then he met Lucy.'

'How would you describe Charlie?' DS Murphy asked.

'He's friendly, inoffensive, kind, generous – just a nice kind of guy.'

'And what else do you know about him? About his family, for example?' DS Murphy asked, turning the page of his notes.

'He didn't talk about his family much. When I first met him, he said his mother was a drunk. That's all. I really don't know anything else. I'm sorry.'

'You've been most helpful, Miss Jones.' DS Murphy got up to show her out.

'And Lucy?' Rachel asked.

'Thank you, Miss Jones. I'm afraid I can't disclose that.' He closed the door.

DI Phillips walked around the car and got into the back. Leaning over to put the suspect's seatbelt on, he took a packet of Benson and Hedges from his pocket.

'Cigarette?' he asked.

Charlie nodded. Taking a cigarette from the pack, he leant forward for it to be lit.

***

Fulham police station was covered from every angle by CCTV. DI Phillips got out first and opened the door for Charlie, taking his arm and walking him through the back entrance. DI Phillips left him at the desk with the duty officers and went through to his department. He called Simon's mobile.

When his phone rang, Simon left the others to go outside.

'PC Mackenzie? DI Phillips here. We have Charlie Wainwright in custody. We arrested him today at thirteen hundred hours at his apartment. My DS is at present searching the suspect's apartment, his vehicle has been impounded, and we have twenty-four hours to interview him. I'll let you know our progress after we have questioned him.'

Lucy's phone pinged. She took it out of her bag.

Lucy I'm worried, where are you? Charlie's been arrested. Rachel.

'Who was that?' Lucy asked as Simon returned.

Simon couldn't lie. She needed to hear the truth. Jo looked at Matt, sensing from his face that something was going down.

'For fuck's sake, guys, it's Charlie, isn't it? He's been arrested, hasn't he?'

Simon looked at Lucy, surprised that she'd guess that. 'Yes. I was going to wait until the weekend was over to tell you. Mrs Pope has ID'd the car. The Met arrested Charlie today; he's in custody.'

Lucy stared across the table at Simon, then blinked and sighed deeply. 'Right, that's fine. I'm fine. I feel relieved, I think. I thought I was going mad, I thought I was imagining being watched, but I haven't. He's been here. I smelt cigarette smoke when I cleared the house. Then again the other day when I came back from the beach. Nobody smokes around here apart from Jo and Matt. That night with the bins – that was him, wasn't it? The delivery guy, it was him, wasn't it? I figured it was my imagination playing tricks on me. But it wasn't. How did he find me?' She paused for breath. 'I need some air.'

Lucy left the table and sat outside on the wall by the water's edge, staring out at the horizon. She thought about how she'd felt when she realised he knew where she was, then she thought of Ben. She lit a cigarette and blew the smoke into the air, she didn't ever smoke alone. It seemed to slow her breathing though, calmed her. She thought only of Ben as she inhaled. She couldn't think of Charlie; he made her skin crawl.

'How d'you think she is?' Simon asked. 'Shall I go outside to her?'

Jo turned to him. 'No, leave her.'

After a while, the door of the pub opened and Lucy came in. She sat at the table and looked at the others. She smiled at Simon. 'Thank you. I just needed five minutes to process this. It's escalated so fast, but yeah, thank you.' She sat at the table and downed the gin and tonic in front of her.

'Another one?' Jo said.

'No.'

Chapter Fifteen

Saturday 23rd December

Ds Murphy brought several transparent forensics bags into DI Phillips' office containing the items retrieved from Charlie's apartment.

'Find anything of interest?' Phillips asked.

'Phone, laptop, delivery note, a packet of cigarettes, a wallet containing several receipts for a bed and breakfast in a village called Bromley, Essex,' DS Murphy replied and placed them on the DI's desk. 'DC Kennedy is still at the property.'

'What was in the locked room?' Phillips asked.

'A wooden chair and some masking tape. That was it.' Kennedy replied.

'Right it's beginning to add up,' Phillips replied.

'What's that guv a fetish d'you think?'

'No, it's a little more sinister than that, this ties with Mackenzie stating Miss Carter being imprisoned, locked in a dark room. This isn't nice.' Phillips said taking up the file with Charlie's mugshot.

'Also, guv, his neighbour Rachel gave me some information when you left.'

'What have you got?' DI Phillips said, twiddling an unlit cigarette in his fingers.

'She gave an account of an argument, a woman's scream, door slamming, before Lucy left. She saw Lucy the morning she left – she was in a hurry, wouldn't chat, she said she seemed nervous, and she had a split lip,' DS Murphy continued, reading his notes.

'Anything on Charlie?' DI Phillips asked.

'Said he was kind, nice, inoffensive. His mother drank, apparently, but he didn't talk about his family.'

'How long has she known him?'

'Seven years, guv,' DS Murphy said, closing his notebook.

'Nice work. Interesting – his mother drank.'

DI Phillips took the phone from the bag. All the messages had been wiped.

'Can you get IT on the laptop and phone and get them to bring up all the data that has been deleted? All messages to a Lucy Carter are what we're looking for, and any other contacts of interest. He thinks he's being clever by wiping them – get them back. I want a list of phone calls made in the last three months or so – all numbers. Also emails to any bed and breakfasts, hotels, motels in the vicinity of the victim's residence. Look into whether he has family in the east of London, Kent, Suffolk, Essex, etc. I also want a list of his movements from October to now. Get a positive ID on his number plate across London on all CCTV and onto the M11, M25 and A12. See if you can find anything on his next of kin, his mother.'

DI Phillips went through the wallet and found a bundle of service station receipts and a torn piece of an envelope addressed to Jo Segal c/o Lucy Carter, 3 Lambourne Terrace, Wrabness, Essex. He placed them back in a forensic bag and paperclipped them to a page in the file that CID had given him. It had a mugshot of Charlie Wainwright on the front.

'Get him into the interviewing room. The CPS has given us twenty-four hours to question him before he's charged, bailed or let go.'

Phillips propped his feet on his desk and perused the file and receipts that had been taken from Charlie's wallet. What did Charlie Wainwright want? he pondered. What was his end game? There had to be one. And where was his mother now?

His phone flashed. Suspect in interview room one two six. Phillips got up, put his cigarettes in his pocket and took the file with him. He walked along the corridor, stopping at the vending machine for a coffee. As he approached the interview room, DS Murphy came out of the observation suite. Charlie was sitting there, a station solicitor by his side. She was Asian, her hair in a ponytail, dressed in a blue suit and roll-neck jumper. DI Phillips and DS Murphy entered the room. A duty officer switched on the recorder and the red light signalled recording in progress. A camera in the room moved into position, a red light flashing above the lens. The lens turned towards Wainwright, who had beads of sweat on his upper lip. His arms were crossed defensively across his chest. Behind the glass screen, other officers watched the monitors and Wainwright in the interview room.

DI Phillips spoke first. 'For the record, Detectives Murphy and Phillips have entered the room at fourteen thirteen hours.'

They took their seats and sat back and stared at Charlie, his gaze fixed, arms still crossed.

DI Phillips opened the file on him. 'Interview commenced at fourteen seventeen hours, today's date twenty-third of December 2015. Detective Inspector and Detective Sergeant Murphy present, legal representative Miss Sawallah present, and the suspect, Charlie Wainwright.' Phillips crossed his arms and sat further back in his chair, watching the suspect. 'If you would state your full name for me.'

Charlie looked at his solicitor, who nodded.

'Charlie Wainwright.'

'And your date of birth?' DI Phillips continued.

Miss Sawallah nodded her approval to her client.

'Seventeenth of July, nineteen eighty-four.'

Phillips turned the pages on the file. 'Do you know why you're here?'

Charlie looked at him and bit his bottom lip. 'No.'

'Where were you, Charlie, on Friday the twenty-second of December?'

'No comment,' Charlie said, not flinching.

'Do you know why you are here, Charlie?'

'For the avoidance of doubt, I have to remind my client that he does not have to answer any of your questions,' Miss Sawallah said, throwing a look at Charlie.

'Thank you, Miss Sawallah. Noted,' Phillips said, taking the pen from the table and twiddling it between his fingers.

'I'll ask you again, where were you on the twenty-second of December?'

'No comment.'

'You see, our road traffic CCTV picked up a silver Jaguar heading east towards the junction of the M11. Zoom in, and the registration plate is that of your Jaguar, Charlie. In fact, we have several sightings of the same vehicle from November to December heading east towards Essex.'

'No comment.'

'Do you have family in Essex?'

'No comment.'

'Was your car reported stolen, Charlie?'

'No comment.'

'Joyriders, Charlie?'

'No comment.'

'Let me help you out here,' Phillips said, taking the file and reading the notes made by PC Mackenzie. 'You are here today because you were seen outside number three Lambourne Terrace, Essex. Why were you at Lambourne Terrace?'

'No comment,' Charlie replied.

'Do you know a Miss Lucy Carter?' Phillips asked.

'No comment,' Charlie replied.

'Again, let me help you out. You know a Miss Carter because she was your fiancée, wasn't she?'

'No comment,' Charlie replied.

'You were at number three Lambourne Terrace because that is where Miss Carter lives, isn't that right, Charlie?'

'No comment.'

'Why were you outside Miss Carter's home? When you live in London and Miss Carter left you in October?'

'No comment.'

'I'm finding this a little hard to understand. Why are you saying "no comment"? Because you don't know Miss Carter, or you're suffering from memory loss? You received a call from PC Mackenzie on Sunday the eighteenth of November 2015 to tell you to not contact Miss Carter again. Do you remember the conversation, Charlie?'

'No comment.'

'Again, I'll jog your memory. You replied "Miss Carter is my fiancée and you have no right to tell me what I can and can't do. Who the fuck do you think you are? She's my fucking fiancée, the fucking bitch." Do you lose your temper easily, Charlie?'

'No comment.'

'Do you have a short fuse, Charlie?'

'No comment.'

'I'd say you do. The text message you sent to Miss Carter on the fifteenth of October says: "Lucy, talk to me, you're making me mad now." Is that why Miss Carter left you? Did she leave you because she was frightened of you? Because you terrified her? Did she make you mad, Charlie?'

'No comment.'

'Did you lose your temper with Miss Carter, Charlie?'

'No comment.'

'You were cautioned by PC Mackenzie on the eighteenth of November to not contact Miss Carter again. Yet you continued to do so. Do you remember doing this?'

'No comment.'

'How many times did you hit Miss Carter?' Phillips asked.

'No comment.'

'I have to advise you, Detective Inspector Phillips, that you have no proper evidence to suggest my client has a temper or indeed showed any violence towards Miss Carter. Why is this line of questioning relevant to this interview?' Miss Sawallah asked.

DI Phillips leant forward in his chair and placed his arms on the table. 'Thank you, Miss...'

'Sawallah,' she said.

'Right, Miss Sawallah. Noted. Miss Carter left you in October. She didn't want to be with you any more, did she, Charlie?'

Charlie stared at Phillips and said nothing, he remained unnerved by the interrogation.

'No comment.'

'You abused Miss Carter, didn't you?' Phillips was cool with his questioning. He wasn't going to let Wainwright squirm his way out of it; he'd seen his type before.

'You knew she couldn't fight you, didn't you, so you hit her. Isn't that right, Charlie?'

'Detective Inspector, you have no evidence that my client has been violent towards Miss Carter. Do not try to intimidate my client.'

Phillips threw a glance at Miss Sawallah. She was young, inexperienced. She hadn't yet met the likes of Phillips and she didn't know how he worked. He was at the top of his game and knew exactly how to get a confession and interrogate. He was the best in the Met.

'You hit Miss Carter, didn't you? Did that make you feel powerful, strong, in control?'

'No comment.'

'Detective...' Miss Sawallah began.

He lifted his finger as if to hush her. 'You see, we know you hit her. Why else would you send a text saying "I was angry – you made me angry. I shouldn't have—"? Shouldn't have what?'

'No comment.'

'How many times did you hit her, Charlie?'

'No comment.'

'Do you know a Miss Rachel Jones?'

'No comment.'

'You know Rachel Jones well, don't you?'

'No comment.'

'She's your neighbour, isn't she?'

'No comment.'

'She heard Lucy's screams. She heard her cries. She heard a door slam.'

'How many times have you hit Miss Carter?'

'Detective, I have to remind you that my client...' Phillips took his hand from the file to silence her again.

'Rachel Jones has stated "Lucy seemed not herself and had a split lip".'

Miss Sawallah swallowed hard, she was sitting next to a man who abused.

'No comment.'

'Your family, Charlie, where are they?'

'No comment.'

'Your mother, where is she?'

'No comment.'

'You told Rachel your mother drank, didn't you, Charlie?'

'No comment.'

'Did she hurt you, Charlie?'

'No comment.'

'Did she reject you, Charlie?'

Charlie's breathing grew louder and heavier.

Miss Sawallah jotted down some more notes and tidied her file. She was feeling under pressure in this interview. She knew she was sitting next to a liar and defending him. She was a woman – how would she react if she was struck by a man, controlled, bullied? Would she seek defence herself?

From the observation room the officers watched him. 'He's as guilty as fuck,' one officer commented. 'Look at his body language. He didn't like that last question – look at him.'

The observation room door opened and DS Kennedy entered, carrying a bag containing three small flat-pack boxes and an opened packet of pink tissue paper. DS Kennedy took a photo of the items and printed them out, then put a sticky note on the printed-out photo. In capital letters he wrote: ASK HIM ABOUT A BOX. DPD?'

'Perhaps you'd like to tell us where you were on Friday the sixteenth of November,' Phillips said. Charlie was going to break at some point, and Phillips needed something to break him. As he sat trying to work him out, how he could corner him, the vent in the room opened.

'Interview suspended at fifteen fifty hours. Detectives Murphy and Phillips have left the interview room.' Murphy switched off the record button and left the interview room with Phillips. They opened the door of the observation room and entered.

'What have you got?' Phillips asked. The vent either opening or closing during an interview was a signal to the detective interviewing to suspend the interview, as further evidence had been found and was being held in the observation room. They watched the room through the one-way glass. His solicitor sat reading her notes while Charlie sat staring, his arms still crossed.

'Guv, we found these in the apartment – masking tape, the chair, which we've taken a photo of, and this box. The box is connected to the DPD parcel he sent for delivery on the thirteenth of November. He sent Lucy Carter a gift – a Dior lipstick in pink tissue paper.'

'Nice work, Kennedy. Can we get a written statement from Miss Jones? Do we have a link with the DPD courier for this?' Phillips asked.

'We do. The driver that day was Tony Polenski. It was a collection delivery,' DS Kennedy replied.

'Right, where was the parcel collected from? PC Mackenzie has a statement from Lucy stating the delivery guy was Eastern European. Polenski is Polish.' Phillips took the photo of the evidence retrieved from Charlie's flat.

'Yes, guv. The drop-off point was Tesco Metro on the Fulham Road, at the junction of Munster Road. A DPD vehicle was caught on the street-view camera parked in a bus lane at fourteen twenty-five, registration AD54 TRM. It also received a penalty for bus lane usage. We've already watched the CCTV footage for that day from Tesco,' Kennedy continued.

'Right, and what have we got?' Phillips stared into the interviewing room. Wainwright was motionless, arms still crossed.

'A positive ID on Wainwright, guv. On Tuesday thirteenth November he was seen on camera withdrawing cash at eleven thirty hours, entering Tesco at eleven thirty-three and dropping off the parcel at eleven thirty-six. Then he bought a packet of Marlboro Gold cigarettes at eleven forty-three.'

'Play it to me.' Kennedy pressed the play button and continued: 'You see, guv, the CCTV picks up a close-up of

Wainwright entering the store with a plastic bag. The camera records him going to the cash machine inside the shop then placing the bag on the counter and paying for the delivery of a parcel. The live street cameras pick up the DPD driver parking on Munster Road, the courier leaving the vehicle and entering to collect parcels a few hours later on the same day.' Kennedy turned off the recording.

'Perfect. Can we link the CCTV up to the screen for viewing? Follow my cue with questions.'

Murphy and Phillips left the observation room.

'Coffee?' Murphy said as he stood next to the coffee machine.

'Strong black,' Phillips replied. The machine spewed out the cups and filled them with steaming black coffee.

'What's his motive, guv?' DS Murphy asked, taking a drink from the plastic cup.

'I don't know, but I want him charged. He's dangerous. A room with a chair and masking tape. I've got a gut feeling about him and it's not good.'

The detectives stood at the window until they'd finished their coffee, then went back into the interview room. Phillips placed the file with the new evidence in front of him.

Murphy pressed the record button. 'DI Phillips and DS Murphy present, interview commenced at seventeen thirty hours on the twenty-third of December 2015.' Phillips leant back in his chair.

'Do you like to shop in Tesco?' Phillips asked.

Charlie looked perplexed. What the hell had where he liked to shop got to do with this? He was confused by the question and looked at his solicitor for support. She had no idea why the question had been asked, and raised her eyebrows.

Charlie uncrossed his arms. 'Tesco?' He asked smirking. 'No.'

He'd walked straight into the trap.

'Do you prefer Waitrose?' Phillips asked.

'What do you think?' Charlie replied.

'You tell me, Charlie. I'm quite partial to a small supermarket for convenience – a quick purchase of milk, a bottle of wine on the way home, a packet of cigarettes.' Phillips lured him in.

'Like I said, I don't shop in Tesco,' Charlie replied.

'On the fourteenth of November, Miss Carter received a parcel delivered by a courier. Know anything about it?' Phillips had changed tack. He had what he wanted – a negative on Tesco, exactly the answer he was hoping for.

Charlie sat forward in his chair. He appeared to be about to say something of value. He looked straight at Phillips. 'No comment.' He sat back in his chair, his left leg trembling under the table.

'A parcel was delivered to Miss Carter by DPD at nine a.m. on the fourteenth November. We have the name of the courier driver and proof that you dropped off the parcel on the thirteenth of November at eleven thirty-six. Miss Carter received the parcel, containing a Dior lipstick and tissue paper. Can you confirm you sent this to her?'

Charlie stared at Phillips, unblinking. The observation room watched. 'He's got him,' Kennedy said. 'He's reeled him in without him even realising.'

'Why would anybody go to all the trouble of sending a parcel, unless it is to intimidate, to frighten? There's no logic to this.' Phillips looked at Murphy. 'Any ideas why, Murphy?'

Murphy shook his head.

'For the record, DS Murphy shook his head.'

'So, you don't like Tesco. I have to say, I'm with you on that. I prefer Waitrose. So we can confirm you don't use Tesco?' Phillips asked.

Charlie uncrossed his arms and again sat forward. 'Yeah, I don't use Tesco, so we share the same opinion.'

Phillips lit a cigarette. 'Cigarette, Charlie?'

Charlie leant across the table and took a Benson from the pack. Phillips held out a light to him. Charlie inhaled and blew the smoke towards the one-way glass, staring into it as he did.

'A smoker and a Waitrose shopper – we have that much in common.' As Phillips lit his cigarette, he pulled the file closer to him.

'Is this interview going anywhere?' Miss Sawallah interjected. 'You have determined you both like the same shop and you both smoke, but you have a choice here, Detective. You can either charge my client or you can let him go. At present it would seem that you are clutching at straws. I'd like to remind you, you have no extension on your questioning time.'

'You're absolutely right, Miss….' He stopped.

'Sawallah,' she replied indignantly.

'That's right. Miss Sawallah. Again noted.'

'It's just that Tesco seems to be the nearest shop to you. I mean, Waitrose is by the Tube station and you live at Waldemar Avenue. Tesco is just a five-minute walk away, Waitrose a twenty-minute walk. I'd say you're more a Marlboro smoker too.'

Charlie snorted and tossed his head. 'Marlboro cigarettes? What the fuck? You're stabbing in the dark here. Is this what my taxes pay for?'

Phillips nodded towards the glass.

'Play the CCTV,' Kennedy said.

'Is this going somewhere?' Sawallah asked.

'Absolutely, Miss Sawallah. You see, Charlie, you went into Tesco on Tuesday, didn't you? Take a look.' On the screen, the CCTV began to play. 'As we see here, on Tuesday the thirteenth of November you were seen entering Tesco on the junction of Munster Road. For the record, Munster Road is a five-minute walk from Waldemar Avenue. You are carrying a full Waitrose shopping bag. Odd that you would take a full Waitrose bag into Tesco. You are seen withdrawing cash from the dispenser inside. You keep the shopping bag between your legs as you take the cash. It's not shopping in the bag – see how it sits squarely on the floor? It's not going to fall over, is it, Charlie, because it's not shopping in the bag, is it? At eleven thirty-six you take the bag to the courier collection point. As I thought – there is no shopping in the bag. It's a parcel. You pay by cash – clever, no trace or link on a card, you've thought this through – and at eleven forty-three you are seen buying a packet of Marlboro cigarettes with cash. A Marlboro smoker, Charlie. Then here we see the DPD courier arriving on the street-view camera and parking on Munster Road to collect – oh look, the parcel.'

Charlie watched the screen, beads of sweat visible on his forehead, his leg trembling uncontrollably under the table. Miss Sawallah watched in silence.

'The camera doesn't lie, Charlie. If we zoom in on this, I'm sure we will see the name of the recipient. But we don't need to zoom in on it to prove it, because my DS has been busy finding further evidence, and what do you think he found in your apartment?' Phillips opened the file. 'Well, he's written here on a sticky note that he found flat-pack parcels and tissue paper. I have a black and white photo of the items seized from your apartment, which are now with forensics.' He turned the photo to face Charlie, and Charlie stared at it. 'The same kind of flat-pack boxes you sent to Miss Carter, filled with the same tissue paper. And what do you think I found in your wallet? Receipts for fuel – oh, a receipt from Harvey Nichols, the Dior counter. But just so we make absolutely sure we haven't made a mistake here, we have a crumpled envelope to Jo Segal with Lucy's address on it. It's a little stained – looks like coffee stains. It would seem you went through Miss Segal's recycling bin to find this.' DI Phillips pushed the photo in front of Charlie.

'Anybody can have parcel boxes and pink tissue paper. That's not illegal,' Charlie said, pushing the photo back towards DI Phillips. He squirmed, knowing that he couldn't explain the envelope so easily.

'We have a positive ID of your car being outside Lucy's property on three occasions and an eye-witness account of a smoker being in the car. You might have thought it clever to wipe your phone, but we have collected the deleted data and your phone has been traced as sending messages from, take a guess, Essex. As for the tissue paper, you're right. Anybody can have tissue paper in their house. I'm sure Miss Sawallah can vouch for that, but who said anything about pink tissue paper? The photo is black and white, and I didn't mention the colour. The parcel sent to Miss Carter, as you have pointed out, contained pink tissue paper.'

'He's got him,' Kennedy said from behind the glass. 'God, I love watching this man work. He's brilliant.'

'Miss Rachel Jones, your neighbour, has stated she heard a woman's cries from the apartment. She heard you shouting.'

'No comment.'

'You have a locked room containing just a chair and masking tape. Why, Charlie?'

Charlie glared at him, his eyes narrowed.

'No comment.'

'You locked Lucy in this room, didn't you? Did you hurt her in this room? Is that what your neighbour heard?'

'No comment.'

'It's now nineteen fifty-six. Charlie Wainwright, I am charging you with harassment under the Harassment Act 1997 towards Miss Carter on the fourteenth, fifteenth and sixteenth of November. I am charging you with common assault against Miss Carter at Mansion House during your relationship in and around the years of 2012 to 2015. I am charging you with false imprisonment of Miss Lucy Carter at Mansion House against her will during your relationship in and around the years of 2012 to 2015. You are charged with controlling Miss Carter and coercive behaviour under Section 76 of the Serious Crime Act 2015 during your relationship. You are charged with stalking under the Protection of Freedoms Act 2012 up to October 2015. You will be taken downstairs to a cell where you will be held in custody or granted bail.'

The interview door opened and three uniformed officers entered. Murphy stood up. 'Take him down.'

Charlie kicked his chair back and stood up. He glared at Phillips, then the officers led him out of the room, down the corridor and to a cell. As the cell door clanged behind him and the bolted shot home, he kicked the door with all his force.

'Fucking bitch!' he screamed. 'You fucking bitch.'

Chapter Sixteen

Matt picked up the ringing phone, 'PC Willis speaking.'

'Good morning, this is DI Phillips from the Met. Could you put PC Mackenzie on the line?'

'Good morning, sir, PC Mackenzie speaking.'

'Mackenzie, no need for sir. Thought you'd like to know that Charlie Wainwright has been charged and is in custody. Details of Miss Carter's address were found in his wallet addressed to a Miss Segal.'

'Has he been granted bail?' Mackenzie asked.

'He applied for bail but was denied, due to the nature of the offences and the necessity for a protection order if he'd been granted bail.'

'Any idea about a hearing date?'

'His hearing will be in the next seventy-two hours, then we'll await a trial date. You can let Miss Carter know that she won't be hearing from him while he's in custody. She can rest easy over Christmas at least.'

'What do you think he'll get?' Mackenzie asked.

'Difficult to say at this stage. You will need to get the witness statement from Mrs Pope to Lucy's solicitor. They'll be questioned in court, which won't be pleasant. But for the time being, your man is in custody until the magistrates, which will be within the next seventy-two hours. Wainwright is going nowhere soon.'

'Right. I'll let Lucy know. Thank you and a merry Christmas, sir,' Mackenzie said, and hung up.

'Good news?' Matt asked.

'Bloody good news, mate. He's been charged and bail denied. I need to call Lucy and let her know,' he said.

'You like Lucy, don't you?' Matt said.

'What d'you mean? She's a friend,' Simon said.

'Yep, but you care a lot more. Tell her, mate,' Matt said, taking a slurp from his mug of tea.

'She likes Ben,' Simon said.

At number three Lucy and Jo were wrapping presents. Lucy's phone vibrated on the table. 'It's a mobile number,' she said as she picked it up. 'Hello?'

'Lucy, it's Simon.'

'Oh, hi, Simon. I didn't recognise your number.

'I'm calling from work,' he said. 'Listen, I've got some good news for you. Is Jo with you?'

'Yeah, she's here,' Lucy replied. 'What's up?'

'It's about Charlie. He's been charged.'

'Charged? What does that mean?' Lucy said, sitting on the sofa to steady herself, not quite believing what she had heard.

'He was questioned by Detective Inspector Phillips yesterday. He's been charged with harassment, common assault and aggravated domestic violence, controlling and coercive behaviour, false imprisonment and stalking. Bail has been denied until his hearing,' Simon continued. 'Luce, are you there?'

She was silent.

'Yep, I'm here,' Lucy said finally. 'I just can't believe it. It's, like, I mean, are you sure, Simon?'

'I told you we would sort this and it's sorted. Charlie is in London in a cell and he won't be smelling or seeing freedom until the hearing,' Simon said.

'So, he was here then?' Lucy said.

'Yes, Gladys Pope saw him or at least his car several times. DI Phillips wants the statement from Mrs Pope to go to your solicitor. He's also going to want to question you, but that'll be after Christmas. All you need to know is that Charlie is locked up and you can rest assured he won't be back.'

'And the parcel, Simon?' Lucy asked, her voice shaking.

'It was Charlie. He was nailed on it.'

'How did he know where I was?'

'Through Jo – he went through her recycling bins and found an envelope. Without realising it, Jo was the source that led him to you.'

'Right. Why don't I feel OK? Why don't I feel euphoric?'

'It'll take time. Let this sink in. The crime bureau can offer you support. Take it, you need it.'

'When will the hearing be?' Lucy asked.

'In the next couple of days, so you need to be available,' Simon replied.

'Will it all happen that fast?' Lucy asked.

'Yes. Magistrates is more likely to hear the case and throw it to Crown Court; the offences are too big.'

'Right.'

Lucy ended the call and stared into space.

'Everything OK, Lucy?' Jo asked.

'They've got him. He's in a cell, so it's kind of over for now,' Lucy said. Jo stopped wrapping presents and came over to her. 'That's good news, Lucy, come here.' She hugged Lucy tightly. 'How do you feel?'

'I don't know ... I feel guilty. Why do I feel guilty? What's the matter with me?'

'How did he find you?' Jo asked.

Lucy hesitated. 'Oh, it doesn't matter. He just did. I feel guilty, Jo.'

'You feel guilty because a guy has lost his freedom, but look, you lost your freedom too when you were with him! You lost your mind being with him. He didn't just control you, Lucy, he hurt you, he physically hurt you. You're going to have to tell the court that. He needs to be locked away so can never do the same to anyone else.'

Lucy looked into Jo's eyes, knowing she was right. She knew him being caught was the right thing; she just didn't like the feeling of guilt.

'Come on, it's Christmas Eve. I can't quite believe it,' Jo said. 'We've almost wrapped all the presents. What time is Ben picking you up?'

'Seven o'clock,' Lucy said. 'I thought we might stay local, pop to the pub in the village. I haven't been there yet and I guess I should. Will you guys come and join me later?'

'Sure, we'll come down for last orders,' Jo said, popping the last of the presents under the tree.

The lights twinkled brightly on the tree, catching the glitter on the gift wrap on the presents beneath it. As the girls sat back and admired the tree, Lucy's phone pinged. She picked it up.

'Who is it?' Jo said.

'I don't know. I don't recognise the number. What if it's him, Jo? What if he's got a phone on the inside?'

'Open it and see,' Jo said. 'He wouldn't be stupid enough to send you a message now.'

Lucy opened the message.

Looking forward to seeing you tonight, I've got my phone fixed. Wear trousers. See you at seven, Ben.

Lucy read the message.

'So, who is it from?' Jo asked.

'Ben – he told me to wear trousers. Why does he want me to wear trousers, though?'

'Beats me,' Jo said. 'I guess you'll find out in about, oooh, an hour and a half. Come on, let's go and find you a knock-out outfit and get you ready for your hot date. The boys will be over soon; they were shutting up shop early.'

The day had disappeared and the evening crept slowly in. Lucy sped up the stairs to shower and wash her hair. Today really did mark a new beginning for her. With Charlie behind bars until the hearing, she could live without fear. She turned the shower off and took a towel from the warm radiator, wrapped it around her body and unlocked the bathroom door. Jo was already in the bedroom, sifting through Lucy's wardrobe.

'Here,' she said, 'your outfit for tonight.' She held up a pair of slim-fitting leather trousers, a tight sheer black top, a pretty black thong, a simple bra with lace detail and her stiletto-heeled ankle boots.

'Do you not think that's a bit OTT?' Lucy said.

'You are kidding, aren't you? You'll look sensational and get his heart beating. Right, you get ready. I'm hopping in the shower now.'

Lucy slipped her underwear on then she looked at her slim, toned figure in the mirror. She peeled on her figure-hugging leather trousers and slipped the sheer top over her head. She looked every inch the sexy, edgy girl she had always been. She stood in front of the mirror and blow-dried her hair straight. She pulled on her ankle boots. Then came the rattle of the door knocker. She raced downstairs. It was Matt and Simon.

'Hi guys, Merry Christmas.' She hugged them both. 'Jo is just taking a shower, Matt. Fancy a drink?'

'Sure, sounds great, Luce. Are you all ready for your date?' Simon asked.

'Yep, kind of. I just need to slap on some make-up and then I'm good to go. Can I leave you guys to it while I finish my face?' She left the boys to raid the fridge for a beer and went back upstairs.

'Matt's here,' she called to Jo as she walked past the bathroom door and into the bedroom.

'You OK, Si?' Matt handed him a beer. He knew how he felt about Lucy.

'Yep, I'm fine, mate,' he said, clinking bottles with Matt.

'Smoky eyes or not so smoky eyes?' Lucy asked, starting to apply a layer of foundation.

'Definitely schhhmokey. Here, let me do your eyes. We definitely need sultry eyes,' Jo said with a devilish look.

'Jo, it's our first date!'

Jo finished Lucy's eyes with a line of black liquid liner, giving them a feline look. 'Gorgeous, take a look.'

Lucy looked in the mirror. She had to admit she looked stunning. Her dark eyes smouldered. Her dark hair was sleek and glossy. The sheer top showed a little of the lace bra she wore beneath it.

'Come on, let's go down. The boys will have drunk us out of house and home if we don't get a wiggle on,' Jo said, pulling on her knee-length boots. The girls walked down the stairs and into the kitchen, where Simon leant against the fridge. He whistled. 'Man, you look killer gorgeous, Lucy. Ben's a lucky man.'

'You don't think I look too much – like I'm trying too hard?'

Matt took a swig from the bottle. 'Er, no, you look sensational. Jo, come here.' He pulled Jo towards him. 'I'm not sure I want to go out seeing you dressed like that. Here.' He poured them both a glass of red. 'Merry Christmas, guys. I've got a feeling it's gonna be a good one!'

The sound of the knocker on the door broke through their laughter and chatter.

'I'll go,' Lucy said, tucking her hair behind her ear. She took a gulp of red wine for Dutch courage. She spied through the peephole: it was Ben. She opened the door and stood silently she stood for what seemed to be an age before she said 'hey.'

'Here, these are few you.' He presented her with a beautiful bouquet of wintery flowers, deep red and white, mistletoe cascading through the deepest green foliage.

'Wow, they're beautiful, thank you.' She smelt them.

'Are you going to ask me in?' He smiled.

'Oh God, yes, please, sorry, I'm just a bit...'

'Nervous?' he said as he searched her face. Her eyes were deep and dark and she looked amazing standing in front of him. 'Don't be.'

She moved away from the door to let him in. 'Come through. Sorry, we were just having a glass of wine in the kitchen. The others are here. Come and meet them and I'll get these beautiful flowers into some water.' She led the way down the hall to the kitchen, where Ben was met by three pairs of eyes.

'Hi, I'm Simon.' Simon stepped forward, his arm outstretched to shake Ben's hand.

'I'm Ben. Good to meet you.'

Jo followed. 'I'm Jo and this is Matt, my boyfriend.'

Matt stepped forward and shook his hand. 'Good to meet you, Ben. Fancy a beer?'

'That would be great, thanks.'

'Gorgeous flowers, Lucy,' Jo said as she helped her find a vase.

'They are, aren't they?' Lucy said, untying the cellophane and cutting the string that held them in place.

'I love fresh flowers. Thank you, Ben.' Lucy placed the arrangement on the worktop. They looked stunning and added a Christmassy feel to the kitchen; it was the only room downstairs that the girls hadn't decorated.

'So, Ben, d'you live nearby?' Simon asked.

'Yeah, in Old Harwich, down Smuggler's Way. D'you know it?'

'Yeah, I know Harwich pretty well. The Facebook crime page is buzzing with activity!' He laughed.

'Is it?' Ben asked.

'He's joking,' Matt said, detecting Ben's uncertainty. 'We're police officers, stationed at Wrabness.'

'Oh right, yeah. Busy this time of year?' Ben asked.

'Nothing too exciting. No high-speed chases, that's for sure,' Simon quipped. 'So what d'you do?'

'I build boats,' Ben said as he took a swig from his bottle of Budweiser.

'You build boats,' Lucy said. 'What kind of boats?'

'Sailing boats mainly – small yachts. I work at the boat yard in Dovercourt,' Ben said, his eyes lingering on Lucy, catching a glimpse of the lace beneath her sheer top.

'Is that Percival and Sons Mariners?' Matt asked.

'Yeah, that's the one.'

'Small world. I was at school with one of the sons. Tom Percival.'

'Tom's a good guy. I was out with him the other night, in fact.'

'Send him my best. He'll remember me. Just say Matt Willis – we used to sail together as kids.' Matt took another beer from the fridge. 'Anybody else want a top up?'

Matt handed Simon another beer and topped up the girls' glasses. 'So where are you taking Lucy?' Jo asked, nudging Lucy as she watched Ben. His eyes looked greener in the light than they had at the beach. His jeans sat just below his waist and he wore a thin sweatshirt tucked loosely in.

'Well, I thought you might like to try the bistro in Manningtree. Have you been before?'

'I haven't, but I'd love to. Shall I book a cab?'

'No need, I'll ride,' Ben replied. He rested his hands on the worktop behind him. His top pulled tighter across his chest, showing the outline of muscles.

'Ride?' Lucy said, looking bemused.

'I've come on my bike.'

'Pedal bike?' Lucy looked even more confused.

'Motorbike.' He laughed. 'I don't think I could cycle here in the dark.'

'Ah, that's why you said to wear trousers,' Jo said. 'You look quite the part, Luce. A hot biker chick.'

Lucy nudged Jo before she got too carried away.

'Shall we make a move?' Ben placed his empty bottle on the table.

'Sure,' Lucy said.

'Meet you back here,' Jo called out to them, then the front door closed behind them. Lucy stood by the bike. 'It's quite big.' She didn't really know what to say. Ben looked at her and winked.

'I've never been on the back of a bike before.'

'You'll be fine. Here, put these in your ears, or it will be too loud for you.' Ben handed her some orange foam balls. 'Ready?' He put the helmet on her head and fastened it. 'Feel ok?'

'I think so. I feel like I'm going to topple over with the weight, though. How do I hold on?'

'Hold on to me,' Ben said, straddling the bike. 'Now hop on.'

Lucy sat on the back of the bike and put her arms around Ben's waist, clasping her hands in front of him like a vice. He switched on the engine. It was noisy. Slowly, he pulled out and took the road towards Manningtree at a steady speed. He touched her hands with his leather glove. She held on tighter. Ben opened up the throttle and let the bike go. Her heart raced as he took a corner, leaning in, pulling Lucy with him, changing gear and taking another corner at speed. Fear ran through her body, she wiggled her bottom back, frightened she'd fall. Sensing her movement he held her hands again as he slowed down to approach Manningtree, where he pulled into a space and put his feet down on the ground to steady the bike. Lucy climbed off first and waited for Ben to turn the engine off. Gently he helped her undo the helmet. Lucy smoothed her hair down and removed the foam buds from her ears.

'Did you like it?' he asked.

'I was a bit scared, but yeah, I loved it. But you can't drink tonight if you have the bike,' Lucy said. She could hardly drink and him stay stone-cold sober. She needed a little more alcohol in her system after the ride and to help her relax and not be so nervous. She had butterflies in her stomach somersaulting like an acrobatic team on speed.

'I've got a mate in Manningtree, I can leave it at his. We can always get a cab home, or have a bite to eat here. What do you fancy?'

Lucy weighed up the options. Have a drink or two in a bistro or bear-hug Ben again? She knew exactly which one she wanted. She wanted to be close to him again: she wanted to wrap her arms around his waist and feel his reassuring touch on her hand. She hadn't felt such a touch by a man in a long while.

'Can we ride home?' she said.

'Sure, let's grab a bite to eat.' He took her hand as they crossed the road, letting it go as they reached the pavement. The bistro was buzzing. The waitress showed them to a table in the corner, handed them menus and took their drinks order. Ben read the menu while Lucy watched the bar. Two guys worked behind it, shaking up cocktails for waitresses. A row of huge aluminium light shades hung above the bar, looking like cymbals. It was clearly a popular, cool venue with a young, vibrant feel about it.

'Anything you fancy?' Ben asked, placing the menu on the table and leaning towards Lucy.

'Um, I think I might go for the field mushroom risotto,' she said. 'I love mushrooms and I can't remember the last time I had risotto.' She took a sip of her water.

'That sounds good,' Ben said. 'I'm going to go for the fish pie.'

As the bar filled with more drinkers, the lights dimmed, making the bar seem intimate and seductive.

'So have you always lived here?' Lucy asked.

'Yep, always. I grew up here, went to school here, work here. Does that make me boring?' he laughed.

'Nope, grounded,' she said, tucking her hair behind her ear and bit her lip. Ben watched her intently. He hadn't met a girl like Lucy before: the way she dressed was cool and edgy, yet she seemed insecure. She bit her lip when she spoke to him, she fiddled with her hair … there was something about her that showed her innocence and insecurity. She looked at him, her eyes even deeper than before.

'You look beautiful, by the way,' he said.

Her eyes widened and a smile spread across her face. Then the waitress brought their plates over.

'Risotto?'

'That's me,' Lucy said.

The waitress placed a shallow white bowl in front of Lucy. 'And a fish pie for you. Enjoy.'

'So, tell me about your boat-making,' Lucy said. 'Have you always been into boats?'

'Yeah, I guess I have. It's what I'm good at. I like tinkering with stuff, making things, fixing things. But tell me about your writing. I've never met a writer before. What do you write about?'

'At the moment I'm writing a love story. I found a load of love letters in the house when I moved in and they gave me the idea. They totally inspired me. I've never written historical fiction before so it's testing me a little going back to the Second World War. I need to do plenty of research, but the letters are so lovely, yet sad at the same time.'

'Do you already know how the story will end? Is it all mapped out in your head?' he asked, finishing the last mouthful of his fish pie.

'Pretty much. I've always got a story in my head. I love watching people and making up stories about them.' She pushed her plate away. 'I'm done. I can't eat another morsel.'

'It sounds awesome. I have a terrible imagination. I think I had a good one as a kid, but I was never great at writing at school – you know, when you had to make up a story.'

'Creative writing, you mean?' she asked, enjoying their conversation. 'I guess people are all good at different things. I can't fix things, I'm pretty useless at it, so there you go. I write, you fix and make stuff. Making things needs imagination too – just a different kind.' She smiled at him. She liked him: he listened to her. Charlie had never listened to her; he had spoken *at* her most of the time, not to her.

'So how come you moved here?'

She thought he would ask her that, and she had planned what to say, but she hesitated. Why would anybody move from London a city that was vibrant, cool, full of culture – and move to a village where most people were white, middle-class and ageing?

J. V. Phaure

'Sorry, it's none of my business.' Ben felt awkward; he could see he had made her feel uneasy.

'It's OK,' she said, crossing her legs and tucking her hair behind her ear. 'I just wanted a change.'

'How was your meal?' The waitress appeared at their table and cleared the plates. 'Would you like dessert, coffee?'

Ben flashed a look at Lucy, who shook her head.

'Just the bill, please,' he said.

'We can go Dutch,' Lucy said, taking her purse from her jacket pocket.

'No, I'm taking you out, this is my shout.' Ben tossed his card on the saucer and waited for the waitress to return.

'Thank you,' Lucy said.

When they left the bistro Ben took Lucy's hand again as they crossed the road, letting it go as they reached the bike. She liked it when he did that. Lucy put the foam balls back into her ears and Ben placed the helmet on her head and strapped it on.

He straddled the bike and let her climb on behind him. This time, he took her arms and placed them around his waist, holding her hands as he slowly reversed. The sound of the bike echoed along the street. He took a different route home until they came to the winding road that led past the estuary. Lucy recognised the road in the dark – it was the way the taxi driver had brought her when she came to look at the house for the first time. This time, though, she was sitting on a powerful bike with her arms wrapped around a gorgeous guy. She held him more tightly as he took a corner. He leant against her and held her hands as he took another corner, forcing her to lean with him. As they neared the village, he slowed down then pulled up outside Lucy's house.

'Would you like to come in?' she asked, smoothing her hair.

'Sure.' He walked up the path with her. She unlocked the door then turned to him. 'If I forget to say it later, I had a really lovely night.'

He moved closer to her and took her hand. He lifted her chin. Cupping her face in his hands, he kissed her, letting his lips search the softness of hers, his tongue feeling hers. She felt the hair on her neck stand up and goosebumps form over her body. She moved away and looked at him. Everything she wanted was right here in front of her. She liked him, but she didn't know how to let go of her past. She opened the door, closing it behind them.

The house was empty. Lucy switched the hall light on and they made their way into the kitchen, where empty beer bottles sat on the side, along with two empty wine glasses.

'I think they've gone to the pub,' Lucy said, opening the fridge and taking out a bottle of Bud. 'Beer?' She stood on her tiptoes to reach for a wine glass then she felt him behind her, his hands on her waist. She closed the cupboard door, glass in her hand, and turned to him. His hands were on the small of her back. She flinched. He lifted her chin and cupped her face. Gently, his lips touched hers and his tongue felt hers. He moved closer to her, his hands brushing up her back, his tongue reaching deeper into her mouth, his lips pressing harder on hers. He pressed his body to hers so she could feel his hardness against her. She moved her lips away and bit her bottom lip, wetting it, then reached up and kissed him. He moved away from her, breathing hard. She looked into his eyes and felt her stomach somersault.

'The others will be back soon. Come through to the sitting room, it's more comfortable.' She poured a glass of wine and handed him his beer.

She took off her boots and left them by the front door, then pushed open the sitting-room door. Ben sat next to her on the sofa.

'Do you like living here?' he asked. She had clammed up on why she had left London but maybe she would talk to him now she was in her own home.

'I think so,' she said, taking a sip of wine and turning to him.

'You think so? Still making up your mind?' he said, resting his arm on the back of the sofa.

'I'm still getting used to it. It's quieter, that's for sure. It gives me head space, though, I need that, and I love the beach.' She gazed at the lights as they twinkled on the tree.

'Head space? How so?'

She felt safe enough to talk, and he was listening. She liked the fact that he wanted to hear her talk. 'I was engaged,' she said, 'but things weren't going well. I guess I just needed to escape.' She took another sip of wine and swirled the wine around the glass. She watched it as it caught the sides and rolled back down. It reminded her of her life in a way: drops clinging onto the side, the rest falling, letting go.

'Did you fall out of love?' he asked.

'I'm not sure I ever really loved him,' she said. 'Anyway, it's over now. He's gone. My life is here and I want it to be here. I'm happier, freer.'

'Does he feel the same way?' Ben asked. Something about her words left him with a sense of unsureness he couldn't quite work out. Maybe she did love her ex; maybe he was a rebound. He didn't want to be a rebound.

'He was arrested,' she said. It was out there. She'd said what she needed to say. He'd find out at some stage – and if she didn't tell him now, when would she tell him? It couldn't be a secret between them, not if she wanted to see him again, not if she began to like him more. She already liked him and she barely knew him.

'Arrested?' Was he a drug dealer?' Ben asked. He had no idea where this was going, but he knew he liked her. He liked her more than he could have imagined. He had seen her so often, sitting on the beach, writing, and he was intrigued by her. He wanted to get to know her better. He wanted to know the girl on the beach.

'A drug dealer? I think that would have been easier. No, he scared me, hurt me.'

'Hurt you emotionally?' Ben asked. 'Sorry – I'm prying, you don't have to tell me. It's none of my business and you hardly know me, but this could be a good time for us to get to know each other. We're sober, and maybe you'd like to get to know me? Maybe?'

'I guess you could say emotionally but also...' She stopped. 'I don't really want to talk about it any more, at least not tonight. You're right, I hardly know you, yet here I am telling you about my ex. I just want to sit next you and not talk about him. Maybe another time, but I just want to forget it all for now and—'

'And what?' He turned to her.

Just then the front door swung open and three drunk Christmas revellers fell through the door and barged into the sitting room.

'Hi, we're back!' Jo said, swinging on the door, almost falling over. 'Anyone fancy a drink? It's almost Christmas Day!'

'You guys look half-cut.' Lucy laughed. 'Had fun?'

'We sure did. We met the locals, told them about you and that you'd be in to say hello with signed copies of your novel,' Jo slurred.

'You are kidding, right?' Lucy questioned.

'Er, she's not,' Matt said. 'Jo let everybody know there was a bestselling author in the village. We couldn't keep her quiet, she was a babbling wreck. Lucy, you'd better get signing. Right, beer. Ben, fancy another one?'

'I wouldn't say no, but I'll need to book a cab. I won't be able to ride back now.'

'Or you could stay the night,' Jo hollered from the hallway.

'Ignore her,' Lucy said. 'She's quite entertaining when she's drunk too much. Stay for a beer and I'll phone Dave's Taxis. You could always pick up your bike tomorrow or the next day. Actually, scrap that; you won't get a cab on Christmas Day. I could pick you up tomorrow to get your bike. You've probably got plans for Christmas.'

'Or he could stay, Lucy, he could stay,' Jo shouted from the kitchen. 'The more the merrier – kip on the floor.'

'Jo! Be quiet,' Lucy said.

Jo stumbled back into the room with three beers, a glass and a bottle of red.

'So how was your night, you two? How was the bistro?' Jo asked, opening the wine.

'Yeah, it was good,' Lucy said, holding out her glass. 'Pretty busy. It was nice.'

'Ben, was it nice or was it *really* nice?' Jo asked, giving him a look that said 'tell me more'.

'Yeah, it was more than nice. It was great.'

'Second date?' Jo asked, falling onto Matt's lap and spilling her wine on her jeans. Ben looked at Lucy then at the others. 'Yeah, without a doubt.'

'Well, cheers to that!' Jo said and clinked her glass with Matt's bottle. 'And cheers to that dick in prison.'

Lucy threw a look of nervousness at Jo. Matt stroked Jo's back. 'Shush, babe.'

Ben looked at Lucy. What did Jo mean, and why had Matt hushed her? To save Lucy embarrassment? She'd said her ex had been arrested but she hadn't mentioned prison; she said he'd hurt her emotionally, but what had really happened? What was Lucy not telling him? Would she have moved here if she hadn't had to run away, or would she still be in London? How could anybody hurt Lucy? She was the most gorgeous girl he had seen.

'So, are you guys here for Christmas then?' Ben asked, trying to end the awkward silence after Jo's comment.

'Yep, the station is closed for the next four days and we're spending Christmas here, aren't we, gorgeous?' Simon said. 'What about you? What are you up to?'

'I'm going to spend it with my sister and my folks. I'll head over to them for lunch and chill for the day, watch Christmas telly and then eat copious amounts of Quality Street and loaf on the sofa.'

Lucy looked at Ben. 'If you fancy coming here at some point, you can – if you'd like to, I mean. I guess, Christmas is special with families and stuff, but we're here if you fancy it. No pressure.'

'Looks like this one has given up.' Matt took the glass from Jo's hand. She'd fallen fast asleep on him and snuggled into his chest, beaten by the alcohol. 'I'll take her up, she's totally sparko.' Matt lifted Jo up. She was out for the count.

'You guys are in my room, Matt. The bed's all made and ready for you, and clean towels are in the airing cupboard,' Lucy called up the stairs to Matt as he wobbled his way up.

'I'll be back down. Grab me a beer, Si.'

'I'd better call that taxi, and leave you guys to it,' Ben said, placing his empty bottle on the coffee table.

'One for the road?' Simon asked as he got up from the leather bean bag.

'Oh, go on then, one for the road would be great.'

Simon left the room.

'So, would you like another date?' Ben asked Lucy, who was struggling to stay awake.

'Would you like to?' Lucy said.

'What do you think? Simon was right, by the way.'

She gave him a quizzical look. 'Right? Right about what?'

'He called you gorgeous, and you are.' He leant forward and kissed her tenderly. 'I'd like to see you again, maybe take you for a longer ride on the bike, show you around the area a bit.'

She was beginning to fall for a guy she barely knew, and she liked the feeling. She liked him a lot.

Chapter Seventeen

Christmas Day

'Merry Christmas, gorgeous!' Simon threw his arms around Lucy. 'Are the others up yet?'

It was Christmas morning. Lucy had sneaked downstairs to prep the turkey for the great British roast-off.

'Merry Christmas, hun. No, I haven't heard the others. I think they're still sleeping off the alcohol. What time did Ben leave last night?'

'Dunno. I think about one-ish. He's a nice guy – a really nice guy. You've picked a winner there,' Simon said, switching on the kettle. 'Coffee?'

'He is pretty lovely, isn't he? He was OK when he left, wasn't he?' She sounded a little unsure. She'd taken herself to bed and left the boys chatting. She hadn't seen Ben leave but the guys had been getting on really well and she figured he'd be OK in their company.

'Yeah, why?' Simon took two mugs from the cupboard. 'What are you worried about? Is it because of what Jo said about prison?' He leant against the cabinet as Lucy smothered the turkey with butter.

'Kind of. I'd told him a bit about Charlie – I said he'd been arrested but that was it, I closed down the conversation. Ben asked if he was a drug dealer.' She laughed as she said it. 'It's just the whole thing is so heavy. I'm trying to process it all myself, and I'm not ready to share it with the world, with Ben, with anybody really. Does that make sense? It's like I should feel relieved, and I do, but I also feel guilty. Does any of that make sense or am I just talking crap?' She stood there, her hands covered in salt, butter and a thyme and lemon stuffing. 'It's Christmas Day, Simon. I'm free to cook my Christmas turkey while Charlie is in prison, and it's my fault he's there.'

'Listen to me,' Simon said gently. 'You're not alone. Everyone feels guilty sometimes. You wouldn't be human if you felt no guilt. But you have nothing to feel guilty about – Charlie does, and that's why he's in prison. He feels no remorse. He hurt you mentally and physically and a court will hear that. DI Phillips knew it when he interviewed him. The room, the masking tape – it's all there. I heard the recording; DI Phillips sent it to me. What you have to remember is you didn't go to the police because you wanted revenge; you did it because you were scared. Charlie knew what he was doing – he had some kind of warped, twisted agenda, but we stopped him. He's in prison because of what he did, not because of what you did. Listen, the crime bureau is there to help you so ask them for help. As for Ben, I think he's a good guy. He'll hear your story and he'll be there for you, just like I am, like Matt and Jo are. Seriously, don't feel guilty.'

Lucy looked at Simon. 'You're a good friend, Simon, one of the best.' Gratefully, she hugged him.

'Ben and Lucy – got a nice ring to it. Right, where are the spuds? I can peel those,' Simon rummaged through the cutlery drawer for a potato peeler.

'I've never cooked a turkey before – in fact, I've never cooked a roast. I hope this works!'

'It's all about timing – that's what my mum used to say. How long does it need?' Simon asked.

Lucy read the instructions. 'According to this, it needs thirty-five minutes for every five hundred grams plus an extra thirty-five minutes at the end, so that's about three hours. Does that sound right to you?'

'If that's what the box says, then yep. So we need to get the spuds, stuffing and parsnips into the oven about an hour before the turkey is finished, so twelve-ish for the roasties.' Simon poured hot water into the cafétière and mug with Lucy's peppermint bag.

'I went a bit crazy with vegetables too,' she said, opening the fridge door. 'Sprouts, red cabbage, green beans and broccoli. Plus cranberry sauce, bread sauce and devils on horseback. We are going to be stuffed by the end of it, just like this turkey!'

As Simon peeled the potatoes and Lucy trimmed the vegetables, there were sounds of life from upstairs.

Lucy poured water into the steamer and tossed the vegetables in. 'I think we're done. The turkey is in and everything else is ready to go.' She looked upwards. 'The shower has been running for ages. They're definitely shagging in there. Nobody showers for that long.' She laughed. 'Is it too early for a bucks fizz?'

She grabbed a bottle of bubbly and a carton of orange juice from the fridge. 'Can you get some glasses, Si? Let's take this into the sitting room.'

The sitting room smelt of stale beer. Lucy pulled the curtains open. The sky was grey, the street quiet. A few cars were parked outside along with a red and black motorbike. She hadn't noticed the colour of the bike the night before; it had been too dark. She thought of Ben and how she had held him, then she remembered his kisses and how gentle he had been with her. Her tummy fluttered as she thought about him. She'd forgotten that feeling. She opened a window and lit a scented candle to disguise the stale smell of the room. Simon popped the cork on the champagne and poured it hastily into the first glass before it overflowed.

At the foot of the stairs he shouted, 'Oi, you two lovebirds, champagne is being served. Get your arses downstairs!'

Then Lucy's phone pinged. Two messages. She looked at the first. There was no name. She was nervous. What if it was him?

She opened her messages and scrolled up to the top.

Hey, last night was great. I had a fantastic night, hope you did too. Happy Christmas. I want to see you again – soon. xxx

She smiled. Her tummy dipped with good feelings when she thought about him. Last night had been fantastic. He'd kissed her and she wanted him to kiss her again. She saved the message and closed it. The second message, from an unknown number, stared at her, the numbers blurring. Quickly, she opened it.

It was from Charlie. She caught her breath as she read his words. A sudden urge to throw up. She sighed in despair.

Matt and Jo came down the stairs. Lucy slid the phone quickly back into her back pocket.

'Morning all,' Matt said.

Jo looked sheepish. 'Lucy, I just wanted to say….'

'Seriously, don't worry, Jo. You were pretty smashed last night. Forget it. How's your head?' Lucy said, handing Jo a bucks fizz.

Simon reappeared, holding two more glasses, and poured the bubbly. 'I'd like to make a toast,' he said, holding up his glass. 'To our first Christmas as friends, to your first Christmas here, Lucy, to Jo and Matt and their new-found love – to the four of us!'

'To the four of us. Merry Christmas!' they said in unison.

The bucks fizz slid down their throats with ease.

'So how was last night?' Jo asked. 'Are you seeing Ben again?'

'Last night was lovely, I am definitely seeing him again,' Lucy replied, trying to think only of Ben and his message. Charlie's hastily read message kept coming into her mind, pushing Ben's aside. She tried to block it out. What was he doing texting her? How had he got a phone? He was playing with fire. She wanted to see Ben again. He would have seen she'd read his message. She hadn't responded, so he'd think she wasn't interested and then she'd lose everything just because of Charlie.

'I'll check on the turkey,' she said and left the room.

'Is she OK?' Jo said.

'I'll go and help her,' Simon said, leaving Matt and Jo in the sitting room. Lucy took the phone from her back pocket and unlocked it. She read Ben's message again, then began to type.

Last night was great, I had a lovely time. Thank you again for my flowers, they are beautiful. Have a lovely day with your family. Merry Christmas, Lucy

The message disappeared into the ether.

Lucy stood staring at her phone. She stared until she couldn't see the number any more. She brushed her finger along it.

'You OK, Lucy?'

Simon's voice startled her.

'Lucy?'

She turned to Simon, looking distraught.

'What's up?' Simon looked at her holding her phone. 'Did you forget to put the timer on?'

She stared at him, speechless.

'Lucy? Say something.'

Lucy said nothing. She just stared at the phone and the message, then she read the words properly.

'Lucy, give me your phone. What's wrong?'

She handed him the phone, her face drained of all colour, her hands shaking. Simon took the phone and read the message.

You bitch – you will pay for what you've done. Live in fear.

'Come here.' Simon held out his arms and she cried against his chest. 'Listen, he's got somebody on the inside to give him a phone – probably paid a huge amount for the privilege, but he's going to pay even more. With his freedom.'

'But, Simon, look what he wrote. He said "live in fear" – what does he mean? Why won't this just go away? What if Ben is part of this?'

'Ben is nothing to do with this. Have you heard from him?' He held her shoulders and wiped the tears from her face.

'He messaged me this morning – well, when this message came in Ben's was there too,' she said, wiping her nose on her sleeve.

'What did Ben say?' Simon asked.

'He said he'd had a really lovely time and wanted to see me again.' She was trying to stay positive and not think about Charlie.

'And you replied with?'

'Oh, I sent a really shit reply. I said I had a lovely night, the flowers were beautiful and have a nice day. That was it.'

'So, you didn't say you wanted to see him again? But I thought you did?'

'I do want to see him again, but I don't know. I can't seem to get it right. I seem to find guys who want to control me and manipulate me. Even if Ben is genuine, he's going to read my message and think I was playing a game and I'm not interested. What if he is connected to Charlie? What if he's being paid to lure me in? What if this is all an act and he's not interested at all? Look what Charlie has written: *"you will pay for what you've done. Live in fear"* – what does that mean? That I'm still being followed? That I'm not safe?'

'All it means is he's grasping at straws to frighten you. He can't touch you. He's behind bars. The judge will not like the fact that he's contacted – what a moron. I honestly don't think Charlie is working with anyone else. You have to try not to think about it too much. I know it's hard, but you have to try and live your life. Forget about him. Here, take this.' He handed Lucy a serving spoon. 'Let's baste the turkey. Try to think positively. It's Christmas Day after all. After lunch, text Ben and ask how his day was. You can make this work. Just say you were busy. He's a bloke – he'll be fine, he won't think too much about it. Us men don't dissect messages like you girls do.'

As Lucy was basting the turkey, her phone rang.

'Can you get it, Simon?' Lucy said.

'It's your solicitor, James Cooper,' Simon said, picking up the phone. 'Hi, Lucy's phone.'

'Is it possible to speak with Lucy, please?' James Cooper asked.

Simon held the phone to Lucy's ear.

'Lucy speaking.'

'Lucy, hi. James here. I'm really sorry to call on Christmas Day but I had to let you know the hearing is set for 2pm tomorrow, twenty-sixth December. Can you get there for about one thirty to go through everything? It's all pretty straight-forward. I'd say we'll be in and out within half an hour. It's highly unlikely that the case will be heard by a magistrate, due to the nature of the offences. It's more than likely Charlie will ask to be heard by a jury,' Cooper said matter-of-factly.

'Right, OK. Thanks for phoning. I will see you tomorrow,' Lucy said.

Simon took the phone and put it down.

'So you've got a date,' he said.

'Yes, tomorrow at 2pm.'

***

Ben walked to his parents' house on the sea front in Harwich. Their house was important-looking with a red ensign hanging above the door. He read Lucy's message again. What did she mean by it? He was thinking of her now – was she thinking of him? Was she letting him down gently? As he approached the front door, he put his phone back in his hoodie pocket. He really liked the girl, damn it, he really liked her. The door swung open and his sister beamed at him. 'Merry Christmas, bro. I saw you from the bedroom window.' She held out her arms to him and hugged him hard. The door closed behind him and he left thoughts of Lucy behind it.

***

Matt lit a fire in the sitting room while Lucy and Simon put the finishing touches to the Christmas lunch. Delicious smells filled the house: the thyme-smothered turkey rested on the side and the roast potatoes, parsnips and carrots turned crispy and golden in the oven. The steamer bubbled as Lucy stirred the bread sauce. Warmth flooded through the rooms as Matt stoked the fire in the sitting room.

'Grub's up,' Simon shouted from the kitchen. Lucy laid Christmas crackers on the table.

'Smells divine,' Matt said, pulling out a chair for Jo. The four friends pulled the crackers. With each pop came the smell of sulphur. The kitchen filled with laughter as they took turns to read the truly terrible jokes from the crackers.

'To our first Christmas lunch together,' Jo said, raising her glass. Then the feast began.

Chapter Eighteen

Christmas Day

Christmas wrapping paper lay strewn across the sitting-room floor. Lucy got up from the sofa to draw the curtains. The moon was a silvery orb in the sky kept company by twinkling stars. The sky was a deep velvety black. She noticed Ben's bike had gone from outside the window. She hadn't heard him arrive. He must have come when they'd been eating or in the kitchen. Strange that he hadn't texted to say he had been over.

'Anyone for more bubbles?' she said. She left the room to retrieve a chilled bottle from the fridge. In the kitchen, she took her phone and typed a message.

Hey Ben, hope you had a great day, I saw your bike has gone – you should have come and said hello.

Lucy opened the fridge and took out a bottle of champagne, then picked up the tub of Quality Street from the worktop. As she closed the fridge door, a message pinged in.

Hi Lucy. Yep, we went for a Christmas walk along the estuary. I got the bike then. Didn't knock, sorry. I just figured….

What did he just figure?

Just figured what?

She watched the three dots dance on her phone, indicating that Ben was typing back.

Just figured you didn't want to see me.

Why?

Dunno. It just felt that way.

What did I say that made you think that? Yesterday was great. I messaged this morning in haste. I'm sorry.

It's fine and yeah, it was a great night.

The dots disappeared. He'd gone. She'd lost him. She stared at her phone stood in disbelief. How did that happen? How could she have lost him before they'd even begun?

She left the phone on the table and took the chocolates and bubbly into the sitting room, deep in thought. Should she message him back? Was that her cue not to contact him again? Why couldn't she get it right? Every time she thought she'd met someone, they turned out to be wrong for her. Did she have a sticker on her forehead that said 'pick me, I like to be treated like shit. I don't need to be loved'?

Would she ever find true love, or would she only ever find love in the make-believe characters she wrote about?

***

Charlie sat in his cell at Wandsworth Prison staring at the four walls. They had been stained a yellowy colour by the cigarettes smoked by past inmates. Bail had been denied on the twenty-sixth of December and the magistrates had passed his case to the Crown Court. His trial was set to start on the second of February. There was nothing else for him to do but listen to the goading taunts of his new neighbours. He stared at the walls. The paint had chipped off in places, or had been gouged by other prisoners. It was a far cry from the comfort of his luxurious Fulham pad. He sat on the edge of his iron bed. The mattress was thin, barely covering the metal struts of the bed's frame.

He couldn't block out the shouts from outside. *Wife batterer, rapist, filthy scum!* He exhaled heavily as the words echoed around the prison and ricocheted off the walls. He scrubbed his hands through his hair.

'Shut the fuck up!' he screamed, throwing his tin cup against the wall. She would pay for putting him in here. She'd got him locked up. He didn't want to be in here. He couldn't stand it. He snarled as he saw his mother in his head: deserting him, leaving him at boarding school so she could be free of him, so she could spend time with her boyfriend. Charlie was in the way, a pest, a nuisance. A mistake.

Now he was no longer a small boy imprisoned in boarding school with no weekend exeats, sitting on the edge of the bed with his adored scruffy teddy bear, wishing his mother had time for him, wishing somebody cared for him, that Matron wouldn't flog him for crying at night. Now the abandoned boy in a man's body sat on the bed. His freedom was lost. No woman would treat him this way, he vowed. Not his mother, not Matron, not Lucy. He was in control now. Lucy was his and, when he got out of this pit, he would find her and she would pay.

The hatch in his cell door opened and the warden shouted through it. 'Wainwright, scrub up. Lunch!'

Charlie tucked the phone between the mattress and sheet. He got up and walked to the basin in the corner of his cell, where he washed his hands and splashed water over his face. His cell door was unlocked and he walked out and joined the other inmates as they walked to the canteen, where the stench of overcooked vegetables permeated the air. The kitchen hand slopped Charlie's lunch onto a plate. Charlie slumped down at a table and pushed his food around, staring aggressively at the men opposite him. As he did, the warden came to his table.

'Wainwright, you've got a visitor – your lawyer. Finish up, clear your tray then make your way to A block.'

Charlie scraped his lunch into the bin and pushed the empty tray onto the trolley.

In the empty visitors' room, he sat opposite his lawyer, Stephen Hatten.

'How are you bearing up?' his lawyer asked as he opened the file.

'You need to get me out of here, Stephen. How do you think I am bearing up? I'm not paying top whack for nothing. Get me out!'

'Charlie, I'm afraid you're here until your trial starts on the second of February. You were denied bail.'

'Right, and then what happens?' Charlie asked.

'Well, that depends on the jury,' Stephen replied.

'So what are you saying? Are you saying I'm guilty? What the fuck is this? I'm paying you good money and you need to sort this!'

'It's not looking good. You've been charged with harassment, common assault with aggravated domestic violence, unlawful imprisonment, and stalking. The judge at the magistrates recommended your case be heard in Crown Court. Lady Scott is the presiding judge – and she's tough. I have to be honest: you're looking at a minimum of five years if you're found guilty.'

'What have you got on Lucy?' Charlie asked. 'She's lying.'

'You need to prove that and at the moment, you can't. I need to be honest with you. Money isn't going to get you off, you have to realise that. We've got Pullman as your barrister and he's good. He can fight for a lesser sentence, maybe go with diminished responsibility. But that's pushing it. You'd need to be checked out by a psychiatrist if you want to go down that route. Now, when did you last speak to Lucy or message her?' Stephen asked, reading the police interview.

Charlie didn't flinch. 'Whenever it says in the file,' he lied. 'Who is this eye-witness who said they saw me, anyway? Seeing a psychiatrist would be like admitting I'm mad. I'm not fucking mental. We were at boarding school together, weren't we? We took too many drugs but they haven't made me go mad.' Charlie slammed his fist down on the table.

'Wainwright! Cool it!' came the stern voice of the prison warden.

'Charlie, you know I can't give you that information. At the moment they have been noted as a reliable source. Lucy's statement will have been submitted, but your messages don't look great. You've threatened her, you've ignored the police caution. They'll throw the book at you. You followed her and sat outside her house – what were you thinking?'

'Will Lucy be questioned in court?' Charlie asked, his leg shaking under the table.

'She can be called but she could also give evidence via video link if wants to. That's more than likely.'

'Time's up, Wainwright.' The warden loomed over him. 'Back to your cell.'

Charlie extended his hand to shake Hatten's hand.

'No contact, Wainwright. You know the rules, move it.'

'I'll be in touch,' Stephen said as he tucked the file back into his briefcase.

Scraping his plastic chair across the floor, Charlie stood up and was led back to his cell. As he walked past the other cells, inmates jeered at him. 'Woman beater, rapist, animal, scum!'

'Simmer down,' the warden shouted, 'or you'll lose the open-door privilege.'

Charlie's cell door closed behind him with a clang.

He lay on his bed, his head pounding. The footsteps of hard boots clashed against the metal grid floor.

Then his door opened abruptly.

'Up against the wall, Wainwright,' shouted a warden, two more wardens entered the cell. They stripped Charlie's bed and threw the covers onto the floor. The mobile phone fell to the floor, the screen smashing as it hit the ground.

'Not your best move, Wainwright, an unauthorised phone.' The warden picked up the phone. 'I'll need to record this in a Security Incident Report. You've got solitary confinement for two weeks. Enjoy.' The wardens left the cell, leaving the mattress on the floor.

Charlie slumped against the wall, his head in his hands.

Chapter Nineteen

New Year's Eve

Lucy constantly checked her phone. Christmas had been and gone. Even the tree looked tired: its needles had turned a silvery grey and were falling from the spindly branches. Jo had left for London, Matt and Simon had gone back to the station, and Lucy was alone. She sat at her laptop in her writing room then took a novel from the cabinet and read the blurb.

In 1942 artist Beth Golding is sent away to Auschwitz. Separated from her family, she endures the unimaginable. When Allied soldiers finally rescue her and the camp is liberated, she is barely alive. A story of love, hope and fear.

Lucy read the blurb over and over again. It had moved her, inspired her. She wanted to learn more about Peggy, with the sweet-smelling auburn hair. She picked up another novel and read the back cover. She shivered. Moving into a writer's house – it had to be fate telling Lucy she had made the right decision in choosing this home. Maybe Peggy knew the right person would buy her home and would cherish what she had left behind. Maybe she had imagined a young writer living there.

Lucy placed the novels carefully back in the cabinet. She would read them another day. Outside, the sun burnt through the grey clouds, which clung to each other. She looked at her phone. It was New Year's Eve. She still hadn't heard from Ben. He had obviously forgotten her – and he had done it with such ease. She opened her laptop and began to type, hoping she could lose herself in her story. Then a message pinged into her phone. It was Simon.

Hey, Luce, Just wanted to let you know, Charlie is in solitary confinement for using the mobile phone and contacting you. DI Phillips said he'll probably get an extra twelve months for that. I'll swing by later and see how you are. Take care. Si x

Lucy closed the message, put the phone back on the bureau and began to type again but she was soon interrupted by another message arriving. She picked up the phone and opened it. It was from Ben.

Hey, this doesn't feel right. I don't feel right. I didn't come in when I collected my bike because I thought that was what you wanted. Maybe I misread your message, but I feel crap now. I miss you. Say it how it is right? Well, there you have it. I want to see you again. Ben

A tear stung her eye as she read the message. It was as if two people were willing her on: Peggy, who she'd never met but felt she knew, and Ben: he messaged just when she felt scared by the prospect of the trial and sharing her darkest moments. It was as if he knew she needed him. She replied.

Hey back. I haven't felt right either. My message was rubbish – sorry. Oh God, why is this so hard? Why can't I say how I feel?

How do you feel?

I feel alone. Tonight's New Year's Eve and I'm here alone.

Why are you alone?

Jo has gone back to London and the boys back to work.

Look, I like you. I like you a lot. I'd like to be with you tonight to see in the new year. If you'd like that, let me know. But if you don't want to hear from me, let me know that too.

Come and see the new year in with me. I'd like that. And I do like you.

The dots stopped bubbling at the bottom of the message, she'd told him, he'd told her, and now she wouldn't be alone, she didn't want to be alone, she wanted to be with Ben, and he wanted to be with her.

She left her phone and went downstairs. The sitting room looked empty and the tree now that it no longer had presents beneath it. Beneath the tree lay a carpet of pine needles. She hoovered around it. Each time she hit the tree, needles cascaded from it like miniature arrows that pierced the carpet. She turned the hoover off. It was a pointless task. Instead she went to the under-stairs cupboard and rifled around for the decorations box. Christmas was over. She pulled the box free, a roll of new, unopened masking tape fell out in front of her. She jumped back. She hadn't seen any masking tape, neither had she bought any. He must have been in the house. She crumpled to the ground and cried. With her head in her hands, her phone rang. She picked herself up and went upstairs to answer it. She didn't look to see who was calling, just answered in a robotic way, wiping her face, trying to appear composed, normal, fine. Would she ever be that?

'Hello,' she said.

'Lucy, it's Ben.' She sank to the floor, the phone to her ear. 'Listen, I thought maybe I could come over now. I've finished work. Maybe we could eat in, watch a movie and see the new year in, how does that sound?'

She was quiet.

'Lucy? Can you hear me, are you still there?'

She sat for a while, trying not to cry. She wanted to see Ben so much.

'Yep, that sounds good, what time is it now?' she asked, tears silently trickling down her face.

'It's five o'clock. Would you like me to come over? Are you OK? You sound like you're crying.'

'Oh yes, Ben, I'd like that. Can you come now? I just feel...' She stopped.

'Sure, I'll see you in a bit.'

Lucy was alone again. She put her phone in her pocket and went back downstairs, where she stared at the open door of the cupboard and a roll of tape. She couldn't do it. Every muscle in her body closed down and froze, every part of her mind screamed out. It was meant for her. It filled her with a sense of sickness. He wanted to scare her, to let her know he knew where she lived, to torment her. He wanted to make her pay for escaping him and wanting happiness again. He wanted to hurt her and keep on hurting her. She walked forward and slammed the door shut. The tape still on the floor. She felt a volcano of fear bubble up inside her: fear of him, his messages, his presence. He'd lurked in the dead of night watching her. She felt overwhelmed. His face filled her mind, returning her to the hell she'd escaped – and now she was alone and trapped.

The front door knocker rattled. She jumped and looked at the door. It could only be Ben.

Lucy ran to the door and opened it. 'Ben!' She fell into his arms. His arms went around her. She tried to stand but her legs gave way. She clung to him. 'Ben,' she cried. A tear trickled down her cheek and the saltiness touched her lips.

'Lucy, what? Shit, what's wrong?' He supported her into the hall and closed the door behind him. He searched her face, expecting to see she'd been hurt, but could see no injury. In her eyes was a sadness he couldn't bear to look at. She looked lost. He sat on the stairs and took her in his arms. 'Lucy, what's happened? You're shaking.' He brushed the tears from her face and tucked her hair behind her ears. 'Talk to me. I'm here now, I'm here.'

'Ben, it's all such a mess and I can't deal with it. I'm not the person you think I am. My life is fucked. I'm not the person you need. I don't even know how to tell you or where to start. I'm damaged, I'm disgusting, I'm vile.' Lucy's eyes were empty.

Slowly, he drew her to her feet and stood with her. 'Hey, hey, hey, you're none of those things. You're beautiful and warm and kind.' He took her in his arms and kissed her head. 'Shall we sit somewhere a bit more comfortable and you can tell me why you're saying this?' His eyes searched her face. She looked withdrawn, scared, unsure. He led her into the sitting room and sat her on the sofa. The hoover was still by the tree, the flex straggling across the floor.

'Where do I start?' she asked, wiping her nose with her sleeve.

'The beginning,' he said kindly, taking her hands. 'Start from the beginning.'

'I was engaged,' she began, 'to Charlie, for one year. We were together for three years in total. I left him in October.' She looked at the tree, which was as dishevelled as she felt.

'Why did you leave him?' Ben asked.

'I was scared of him. He was controlling and abusive. I couldn't take it any more, I simply couldn't.'

'So, you moved here,' Ben said, 'to escape?'

'In part, yeah, to escape him, to escape my life with him. I could only escape thanks to my grandfather leaving me money – enough to put down a deposit on a house. It was like he knew I needed it. I took the opportunity while I could. But he followed me here. He found out where I lived, he messaged me, he sent me a parcel to frighten me, to let me know he knew where I was. I went to get the Christmas decorations box. It fell out of the cupboard in front of me and I just thought, it's there and he's there, he's always there.

'Hey, hey, slow down. What fell out Luce?'

'Masking tape, he's been here,' she sobbed.

'Lucy, I don't understand, what masking tape?' Ben asked concerned and trying to figure out what Lucy was talking about.

'He used to lock me in a room and gag me with masking tape,' she said her heart breaking inside her.

'What the fuck! Where is he now?' Ben asked.

'In prison. He was arrested just before Christmas, but he contacted me on Christmas Day, sent me a message from a mobile in prison, threatening me, telling me to live in fear,' she said.

'So that's who Jo was talking about when she was drunk? He's the dick in the prison, right? That's why he was arrested?' he asked.

'Yeah, she was talking about Charlie. He'd been here, watching me, for months. The police arrested him and he's in Wandsworth Prison. I thought it would stop, that it would end, but then the message on Christmas Day made me realise it's never going to stop. It won't stop until he ends it – ends me.'

'Lucy, come here.' He pulled her in even closer to him. She could feel the strength of his arms around her, hear the beating of his heart. 'Did he ever hurt you?'

'You mean like hit me?' she said, turning further into him. 'Yeah. He hit me. He hit when he thought I'd done something wrong, when he thought I'd behaved badly, but I never knew what I'd done wrong. He had this locked room in his apartment and he'd lock me in there. It was always dark. Sometimes he would put masking tape over my mouth. He'd bring in water and throw it in my face. And then, when I thought everything was OK, I'd make supper and he'd throw it on the floor and make me clear it up. And then, just before I left, he … he … he…' She stopped, tears falling from her bloodshot eyes.

'What did he do Lucy, Lucy?' he cupped her face.

'He raped me. He pulled me across the floor, I remember trying to run from him, but he punched me and I could feel blood running into my mouth, intense pain. He dragged me by my hair into the bedroom and ripped my top off. He bit me, he groped at me, then he hit me again. I fell onto the bed, begging him to stop, then he tore my tights. Like an animal, he pinned me down. I screamed no, I screamed no, but he didn't stop, he forced himself into me, hurting me, his hand across my mouth. I couldn't breathe, and then it stopped. I could feel his weight on me, the smell of his sweat. I lay still. I couldn't breathe, I wanted to die right there and then. Then he let me push him off me and I crawled to the shower. I sat in the shower and let the water run over me, watching the blood-stained water trickle away. I wanted to disappear, to wash away. That's why I am damaged.'

'Lucy, you are not damaged. He's sick – he's a sick bastard, an animal. I'd like to break his kneecaps. My God, come here.' He pulled her in and held her tightly.

Lucy was in shock. She'd finally told somebody that the relationship hadn't just been about control, manipulation, narcissism; it had been more than that. She had been raped and lived with her rapist. Lived with the person who had violated her. Now she was running, running like a scared deer from the wolves in the forest. Would she ever stop running?

'Why didn't you report him?' Ben asked, cradling her to his chest.

'I couldn't. Who would believe me? We were engaged. I haven't even told Jo. I still can't now. I want to, but something stops me. She's my best friend, but this is more than a friend should have to hold, deal with. Where do they go with that? I can't tell her Ben. Nobody saw what he was like indoors. To everyone else, he was always lovely Charlie – cool, calm, perfect. But Jo saw how he'd twist the skin on my wrist or hold me back when we were out. But nobody would believe me if I told them. Nobody.'

'You've told me, and I believe you. That's the first step. I'm not leaving you tonight, I'm staying. I'll crash on the sofa, but I'm not leaving you alone. Come here, baby.'

'Do you promise? You won't leave in the night when I'm asleep, will you? I can make the writing room up for you.' She clung to him.

'I'm staying with you. Do you feel better now you've told me? I mean, not better, that sounds crass … I mean, how do you feel?' He stroked her hair and kissed her head softly.

'I feel better I've said it out loud. I've let myself remember it. But it never goes. I can sit and write at the beach and watch the waves. It's quiet but it's there – it's always there. I can try and clear my head, but it's like a recurring nightmare, but a nightmare isn't real. Time doesn't heal it; it pushes it further away, but it never goes. It won't ever go. I'm scarred, but I hope that one day the scars won't be like open wounds; they'll fade. I feel damaged. I don't trust men – I didn't trust you.' She looked at him, her face expressionless.

'I understand that. In time you will trust me and men again, but that's not going to happen overnight. You trust Simon and Matt, right?' he said.

'I trust them because they're different – they aren't attracted to me, they have no agenda, but now I don't know how to deal with my feelings towards a guy. I want to let them free but I don't know how to any more. I don't know how not to be scared. I don't know how to let you into my life and feel safe, and I want to.'

'You've taken the first step. You're here with me now, you fell into my arms at the door, you cried, you told me your story and I'm still here. I haven't run. You're not damaged to me. You've been...' He couldn't bring himself to say the word. 'I can't imagine how you feel. I know how I feel and what I want to do to him, but that's my anger to deal with. I'm glad you've told me. Have you told the police any of this?'

'No, I can't. I can't admit that the man I shared a bed with did that to me. Who would believe me? The jury will say I asked for it, it was just rough and playful, but it wasn't. They'd never believe me. Nobody will.'

'I believe you.'

She let him hold her tighter.

'When's the trial?'

'It starts on the second February. I'm dreading it. I don't want to see him in court. Simon said I can maybe give evidence by video link...' She looked at him. 'Oh my God, I've just poured everything out to you, landed it all on you. You've just finished work and I haven't even offered you a drink.'

'Lucy, shhhh, that can wait. Shall I put the hoover away? I feel like it's watching us,' he said. 'And Lucy, you haven't landed me with anything.'

Ben carried the hoover into the hall. 'Where shall I put it?'

Lucy looked out from behind the fridge door, her face telling him without the need for words.

'In here?' he said. 'Is this masking tape? Why don't I put it in the car it will be needed as further evidence? Maybe knowing it's not here will help you.'

'Can you do that?' she asked.

'Yep. I'll take it. Pass me a carrier bag and I'll put it in the boot. And Lucy…'

'Yes?'

'I will come to court with you if you want me to be there.' Ben took the carrier bag and carefully placed the masking tape in it, then went out to his car and put the bag in his boot. He locked the car, closed the gate and shut the door. He put the hoover in the cupboard. 'Job done.'

Lucy handed him a bottle of Bud and the local Chinese take-away menu.

He took the menu and beer, placed them on the table and turned to her. 'Come here, you need a hug.' He held her tightly – an honest hug from the man she was beginning to trust.

Chapter Twenty

Lucy's phone buzzed and jumped on her bedside table. She stretched out her arm and turned it off. Her bedroom was still in darkness; even the birds outside hadn't stirred yet. The darkness made her want to stay in bed forever, warm and safe. Sighing, she picked up her phone and looked at the screen, still trying to focus. Eight thirty-five. She closed her eyes, dreading the day ahead. She felt sick.

A message pinged in from Ben.

I'll be with you at ten. Keep calm, have breakfast, and think positive thoughts.

She smiled wryly. Think positive? She still hadn't shared the full story with the police, and she hadn't told her lawyer, James, everything. She couldn't. She'd only told him that Charlie had been abusive, that he had hit her, hurt her physically. She had told him about the room and being locked in it, sometimes too frightened to move from where she'd been pushed to the floor, sometimes tied to the chair and gagged. She couldn't bring herself to tell him what Charlie had done the night before she left; that had to remain her deepest, darkest secret. She'd shared it with Ben, but she wasn't ready to tell anyone else. It felt like a nightmare she had to live with. She opened Ben's message again.

I'll be ready, Lucy.

She didn't know how she would ever feel ready in her head, but today was D-Day. The month had gone by so fast. She'd spent her days on the beach writing and now it was here. At midday she had to go. If she was going to let Ben into her life, she needed to let go of her past and move on. She knew Ben was right: she needed to muster every bit of positivity she had in her to get through it. As she read his message again, another message pinged in. It was from Jo.

I'm thinking about you – be strong and don't be beaten. You've got it in you, my gorgeous girl, you are going to win this. Love you. Xxx

Lucy smiled. She knew she could be strong. Eight forty-eight. She had to get up and do exactly what Ben had said: a good breakfast and think positive thoughts, Ben would be with her at ten.

She showered. As she dried herself, she thought about the day ahead. The letter box rattled as a pile of letters fell through. After thinking about what to wear, Lucy chose skinny black trousers, a black ribbed polo-neck and Chelsea boots. She looked at herself in the mirror. She looked pale and scared. As she blow-dried her hair, she thought about how she would remain focused; she knew the defence lawyer would try to unbalance her. Her solicitor, James Cooper, had advised her how to act, how to behave on the witness stand. He had explained that the defence would try to find her weaknesses, try to rattle her, but she was just to tell the truth and remain calm.

She unplugged the drier, threw the duvet over the bed, plumped the pillows and opened the curtains. She closed the bathroom door and went downstairs. When she opened the front-door curtain, letters that had got caught behind it tumbled to the ground: bill, bill, junk, and not sure. She opened the bills and left them on the side, threw the junk mail into the wastepaper basket by the door, and ignored the other letter. Nine fifteen: time for breakfast and tea, she thought. She opened the sitting-room curtains and plumped up the cushions on the sofa. The room seemed bare now that the Christmas tree had come down. The smell of toast wafted through to the sitting room. She tidied the cushions again and made her way to the kitchen, where she ate her toast, trying to stay focused. Every mouthful tasted like cardboard. She wasn't hungry. She pushed the plate away. She wanted the day to end before it had even started. She left her plate and half-eaten toast and went back up to her bedroom.

She sat at her dressing table. The face that looked back at her from the mirror wasn't the face of a strong, confident writer. It was the face of a scared girl, full of doubt.

As she applied the last touches of eye make-up she heard a car pull up. She walked to her writing room, opened the cabinet and took out one of Margaret Arthur's novels. She read the back cover, which told of a story of mindful power, love, hope and fear. She read the words over and over again until the sound of the knocker made her stop. She left the cabinet open and walked down the stairs.

Ben stood outside.

'Hey,' she said, beckoning him to come in. 'I just need to grab something.' She ran back upstairs and grabbed the novel, closed the cabinet door and ran back down the stairs.

'How are you feeling?' Ben asked.

'OK, I guess. Well, not great, but I keep reading the back of this novel and it's how I need to be,' she said, handing the novel to Ben. 'I don't know how much of it is based on truth but I can use these words to make it all go away. The memory will always be etched in my mind, but hope is what I need to keep with me. Shall we go?'

She left the book on the side with the unopened letter and locked the front door behind her.

The journey seemed to take forever. Nothing looked familiar; the buildings, the landscape, all just blots on the landscape. The town centre confused her as she watched people milling about; she'd got used to the silence of the countryside and now she was surrounded with noise and traffic. It overwhelmed her. Ben turned left into the NCP car park. He looked over at Lucy, who looked scared, nervous, lost in thought. He placed his hand on her leg and gently squeezed it. 'Stay positive. I'm here.'

She turned to him and smiled; she was glad of his company. They left the car park and walked through the throng of people. Lucy grabbed Ben's hand when a man jostled her, hitting her shoulder.

'Sorry, love,' he said, turning to her. Ben held Lucy's hand as they reached the main road. Lucy stepped out. A car horn blared and she jumped back, startled. Everything moved too fast for her: she felt like everything was moving and she was standing still, buffeted by people, traffic, noise.

She couldn't see straight. The beeping of the pedestrian crossing penetrated her mind, the green man flashed in front of her face, and a woman behind pushed her in the back. Ben took her hand and pulled her closer to him. The people she passed stared and glared at her. Then there it was – the Crown Court. It looked austere, important. Three storeys high with large columns at the front. Ivy grew up one side of the building and a Union Jack fluttered in the wind. Above the double doors was the Royal Coat of Arms and on either side the words 'Crown Court' were etched into the stonework. This was somewhere where Lucy should feel safe, yet she was overwhelmed with fear. The building was colder inside than she'd expected, and she held Ben's hand tighter. A sweeping staircase led to a gallery above, where a petite blonde woman talked to a circuit court clerk who clutched a bundle of papers and files. Men in black robes glided past, their heels clipping the stone floor, their wigs hiding their hair.

'Ah Lucy, you're here.' Lucy turned to see Detective Inspector Phillips, James Cooper and Christopher Hardy, her barrister, standing behind her. Hardy wore a wig and black robe.

'How was your journey?' Hardy asked.

'OK,' she replied.

'Lady Scott is the judge today, which is good. We hope to win this, Lucy. You just have to be strong, stay unrattled by the defence's questions. Charlie has one of the top barristers on his case, but money cannot buy freedom. The jury will be called at midday. I expect a very positive outcome.'

Lucy felt the knot in her stomach tighten. How could she stand up in court? How would she get through this? She'd expected to give evidence via video link, not to see his face across the courtroom, but now she was faced with just that. Hardy led Lucy down the corridor. Offices and rooms channelled off it.

'Lucy, take a seat.' Hardy beckoned to her to sit with DI Phillips and Ben, then he left them. She watched him talk to a young guy in a grey suit holding a box of files. His robe swishing behind him, he took a file from the clerk and returned to Lucy.

'The accused has arrived; we will be called shortly.'

A voice called from behind the desk. 'The trial for Carter v. Wainwright, courtroom five.'

'That's us.' Hardy stood and waited for Lucy to stand. Her legs felt like jelly beneath her and she could no longer feel her feet. She turned to Ben and her eyes searched his. He smiled reassuringly at her and squeezed her arm. 'You'll be

OK.' Hardy led Lucy through to the courtroom. She sat in a wooden pew behind James, her solicitor, on the right-hand side in front of the judge's bench. Ben and DI Phillips took seats in the public gallery above.

'DI Phillips isn't it?' Ben said.

'It is,' he replied.

'I think you need this.' Ben handed him the bag with the masking tape. 'It was hidden in Lucy's house, in a cupboard.'

DI Phillips nodded his head. He left the public gallery.

As she sat there in silence, the door above opened, squeaking in the silence. People turned to look. Matt, Jo and Simon walked in and took seats by Ben. Then a door to the other side of the gallery opened and Gladys Pope walked in, wearing a navy skirt, flowery blouse and a blue cardigan with a large brooch resting on her ample bosom. She took a seat and perched her black handbag on her lap. Another door opened. From the steps below, a barrister emerged. Behind him was Charlie, staring straight ahead, his wrists cuffed, accompanied by a prison officer. He was led to the dock where the whole courtroom could see him. A court artist began to sketch on his pad. Jo glared at Charlie. His look defiant, he smirked at her. A petite lady came in and placed the bag on James Cooper's table and whispered in his ear. James stood up and gave the bag to Hardy. The door of the public gallery opened, and DI Phillips took a seat.

To one side of the courtroom, a lady in a grey tweed suit opened the door for the jury. The twelve men and women filed in and took their seats in the jury box.

'All rise,' the lady in tweed said.

The side door opened. Lady Scott entered and took her seat at the bench. She glanced around the courtroom and took her glasses from their case to read the notes handed to her.

Her face stern, she looked over her glasses at Lucy and then Charlie. She wore a soft pink lipstick, which softened her austere manner. Lucy watched her. She reminded her of a feared schoolteacher.

Lady Scott began to address the court. Lucy felt the knot in her stomach tighten. Her legs shook beneath the table and she clasped her hands more tightly than ever. She turned and looked up at the gallery. Ben, Matt, Jo and Simon gave her supportive smiles.

The court clerk stood up, the lady in the tweed suit, hair neatly scraped back in a tidy chignon. She took a name from a box and called it out. A member of the jury stood. The court sat in silence as the first juror spoke. 'I solemnly, sincerely and truly declare and affirm that I will faithfully try the defendant and give a true verdict according to the safe evidence.' As each juror stood and swore themselves in, Lucy was oblivious to the indentations her nails made on her hands.

'Members of the jury, your duty will be to determine whether the defendant is guilty or not guilty, based on the evidence provided in this case. The prosecution has the burden of proving the defendant guilty beyond a reasonable doubt. However, if you feel you are not satisfied of the defendant's guilt to that extent, then reasonable doubt exists, and the defendant must be found not guilty.' Lady Scott looked around the court. She looked intently at Lucy then turned to the bench. 'Please call the first witness.'

'We ask that a Mrs Gladys Pope please take to the stand,' Hardy said. Gladys Pope rose to her feet and pulled her cardigan over her blouse, adjusted her brooch and made her way slowly and steadily to the witness box.

'Would you state your name and where you reside to the court,' Hardy said, adjusting his robe.

'Mrs Gladys Edith Pope of number eight Lambourne Terrace, Wrabness, Essex,' Gladys said in her broad Essex accent.

'Mrs Pope, do you know this young woman here?' Hardy asked, turning to Lucy.

'I can't say I know 'er, no. I know of 'er and that she moved in opposite me a few months ago, but no, I've never made 'er acquaintance.'

'You say moved in opposite you – where exactly, Mrs Pope?' Hardy asked.

'She moved into number three, she did, what used to be Mrs Arthur's 'ouse. She died a while back. She was an author, well known too.'

'And number three is where in relation to you, Mrs Pope? Your neighbour, opposite, down the road?'

'It's opposite me. Red door, roses lining the path,' Mrs Pope said and smiled at the judge. 'She was a re-pew-ba-bul author, your excellency,' she said, addressing her comment to the judge. Lady Scott smiled wryly. Hardy smiled inwardly at Mrs Pope's words.

'Thank you, Mrs Pope for enlightening us about her reputable status. So, you can see my client's house clearly from your house?' Hardy turned to the gallery.

'Well, I can see if I'm looking, yes, from my 'ouse, but I wasn't looking, if that's what you're asking, I'm a re-spec-ta-ba-ble part of the community, I am,' she said. 'My Stan can vouch for that. I never pry.'

'Mrs Pope, what I am asking is, from your house, are you able to distinguish clearly people coming and going from my client's house?'

'I am, your worthy.'

Hardy gave a wry smile. He'd never been called 'your worthy' before. Her naivety and malapropism added a lightness to the solemn courtroom air.

'Do you have any pets. Mrs Pope?' Hardy asked.

'Irrelevant!' Mr Pullman QC, the defence barrister, stood up and interjected. 'Whether Mrs Pope has pets is irrelevant, My Lady.'

Hardy looked at Lady Scott. 'On the contrary, My Lady.'

'Overruled. Continue, but keep it relevant, Mr Hardy,' Lady Scott said.

'Mrs Pope.' Hardy moved from behind the bench and closer to Lucy. 'Let me ask you again, do you have any pets?'

'I do. I 'ave Barry,' Mrs Pope replied, brushing her skirt.

'And what is Barry?'

'Barry is a pedigree Bassett 'ound,' Gladys replied with a sense of certainty about her statement,

'How often do you walk Barry?'

'Twice a day, your worthy. Once in the morning and once late at night for a last whoopsie.'

'When you have walked Barry, have you ever noticed anything odd or out of place in your road?' Hardy continued.

'Objection, Your Honour. The prosecution is trying to lead the witness.' Pullman interjected standing up and leaning across his desk.

'Overruled,' Lady Scott said. Hardy bowed his head and continued. 'Thank you, My Lady. Mrs Pope, when you walked your dog late at night did you ever notice anything out of place?'

'Yes, your worthy, a few times I saw a silver car parked in the road – a flash silver car.'

'And why was this odd, Mrs Pope? Many people drive silver cars, many people drive flash silver cars. I myself drive a silver car – it's a common colour,' Hardy continued, his approach, calm, clever, unwavering.

'It was odd because it always parked outside number seven and it always drove away at speed from the same spot. Nobody in the village owns such a car,' Mrs Pope said.

'Number seven? And where is that in relation to my client's house?' he asked.

'It's next door but one,' she said, pulling her cardigan over her blouse.

'Would it be odd to drive at speed in the village, Mrs Pope?' Hardy said, turning to the jury.

'Well, yes,' Mrs Pope said. 'It was dangerous. It was dark – 'e nearly knocked me down the first time, me and my Barry.'

'Driving at speed in the dark is not dangerous, Mrs Pope. Would I be correct to say that the driving was dangerous because the car had no lights when it drove, Mrs Pope, and the driver did not see you?'

A member of the public sniffed from the gallery. Mrs Pope looked up.

'Yes, it 'ad no lights on, for quite a while too,' she said.

'Mrs Pope, you said you saw this car on a couple of occasions. Did you see the driver when he almost hit you?' Hardy asked.

'I never saw the driver, but my Barry barked at his car one night. He startled my Barry.'

'And you were not close enough to see the driver?'

'No, I didn't see the driver,' she said, seeming flustered. 'As I approached the car, the driver put his window up. I saw a man's 'and. He was smoking – 'e threw the cigarette out of the window.'

'Mrs Pope, were you close enough to see the make of the car?'

'Yes,' she replied.

'And, Mrs Pope, can you tell the court the type of car it was?'

'It was a silver Jaguar.'

There was a gasp from the gallery.

'No further questions, My Lady.' Hardy took a seat and Mrs Pope left the witness box.

Lucy sat and watched Mrs Pope walk back to the bench and retrieved her handbag.

The woman in grey stood once more.

'The prosecution call a Miss Carter to the stand.'

Lucy heard her name and froze. How long had she sat before she stood up seemed like hours. Her legs shook. She placed her hands on the table to balance herself, and took a sip from the glass of water on her table. She looked up to the gallery, feeling sick. Jo smiled down at her, willing her on, her fingers crossed.

Hardy looked at her, his face softening. 'Would you state your name to the court?' he said.

Lucy tucked her hair behind her ear and bit her lip. 'Lucy Emma Carter,' she said, her voice trembling. A bead of sweat formed on her upper lip.

'Miss Carter, would you tell the court where you live?' Hardy continued gently.

'Three Lambourne Terrace, Wrabness, Essex,' she said, clasping her hands together as they shook uncontrollably.

'Miss Carter, when did you move to Wrabness?' Hardy asked.

She searched her mind. Why did she not know immediately? She looked up at the gallery again. Jo threw her a look as if to give her strength. Lucy turned to the jury and looked at their faces: twelve faces that gave nothing away, solemn, emotionless.

'Miss Carter?' Hardy asked reassuringly.

Lucy looked at her barrister. 'Last year on the fifteenth of October,' she said, and a tear fell down her cheek.

'Yes,' Jo said under her breath.

'Miss Carter, why did you move to this address?' Hardy asked.

'I moved to escape my boyfriend,' she replied.

'Who was your boyfriend, Miss Carter?' Hardy pushed.

Lucy looked up at the gallery and saw Ben, leaning forward. She saw the man she had opened her heart to. She barely knew him, but she felt safe to tell him her story. She saw the man who had been supportive and kind to her. The faintest of smiles appeared on her face as she looked at him. She turned to the dock and saw the man who'd beaten her, played with her mind, abused her mentally, stalked her. She saw a man who had never loved her, just controlled and taunted her. She looked at her barrister and saw the words from Margaret Arthur's novel like a photo imprinted in her mind: 'a story of mindful power, love, hope and fear'. It was as if she had been destined to find that novel, the house, the words from one writer who'd lived through hell. Without flinching she stared at the jury and words came out of her mouth.

'Charlie Wainwright. I left London because he abused me, battered me, controlled me, frightened me, was forceful in bed. I escaped but he stalked me at my new house, he texted me, he wouldn't leave me alone.'

Hardy looked at Lucy, impressed. He had never seen her act with such strength, he had never seen her assert herself so strongly. She had been scared and insecure when they had discussed the case; she was a mess emotionally. Yet now here she was, standing up to Charlie with her love for Ben, hope for happiness and fear of letting herself be loved.

'I have no further questions, My Lady.'

Mr Pullman QC stood up and looked around.

'Miss Carter, you say the defendant was your boyfriend. Is it not true he was in fact your fiancé? Why would you become engaged to a man who scared you?'

'Because I loved him,' she replied.

'Miss Carter, I am finding this hard to understand, I love Mars Bars, but I don't eat them daily because they are bad for me. Yet to become engaged to a man who you paint as a monster seems a little absurd,' Pullman said, his voice full of cynicism.

'I got engaged to him because I loved him, but then he changed,' Lucy said, clenching her fists. Her nails dug into her palms.

'You say he was forceful in bed, this man. Yet he is a businessman in the City, a philanthropist, an upstanding part of the community. You say he was forceful and controlling in bed, really? I put it to you that he was behaving like a healthy, red-blooded man. I put it to you that experimental sex is just that, and you are crying wolf?'

'Objection, My Lady. This line of questioning is intrusive and unpleasant, and to use an ad hominem approach is disingenuous.'

Lady Scott looked at Pullman. 'Sustained. Mr Pullman, please keep to the evidence given.'

Pullman bowed his head in acknowledgement. 'I'm sorry, My Lady,' he said in an apologetic manner. 'Miss Carter, I put it to you that the defendant loved you and that you confused fun with something else. After all, you are a writer and have an imagination that can perhaps run away with you.'

'Objection, Your Honour! The defence is leading with the exact same question.'

'Sustained. Mr Pullman, I will ask you to rethink your questioning. That is a leading question,' Lady Scott said, scribbling his line of questioning on her pad.

'Indeed. I'm sorry, My Lady. Miss Carter, you are a writer, is that correct?'

'Yes,' Lucy answered.

'And how long have you been working as a writer?' Pullman asked.

'About eight years. I worked on magazines straight after graduating from university,' Lucy said, keeping her hands still. Hardy had warned her if she touched her hair the jury might think she was lying.

'So, can I assume you've written many novels?' Pullman asked, his voice drenched in cynicism.

'I have written five. One was televised for the BBC,' she said, looking at the judge.

'We can assume you live in a world of words and imagery, would you agree?'

'I would agree, yes. I love writing,' she said hesitantly.

'Would you believe you have a vivid imagination – more than most people, perhaps?' Pullman asked.

'I am a writer so I'd say yes, I have a vivid imagination,' Lucy answered.

'More than most, Miss Carter?' Pullman asked mockingly.

'I don't know what you mean.'

'Miss Carter, is your imagination more vivid than mine, for example?' he said.

'I write. I make up stories; they are not real. They are fiction.'

'Perhaps you imagined this fictitious controlling relationship?' he said, brushing his hand over his notes.

'No, that's not true!' she said.

'Miss Carter, you say the defendant controlled you. In what way did he control you?'

Lucy looked at her barrister. 'He controlled who I saw, when I went out, how I dressed.' Lucy was starting to feel overwhelmed by his line of questioning.

'Miss Carter, is that not normal for a couple who share a home together, to show interest in where you are, how you look, who you see? Is that not simply the norm?'

'No,' she said defiantly.

'Miss Carter, did you tell my client that you were unhappy with his control, as you perceived it?' Pullman said.

'No, I didn't,' Lucy said. Her stomach churned and she felt trapped again.

'Miss Carter, forgive me for sounding ignorant, but if you were unhappy with a meal in a restaurant would you not tell the waiter?'

'Yes, I would, but I'd—'

Pullman cut her off. 'But you were unable to tell the man you lived with that you were unhappy.'

'But it wasn't like—'

He cut her off again.

'He didn't control you. One can assume your imagination let you believe that,' he said loudly, almost as if he was playing to an audience, not a jury.

'No, that's not how it was.' Lucy's voice was almost a whimper.

'Miss Carter, did you maintain a sexual relationship with my client up and until you left him?'

Lucy's legs trembled as memories of her last night with him came flooding back: a night of horror, fear, violation.

'Yes,' she said.

'No further questions, My Lady.' Pullman smoothed his robe beneath him and sat back down. Lucy stood in the witness box, confused. Was that it? She looked up to the gallery. Jo looked as confused. Her barrister beckoned her to leave the witness box. She took her seat again behind Hardy. She'd lost. She had no chance against his barrister; he was as brutal as Charlie.

The court clerk stood up. 'The court summons the defendant,' she said.

Charlie stood in the dock; he was not led to the witness stand where Gladys and Lucy had been questioned. Instead he stood, handcuffed and defiant, in the dock.

'Would you please state your name to the court,' the clerk said.

'Charlie Wainwright,' he said.

Pullman stood up. 'Mr Wainwright, when did you become engaged to Miss Carter?'

'On the fourteenth of February 2014 in Vienna.'

'Did you live with Miss Carter before you got engaged?' Pullman asked, his questions simple and to the point.

'Yes, for about two years,' he replied.

'Where did Miss Carter live before moving in with you?' Pullman asked.

'She lived in a shared rented flat,' Charlie replied. That much was true.

'Did she pay towards the flat that you lived in, Mr Wainwright?'

'We divided the bills, but I own the flat,' Charlie said, scratching his cheek with his cuffed hand.

'And would you say you had a happy relationship with Miss Carter?' Pullman continued.

'We had our arguments like any normal couple, but yeah, I loved her. We were happy,' he said.

'Did you ever feel Miss Carter was unhappy in the relationship?' Pullman asked, shuffling his notes. 'You were set to marry early next year, is that correct?'

'No, I never thought she was unhappy. Yeah, we had planned to get married in June.'

'Were you aware Miss Carter had money for a deposit on a property?' Pullman asked.

'No, I was not,' Charlie responded.

'And were you aware that her grandfather had left her a sum of money?'

'No, I had no idea. I rarely went to see Lucy's grandfather with her.'

'Do you believe that Lucy had no intention of marrying you but instead was using you?' Pullman questioned.

'Objection, My Lady. My learned friend is leading his client into an attack on the prosecution.'

Lady Scott peered over her glasses. 'Sustained,' she called. 'Mr Pullman, please be aware that this is a courtroom. Your questions must not mislead the jury when they retire. Please refrain from this line of questioning.'

Pullman shuffled the papers on the bench, looking annoyed.

'Mr Wainwright, do you love Miss Carter?'

Charlie looked at the judge and then towards the jury. 'I have never stopped loving her. I just want her home where she belongs,' he said.

Jo watched him with disgust, back at home with him where he could hurt again, bully her, he was a liar and now he seemed to be fooling the jury. If it wasn't a contempt of court, she would have spat at him.

'I have no further questions, Your Honour.'

Hardy took to the floor. 'Mr Wainwright, my client left you on the fifteenth of October, is that correct?'

'Yes,' Charlie replied.

'And she wrote a letter to explain why she was leaving and asking you not to contact her?' Hardy continued.

'She wrote a letter, yeah.' Charlie coughed.

'Yet you texted her abusive messages on the sixteenth of October, left abusive voicemails and proceeded to contact her for the following months, even after PC Mackenzie advised you not to contact her on Sunday the eighteenth of

November?' As Hardy put forward his attack, Lucy watched. As much as she wanted it all to end, she also wanted the floor wiped with him. He'd hurt her enough.

'I sent a couple of messages. She is my fiancée,' Charlie said stubbornly.

'She was your fiancée, but the letter I believe said: "I will be long gone from your life and it will be too late to tell me you are sorry, sorry is just a word, meaningless to you. Today I want to be free". My learned friend, members of the jury, would that not tell you the relationship was over? The fact you were engaged is irrelevant. When Lucy sent that letter, it marked the end of your relationship. She was no longer your fiancée, would you not agree, Mr Wainwright?'

Charlie stood defiantly in the dock. He glared at Hardy he said nothing.

'Mr Wainwright, for the court, would you please answer the question? Would you not agree that the relationship was over?'

Charlie said nothing. Instead he smirked and threw a look at Lucy.

Hardy turned to the gallery, twiddling his pen in one hand.

'Mr Wainwright, I'm going to ask you again. Would you not agree the relationship was over?'

Charlie didn't flinch.

'Perhaps the reason you don't want to answer that question is because you have no reasonable explanation to give for your behaviour.' Like a man on stage, as if the jury was his audience, Hardy turned to the jury. 'As you are unable to answer this very simple question, one can only assume that the relationship was over. Miss Carter left you because you bullied her, you manipulated her, you hurt her. She feared you, is that not right, Mr Wainwright? The woman who you purportedly loved, feared you so much that she was unable to tell you to your face it was over. Instead, she left without a trace. She left to be free. Is that not the true version of events?'

Charlie said nothing.

Lady Scott cast a glance at the barrister and then at the defendant. 'Mr Wainwright, are you able to give my learned friend an answer?'

Charlie glared menacingly at the judge. 'She's a liar!' he snarled.

'Mr Wainwright on the twelfth of November you sent Miss Carter another text. It reads: *talk to me I was angry — you made me angry.* On the thirteenth of November you dropped off a parcel to be delivered to number three Lambourne Terrace, containing a Dior lipstick, to frighten my client. I put it to you that you that this was a premeditated act. Why would you send such a gift to a girl who clearly made you angry? You knew my client lived alone, in the countryside, and had not disclosed her address to anybody but her best friend and literary agent, Miss Jo Segal. Is it true that you went through Miss Jo Segal's recycling bin and found Miss Carter's new address?'

Lucy sighed. She hadn't wanted Jo to find out she was the reason Charlie had found Lucy.

Jo shot a look at Lucy and gasped.

Charlie began to sweat. 'Lucy is my fiancée. I didn't go through any recycling.'

'Correction, Mr Wainwright, she *was* your fiancée,' Hardy fired back. 'So how did you know where to send the parcel, Mr Wainwright? Did you follow her?'

'She's my fiancée. I don't need to follow her,' Charlie responded, his hands sweating.

'Perhaps you'd like to explain to the court why you sat outside my client's house on Friday the sixteenth of November, why you were in her front garden that night, why she heard a dustbin lid falling and footsteps running away. Was your plan foiled because you heard two voices in her garden and knew she was not alone?'

'I wasn't there,' Charlie said, his look smug.

'You recognised the second voice didn't you, Mr Wainwright? Is it true you ran from the scene because you weren't expecting two voices?'

'Your imagination is as vivid as Lucy's,' Charlie snarled.

'I believe you recognised the second voice and knew she would be a credible eye-witness. Isn't that right? What were you going to do that night, Mr Wainwright? Was my client in danger?' Hardy lashed out without a pause.

'Objection, Your Honour. My learned friend is misleading and twisting the evidence.'

Lady Scott turned to Hardy. 'Do you have a plausible reason for these questions? Is it true that the defendant was allegedly trespassing? I must remind you that evidence is just that; it cannot be elaborated on. Sustained.'

Pullman sat down looking triumphant.

'Mr Wainwright, it was noted in a statement made by Mrs Gladys Pope that she saw you racing through the village that night with no lights on. That's the same night you were heard running from the garden of number three Lambourne Terrace.'

'I wasn't there, I was in London. I live and work in London,' Charlie replied.

'Mr Wainwright, it is noted that it was a pleasant evening – a little chilly, with a slight breeze but not gale-force winds. This is what Mrs Pope wrote in a statement dated the twenty-first of November. It would be incredible to suggest that such a wind could move a metal dustbin lid from its container or indeed open the latch of a gate. We have a statement by Miss Jo Segal stating that, on returning to the house, the gate was closed but when she checked through the window after hearing footsteps run away, the gate was open.'

'And that means what? So what? The gate was open – is that all you've got?' Charlie said. The prosecution was hammering him from every angle. Hardy pulled no punches with his cross-examination.

'Mr Wainwright, the gate was open because you fled from the scene, and in your haste did not close it. The lid fell because you knocked it in your haste – or perhaps you were climbing on the bin to scale the wall into my client's garden, but you were stopped in your tracks because you heard two voices. You hadn't planned for two people being at the scene. It was my client you had come for, wasn't it?'

'Objection!' Pullman rose. 'My learned friend is leading my client to an untrue account of the facts.'

Lady Scott sat and deliberated for a few moments. 'Mr Pullman, I feel that the evidence of the defendant being on the property is reasonable enough to question why. Overruled.'

Pullman sat back down, his frustration showing in his face. He muttered to himself as he ruffled the papers on his table.

'Mr Wainwright, would it not have been easier to have used the front door?'

Charlie glared at him. Twelve sets of eyes watched him from the jurors' bench. 'On the twenty-second of December you were seen again outside my client's house.'

Hardy pulled the new evidence closer to him, this would nail him, he looked back on his notes.

Hardy browsed the public gallery, 'You see on the twelfth of November, in your bombardment of abusive texts you sent one stating: *"you can't just leave, you fucking bitch. I'll get you!"* Unpleasant to say the least. Would it be then that on the fifteenth of November you entered the house of Miss Carter, through a window at the back of the property, unnoticed. It is then is it not that you hid a brand-new roll of masking tape in a closed under-stair cupboard.'

'Objection your honour,' Pullman thrashed his cloak behind him, where the hell had Hardy got this from 'there is no evidence shown by the prosecution.'

Lady Scott peered over her glasses. 'Mr Hardy are you able to support this?'

'I am, My Lady, we are in receipt of evidence only given today. Under the circumstances it is paramount I address it.'

'Overruled.'

Pullman muttered under his breath. This threw the defence into a catastrophic mess.

'Thank you, My Lady.' He took the tape and held it in his hand. 'I put it to you that you came to Miss Carter's house with an intent to hurt her, imprison her, gag her. The tape I have here, with a stamp on the inside reading Fulham HSS Hire is similar to the tape used in London, where you gagged and imprisoned her. I put it to you that, that day Miss Segal saw what she thought was a menu delivery canvasser was in fact you. You were seen leaving the property, where you had gained entry and hidden the tape, in a small cupboard where Miss Carter could be locked away. You had come to hurt Mis Carter, hadn't you? Your promise of, *'I'll get you'* was exactly what you were going to do. Isn't that right Mr Wainwright?'

Charlie stared at Hardy his upper lip curling he was being cornered.

'Isn't that the truth Charlie you had come to hurt her again and again, just like you did in London.' Hardy had him pinned down, nowhere to go. 'On the twenty-fifth of December, while you were in custody, you sent my client a message from a borrowed mobile stating she should *"live in fear"*. Why, Mr Wainwright? What were you going to do to her?' Hardy quipped. 'Is that why you needed the masking tape?'

'Objection, Your Honour. My learned friend is insinuating an act of violence again.'

'Overruled. Please continue with your question,' Lady Scott replied.

'You see, Mr Wainwright, I believe you came to my client's house on the sixteenth November to seek revenge, but your plan was foiled because you weren't expecting my client to be with somebody. You fled, and in your haste let your presence be heard. You see, if you had wanted to perhaps see my client and talk, which is indeed credible, would you not have simply knocked on the door?'

Charlie could only watch as Hardy wiped the floor with him.

'I have no further questions, My Lady.' Hardy sat. If the jury didn't see Charlie as the man he was, and what he was capable of, then he would have failed as a barrister.

Lady Scott peered over her glasses. 'Mr Hardy, Mr Pullman, we have heard the evidence and I ask you now to sum up. The time is now two o'clock. Once both summaries have been made, the court will adjourn until the jury have reached a unanimous decision. If the jury are unable to reach a decision today, this case will be adjourned until tomorrow at ten o'clock. The court hearing will not continue beyond four thirty this afternoon. Members of the jury, it is your responsibility to listen to the cases Mr Hardy and Mr Pullman put to you. On this evidence, and on this alone, you must reach your decision. If there is any doubt in your minds, the defendant must be found not guilty.'

Hardy stood up and turned to the jury. 'Members of the jury, today you have heard how my client, Lucy Carter, has been subjected to the controlling and manipulative actions of a man she thought she could trust. A man she was set to marry – yet instead of treating her with kindness, compassion and the protection any woman would expect from their partner, she instead experienced a living nightmare. You have heard today how Miss Carter feared the man she shared her life with, how he abused her mentally and physically, how the only way she could escape was to leave when he was at work. On the fifteenth of October 2015, Miss Carter fled London, where she had moulded a successful writing career and built a life for herself. Instead she bought a new home with the funds her grandfather had left her in a place she was not familiar with, where she was alone. Why would a woman flee and not tell her fiancé where she was going? Is it normal for a relationship to finish in this way? Miss Carter is a woman who has a passion for writing and is well regarded in the publishing arena, yet her life was turned upside down when she met the defendant, Mr Wainwright. She was subjected to abuse throughout her relationship and even after she ended it, he taunted and tormented her. The defendant watched her and stalked until she feared living in the new home she had bought to escape this ordeal. The defendant, as we have seen, has shown no remorse over the way in which he treated Miss Carter. Instead, he set out to deal with her in a way in which could have resulted in an act of violence or harm. It is crucial that this abuse must not be allowed to continue. I advise that the jury finds the defendant Mr Wainwright guilty.'

Pullman sighed as he stood to address the jury. A brilliant performance by the prosecution to damage the credibility of his client, he thought.

'Members of the jury, we have heard today how my learned friend has tried to sabotage the character of my client, Mr Wainwright. A man who is at the top of his career in the City and has an outstanding reputation with businesses and friends alike. Would a man who was a philanthropist himself really be capable of the acts you have heard about today? Is it not simply a case of a woman with a vivid imagination, a writer, who is unhappy in her own skin and with her own insecurities, has seemingly tried to blame a man who loves her passionately? Does this man really look like he has set out to hurt her or abuse her? He hasn't controlled a woman he loves; it is disingenuous to state such a thing. It is reasonable for any person to want to know why they have been left, to be given a chance to talk. The man before you, was set to marry the woman he loved in June next year. He has tried hard to get the woman he loves back, yet he has been vilified for these actions of love and devotion. This isn't a monster in front of you; this is a man who has lost the woman he loves. It is with this thought that I urge you to see beyond the slanderous attacks and realise the correct verdict: that is, that my client, Mr Charlie Wainwright, is not guilty.'

Lady Scott cleared her throat and addressed the court. 'Members of the jury, you have heard the prosecution and the defence give their evidence. It is now for you to determine a verdict based on the facts that you have heard, and only on those facts. I will ask you now to retire and discuss between yourselves the verdict. The court is now adjourned until you reach your verdict.'

'All rise.'

Lady Scott left the courtroom and the jury filed out. Charlie was led back down the stairs, the prison officer by his side.

Lucy sat motionless. Hardy turned to her. 'The worst is over – now we have to wait.'

'They didn't believe me, did they? They think I am imagining it all. It's never going to end, is it?' Lucy said, a tear falling down her face.

'Lucy, we put forward a strong case. We cannot do anything else now. As hard as it is, we must wait. I have every faith that the jury will reach the right decision.'

The courtroom was empty, the public had left the gallery.

'Let's grab a coffee and chat about this. DI Phillips will be waiting for you and I imagine your friends will be there too. I'd like to discuss some things with James. James, could we do that now before the jury are called back?' Hardy said as he collected his files and slid them into an envelope.

'Absolutely, no problem. Pullman tried to pull some punches,' James said.

Hardy shrugged. 'He did. He's a good barrister and he probably didn't like what he had to do, but he was always fair when we trained at the bar together. Let's talk this through over a coffee in the lobby.'

They left the courtroom and walked along the corridors to the main hallway. Jo was standing with the boys. She saw Lucy and put out her arms. 'Come here,' she said. 'You were so brave, Lucy. I'm so proud of you.'

'Could we get a tea?' Lucy said. 'I'm exhausted and drained. That was just horrible.'

Jo slid her arm through Lucy's and together they walked towards the coffee shop in the corner of the main hall. The boys followed them with DI Phillips and Lucy's legal team.

'How do you think it went?' Simon asked Hardy.

'As well as can be expected. Pullman tried the vivid imagination card – the writer's creativity, whimsical approach. I knew he would, but we can only hope now. He didn't go as heavily as I thought he would with his cross-examination, but Lucy was strong out there, even though she doesn't agree,' Hardy said.

'Why d'you think Pullman held back?' DI Phillips asked.

'Between you and me, Tony, I'd say because he didn't believe his client,' Hardy said.

'There's something off about Wainwright,' DI Phillips said as he ordered a large espresso and caramel slice. 'I've got a gut feeling about him and it's not good.'

'What do you mean?' Simon asked. 'D'you think he'd come to do something on the sixteenth?'

Hardy stirred two sachets of sugar into his flat white. 'I believe that if Jo hadn't been there, we would be dealing with a very different case. The masking tape find was something else.'

'Are you saying what I think you're saying?' Simon asked.

'Homicide,' DI Phillips said gravely. 'I think the same, Christopher. I believe he came to the house with intent. He needs to be sent down, we've got a dangerous man on our hands with an agenda. The problem is, Lucy won't be the only woman he'll treat badly. I wonder if she was the first. Might be worth finding out about his ex-girlfriends and mother.'

'Don't tell Lucy that,' Simon said. 'She's scared enough as it is. If the jury come back with a not guilty verdict, then what? He's not going to go away. We've seen what he's like. He'll want revenge.'

Ben listened to Simon. 'I think Simon's right. I have just started to see Lucy – I mean, I'm not her boyfriend. I'd like to be, I'm crazy about the girl, but I can't protect her day and night. She needs protection if he comes back. She was terrified the other night because the masking tape fell out of the cupboard in front of her. She was a mess. I stayed the night in the spare room – I couldn't leave her.'

'Ben, isn't it?' DI Phillips said, sipping his cappuccino. 'I believe you're right, she does need protection. I don't know whether she'd allow herself to be moved to a safe house. If he's sentenced it won't be forever, will it? What do you think, Chris, two years, three years max, out early on good behaviour?'

'The longest sentence would be five years, I suspect, out on licence after that. If he had raped her with other offences he could have got fifteen plus years, but with what we have put forward, five years max,' Chris Hardy said. 'With these sorts of cases it's the burden of doubt. If there is any doubt in the jury's mind – well, he goes free. Doesn't matter what you, I or even the judge thinks; the jury has the final word. If they come back not guilty then we have an acquittal and that's it.'

'I'm going to ask her out. I need her to stay alive. Jesus Christ, I'd fucking break his kneecaps if he came anywhere near her,' Ben said angrily, his fists clenched.

'We'd all like nothing more than to do that,' Simon said, 'and I'm a police officer, but don't even go there. You'll be charged with ABH and that won't help anybody, certainly not Lucy. She needs you more than ever now.'

'Yeah, I know, mate, but fucking hell – what he's done to her. It'd be crazy if he got away with it,' Ben said, glancing over at Lucy who sat at the corner table with Jo. She was so beautiful and gentle – how could anybody hurt her the way Charlie had? He thought about what she had told him, what Charlie had done to her, and how she wouldn't tell anybody else. He *had* raped her, he'd beaten her. Because she was afraid that nobody would believe her, she'd said nothing, but it was a game-changer. Charlie would get a longer sentence if she had told her solicitor he had raped her – and if the jury believed her. If he was found not guilty, she would have been right; she needed the jury to believe her. Should he break her confidence, tell somebody? Simon, DI Phillips? Should he tell them the whole truth and nothing but the truth – wasn't that what justice was about? But then she'd never trust him. He'd be like all the other men she'd got close to; she would see him like Charlie, he would become like Charlie. She trusted him.

'I'm going to see how she is,' Ben said, pushing his coffee cup to one side.

'He likes her a lot,' Simon said. The four men sat at the table. It was ten to four. The jury had been out for two hours. As Simon was about to order more coffees, the court clerk came into the hallway.

'Would the trial for Carter v. Wainwright please return to courtroom five.'

Hardy stood up. James followed him. They walked to where Lucy sat with Ben and Jo. 'Are you ready, Lucy?' Chris said.

She nodded and left Jo and Ben. 'We'll be in the gallery, Lucy. Hang in there,' Jo said as Lucy was led away with Chris and James.

'This will be like before but there will be no further questions. The jury will be asked for the verdict. Depending on the outcome, the judge will then make the decision on sentencing if found guilty. You need to stay positive, Lucy. Whatever the outcome, you need to stay positive. Can you do that?' Hardy said as he opened the door that led to the benches. He touched her arm and left her by her seat. James sat in front of her and Hardy sat at the bench.

The door of the gallery opened and the public took their seats. Jo sat first, her fingers crossed. Ben sat next to her, followed by Matt and Simon. As they waited for the defence to arrive, the door opened again. Gladys Pope came in, clutching her bag. She took a seat next to Simon.

' 'e sounds like a wretch,' she whispered to Simon.

Simon faced her. 'You're right there. Let's hope it's a positive outcome.'

Then Pullman walked into the courtroom followed by Charlie, still cuffed and accompanied by the same prison officer. Behind him was his solicitor, Stephen Hatten.

' 'e looks as guilty as 'ell,' Gladys Pope piped up, nudging Simon. Simon acknowledged her with a shrug.

The prison officer led Charlie up to the dock. He looked up to the gallery and smirked at Jo and the boys. He looked at Lucy and glared.

The jury filed their way in once more.

'All rise.'

Lady Scott entered the court and took her seat.

The court clerk turned to the jury. 'Members of the jury, could I ask the foreman to please stand.'

A slick-looking Asian man stood up. He was tall, clean-shaven, dressed in a charcoal-grey suit and navy tie. He stood with his hands in front of him, silver cufflinks visible.

'Have you reached a verdict in respect of the accused, Charlie Wainwright?' the court clerk asked.

'As the foreman of the jury, I can say we have reached a verdict.'

Lucy sat and watched. Her hands were clenched, her stomach turned over, her legs trembled. Jo took Ben's hand and held it tightly.

'Can I ask you to tell the court your verdict,' the clerk said.

The foreman stood, his face expressionless. Well-practised in his duties, he turned slightly to the judge. 'We find the accused...'

There was silence. Lucy closed her eyes. She felt as if she would collapse.

'Guilty.'

Lucy gasped. She couldn't control her breathing: she felt her pulse racing. Her head dropped into her hands, her eyes still closed. She felt herself let go.

Lady Scott looked through her notes, placed her pen on the bench and turned to the jury.

'Members of the jury, today we have heard the case of Miss Carter v. Mr Wainwright. I have listened to both sides.' She looked at Charlie, who stood unmoved by the verdict.

'Mr Wainwright, in October Miss Carter was starting a new chapter in her personal life, and that included bringing to an end her relationship with you. The jury are satisfied that, from the evidence they have heard, you tormented Miss Carter while you were in a relationship with her, and you proceeded to torment her further when she left you. You have calculatedly tried to make Miss Carter feel as if she was going mad, and have subjected her to a life of mental and physical abuse. You used your high-standing reputation to your advantage. You, cleverly and with premeditated actions, frightened Miss Carter throughout her relationship with you. You used various ways to establish and achieve emotional and physical control over Miss Carter. You bullied, controlled and abused her until she had no choice but to flee London, with the help of a close friend. Your actions were planned, determined and malevolent. You destroyed her mentally. You controlled her body and mind. This is worse than violence. Miss Carter will never recover fully from this. Having considered all the circumstances, I sentence you to five years, with a minimum of three being served fully. Take the accused down.'

Lady Scott gathered her notes and left the courtroom.

'All rise.'

Hardy threw his head back and drew his lips together in triumph, then turned to James and shook his hand.

'Good work, Chris. You did it,' James said, gripping his hand firmly. Chris Hardy walked over to Lucy, whose face was drained of all colour. She stood up, tears streaming from her eyes.

'Thank you,' she said. 'Thank you.' Her voice was soft.

Chris held her arms. 'It's over, Lucy.' He smiled, looked up to the gallery and nodded at the people he recognised. 'Go to your friends now. They are there for you.' He led her through the doorway and out into the hall.

Jo ran towards her and held her tightly. 'My God, Lucy – it's all over.' She held Lucy so tightly that she could feel her ribs.

Simon walked over to James and Chris. 'Thank you,' he said. 'For a moment I thought it would be a different verdict.'

'We proved everything beyond reasonable doubt,' Chris said.

Matt put his arms around Jo and Lucy. Lucy broke away. 'Where's Ben?'

'I don't know. He was with us a minute ago,' Jo said.

'I'll go and look for him,' Matt said.

'I'll go,' Lucy said. 'It needs to be me.' She left the three of them with Chris and James. As she climbed the sweeping stairs, her hand brushed along the highly polished banister.

At the top she saw Ben sitting on the floor, his knees bent up and his head in his hands.

'Ben?' she said, sitting next to him. 'I wondered where you were.'

'I'm here. I just had to get some air. Man, that was hard to hear. And seeing the guy who did that to you...'

'I know, I felt the same, but I think it's over,' she said as she took his hand.

'Lucy,' he said.

'Yeah?' She looked at him, exhaustion in her eyes, and bit her lip.

'I love it when you do that,' he said.

'What?' she said, a smile returning to her eyes.

'You bite your lip,' he said. 'You always bite your lip.'

'Do I? I hadn't noticed. Must be habit. Was that what you were going to say?'

'No, I was going to ask you to be my girlfriend.'

Lucy took his hands in hers and kissed his nose. 'Oh, Ben, I'd like nothing more.' She stood up from the floor and took Ben's hands to haul him up. 'Come on – let's go and see the others and get ourselves home.'

As they walked along the gallery that led to the staircase, Ben took Lucy's hand and pulled her to him. He held her tightly as they descended the staircase. Lucy walked over to the others, who were still in conversation with Chris Hardy.

'We are going to make our way home,' Lucy said, interrupting their conversation. 'Detective Inspector Phillips, thank you for everything you have done for me. I'm eternally grateful.' She took his hand and shook it.

'Look after yourself, Lucy – and I'd like a signed copy of that novel when it's written.' DI Phillips shook Ben's hand. He had grown to like Lucy a lot and he had a feeling that Charlie was bad news. He'd had a gut feeling about him. When he returned to the station he'd dig deeper into his previous relationships.

'Lucy,' Chris Hardy said, 'I'll be in touch. In the meantime, finish that novel.'

'I will. Thank you again, Chris, for everything – and for believing me.' Lucy went to take his hand. Instead instinctively the old Lucy returned, and she hugged him.

DI Phillips turned to Chris Hardy. 'Well done, Chris. Justice prevailed.'

'It did on this occasion. I'm wondering how many other Lucy Carters there are out there,' Chris Hardy replied.

'That, my friend, I am about to find out. I'm going to investigate Charlie Wainwright further. I've got a hunch about him.' DI Phillips shook Hardy's hand and left the Crown Court.

***

The squeak of the gate's hinges was a welcome sound. It had always annoyed her in the past – like the scratching of nails on a blackboard – but now, after the long drive home from Chelmsford Crown Court, it was a familiar and welcome sound. She would get it oiled, though, she thought. Maybe she'd ask Ben to do it now they were going out. She smiled at the thought. The guy on the bike who she'd noticed when she first wrote on the beach was now hers to think about freely as she wrote.

As Ben closed the gate behind him, the headlights from Simon's car dazzled him as he pulled up with Matt and Jo. Lucy opened the front door and switched on the hall light.

She threw her keys onto the table and picked up the unopened letter. As she slid her finger under the envelope's seal to open it, she called out to the others, 'Coffee, tea, or something stronger?'

She put the letter on the worktop and flicked the kettle on. 'Ooh, something stronger for me,' Jo said, opening the fridge door and taking out the slimline tonic. 'Point me to the gin, Lucy.'

'Are you staying, then?' Lucy asked.

'Yep. I've taken two days off – well, working from home, but I'm staying with Matt tonight. Will you be OK on your own?' Jo rummaged in her bag for her cigarettes.

Jo opened the back door and the smell of tobacco wafted into the kitchen.

'Beer, guys, or gin?' Lucy asked as she opened the fridge and took out bottles of Budweiser, a pot of hummus and olives.

'You know that Mrs Pope?' Jo said, one arm extended into the garden as she blew a plume of smoke into the cold night air. 'She seemed genuinely nice and concerned for you. How come we've never met her? She lives opposite you!'

'I don't know. I've seen her curtains open and close a few times, that's all. I need to take something over to say thank you – a card, maybe. Her witness statement was vital.'

'Yeah, she sat next to me in the gallery,' Simon said as he opened his beer. 'She called Charlie a wretch. It's probably best not to send a card, though – she was a witness and had a legal obligation to appear in court. A card might look like it was a favour, or you had sweetened her into doing it. Maybe just let it go.'

'Right, Jo,' Matt said, 'we need to make tracks after these drinks, I am in early tomorrow.'

Jo put out her cigarette in the flowerpot. A draught blowing through the open door lifted the letter from the worktop and blew it onto the floor, where it slid under the cupboard, unnoticed. 'Sure. I'm ready to go after this. Are you sure you'll be OK on your own?'

'Yep, I'll be fine. I'm going to start reading Margaret Arthur's novel tonight,' Lucy said as she locked the back door.

'Are you ready, Simon?' Matt asked.

'Yep, I'm good to go. Ben, maybe we can catch up for a beer at the weekend if you have no plans?' Simon said, placing his empty beer bottle on the kitchen table.

Lucy led the way to the front door. Jo hugged her.

'Call me tomorrow, kiddo,' she said.

Lucy closed the door behind her and pushed the bolt across.

'You've locked me in,' Ben said as he heard the lock and came up behind her in the hallway.

'Habit, I think. I always lock the door. You're free to go, though.' She pulled the curtain across; she could feel a draught from under the door.

'D'you want me to go?' he asked.

'Um, well, I'd like you stay for a bit at least. We can snuggle on the sofa, finish the olives, maybe. Have another beer?' Even though Ben was now her boyfriend, she was still tentative. She was still learning about him. She needed to trust him – and more than anything she didn't want to be hurt again.

'Sofa it is, then,' Ben said and took Lucy's hand.

Chapter Twenty-One

Friday, 19th March

Lucy sat on the beach in her favourite spot. The stone steps leading down to the beach were as cold as ice. The sea lapped onto the beach. The steel cranes on the horizon loomed across the Maersk freight ships; she still thought they looked like giant giraffes. Forlorn fishing boats bobbed on the murky grey water and a RNLI boat chugged out from the pier. Lucy took her journal from her satchel and began to write. She loved nothing more than being here in her space and letting her thoughts run wild, her imagination filling the crisp white pages. Today was the start of a new chapter: both in her life and in her latest novel.

She looked out to sea, at the waves cresting and falling. Seagulls swirled about the sky, darting down into the cold water for food. As she watched, she let her mind drift. An old collie dog, with grey eyes and a bedraggled black and white coat, came sniffing around her. She recognised him from when she first wrote at the beach. She didn't see many dogs there but this one looked familiar and always sniffed about her.

'Archie!' a harsh voice said. 'Here! Don't mind him, miss, he's harmless and half-deaf.' He stood by the wall and let Archie sniff about the beach. 'Never goes in the sea – he's scared of the water. Where are the children today?' He leant over the wall and looked around the beach below. The sand was empty.

'Children? I don't have any children,' Lucy said, turning to him.

'I thought I heard the voices of children beneath the wall. You sit here a lot. I thought you were with the children,' he said. His face was unshaven, his chin covered in greying bristles. His hands young, manicured, they didn't match his face or attire.

'Nope, no children, just me and my journal. I don't have children,' Lucy said as she turned back to the sea.

'So, what are you writing? Your thoughts?' he said, sniffing.

'I guess you could say that.' She smiled and watched the collie sniff the side of an upturned rowing boat before cocking his leg against it.

'Writing a diary?' he said, leaning against the wall.

'I'm a writer,' Lucy said. 'I've been writing parts of my novel here. I like to sit here by the sea and watch life passing by. It's a good spot for me, even when it's cold. But today I'm writing my diary, yes.'

Archie limped over to her and sniffed at her boots.

'A writer? I knew a writer once – a poet, in fact. He wrote about the sea mainly. Writing helped him free his mind.' He called Archie to heel and tied the rope around his neck.

'And now, where is he?' Lucy asked.

The man seemed sad. 'He lost his mind.' Abruptly, he turned and left Lucy. Archie walked on his rope a little ahead, cocking his leg every few seconds. The man had a limp. His grey trousers were tied with a piece of cord, and he wore a shabby coat and shoes that had seen better days.

Lost his mind? she thought. What did he mean? She pondered his words. They sounded as melancholy as the sea looked. So many people had hidden, secret pasts. She was curious about them; she wanted to learn about this ragged old man who thought he'd heard children when the beach was silent. Other than the shrieking of gulls whirling in the grey skies and the chugging of a boat engine, there was not a sound. Yet he had heard children and knew a poet who had lost his mind. When he talked about the poet, it was as if the man had been special to him, not simply an acquaintance. There was a melancholy rawness in his words.

Lucy shivered in the cold wind. It whistled around the clinking halyards on the forgotten boats. As she listened to the wind, a message pinged into her phone. She took it from her satchel.

Hey you, how are feeling?

She smiled. Ben.

I'm OK. At the beach writing. I met this guy.

Hmm, do I need to be worried?

Well, he had a toothless smile, he's unshaven, a bit dishevelled and a lot older than you. He has a half-deaf dog called Archie. So you definitely need to be worried. LOL.

Sounds like a catch – although I think that sounds like Bob. He has a few tales to tell. And he's not as old as he looks.

Is he a tramp?

LOL no but….

But what?

I'll tell you in person; it's too complicated by text. Plus I want a snuggle with you.

Tonight?

Perfect. See you then, gorgeous girl. xxxoooxxx ☺

She put her phone away and scribbled in her journal: Harwich Beach, March 2016, old man, a bit raggedy and dishevelled, toothless smile, dog called Archie, knew a poet/lost his mind, heard children, there were no children, a soullessness in his face. She underlined 'soullessness' twice.

The cold bit at her face as the light dwindled and dark skies rolled in across the seafront. The sound of a foghorn pierced the quietness. She picked up her bag and walked back to her car, parked by the old museum. She always used to wonder whether the guy on the bike would cycle by – now she was going out with him. She smiled as she climbed into the car and threw her satchel down beside her. The guy on the bike was coming to see her for a snuggle and she could think of nothing nicer than having his arms wrapped around her. Warm air blasted out of the heaters and her toes tingled as they came back to life. She drove back to Wrabness, feeling content.

She opened the door to the dark hallway. The sun had set. She undid her coat and threw it over the newel post, then drew the curtains in the sitting room, lit a scented candle, left her satchel on the stairs and went through to the kitchen. It was quarter to five and Ben would be over soon.

Lucy ran up the stairs to her writing room. The lamp on the bureau threw a circle of light over her laptop. Lucy opened the last chapter she had written and began to type up what she had written that day. Then she heard the squeaking of the gate and the door knocker rattle. Smiling, she raced down the stairs and flung the door open. He stood at the door smiling at her. She closed the door and let his arms envelop her, his hold tight, then he lifted her chin and kissed her. He hadn't kissed her properly since the first night he'd taken her out. Today his touch was warm on her lips. His tongue found hers and he kissed her harder, his arms banded tightly around her back.

'Hello, by the way,' she said. 'Is lasagne OK for supper?' she asked.

'Sounds perfect,' Ben replied, unzipping his jacket and leaving it on the banister with Lucy's then turning to lock the door and draw the curtain.

'Locking yourself in, Ben?' She laughed.

'Yep.'

Lucy went into the kitchen and put on the oven. As the fan on the oven whirred, she slid in the pre-made lasagne to heat through and took some drinks through to the sitting room.

'Come here,' Ben said, taking her hand and pulling her down onto his lap. 'I hadn't finished.' He took Lucy's face in his hands and kissed her nose, then each eyelid, then her forehead, then he moved back to her lips. His tongue slipped inside her mouth and touched her tongue, twisting against it, his mouth moving deeper on hers. His hands moved down to the small of her back and then ran up her spine. He moved one hand up her side until he reached her breast and cupped it. She whimpered in pleasure. He lifted her top and she felt his hands on her bare skin. She sighed and pushed her hands through his hair. He nuzzled her neck and, moving her hair back, kissed her neck. He undid the clasp on her bra and let it open up away from her body. He caressed her bare breasts. She kissed him harder as she felt his touch.

After a while she pulled away and stared into his eyes, before letting him touch her all over. She wanted him more than she could have imagined but it was too soon – too soon for her to let him be so close.

She moved away from him.

'Shit, the lasagne!' she said suddenly, jumping off him and doing up her bra.

He looked at her, disappointed. 'Damn the lasagne,' he muttered. As she left the room, he adjusted his jeans, but he understood that she needed time.

It was nice sitting with Ben on the sofa eating the lasagne; she hadn't felt so happy in a long time. She'd been going out with him for a month and a half now and they had talked more than anything, they'd got to know each other a little more, and now he had kissed her – a kiss like on the first night, yet he'd been patient this time, he hadn't pushed her. She'd been through a harrowing time and he obviously wanted her to feel ready with him. Now he was at hers, the front door was locked, they were eating lasagne on the sofa together, and she thought they felt like a unit.

'Tell me about this Bob guy, Ben. You said he had a tale to tell, and who does he know who's a poet?' Lucy said as she placed the empty plates on the table and curled her legs under her on the sofa.

'Bob – he's a misunderstood old chap, I'd say,' Ben said, taking a swig from his beer. 'He used to be in the Navy – an officer, married with two young children. He lived in the big house on the sea front, Artillery House, until it was destroyed in a fire.'

'That's awful,' said Lucy, 'but he was OK, wasn't he? I mean, obviously he was, he's here now.'

'He survived, yes, he was away at sea at the time, Portsmouth, I think? But his wife Olivia and his children, Robin and Charlotte, died in the fire. There was nothing anyone could do. It took hours to get the fire under control and by that time his family were dead. They would have died from smoke inhalation. Pretty horrific.'

'And Archie his dog?'

'He was just a puppy at the time. He was injured in the fire – that's why he's half-deaf now, due to the trauma. Bob was helicoptered back from the ship, he ran into the blaze to rescue his family, and a huge beam from a ceiling collapsed on him and crushed his leg.'

'Oh my God Ben, that's awful. Is that why he limps? How long ago did this happen?'

'Fifteen years ago I think. Bob isn't as old as he looks – I think he's about fifty something, if that? Losing his family devastated him. I was about twelve at the time, and my sister used to babysit for them. He was called back from sea: I can remember the helicopter landing on one of Trinity House's ships, they are all Merchant Navy ships with helipads and anchored along the pier. I can remember him running to the house. He ran through the streets, pushing past people, not even looking to see if the road was clear. I remember watching him from my bedroom window, but it was too late. He'd lost everything. The only thing that survived was Archie. The bodies were found later. Olivia's body was found on the landing outside Robin's bedroom, and the two children were in bed asleep.'

'So Olivia had tried to reach them?' Lucy felt the hairs on her neck stand up on end.

'That's what the fire crew said,' Ben said. 'It was a bad day for Harwich. Nobody really talks about it. Bob left the Navy and sold the land and his home to a developer. He lives in a flat down by the harbour, a dilapidated place, and he's sort of let himself go.'

'And the poet?' Lucy asked.

'That was him – he used to write poems for his children about the sea. He used to take them to the beach when he was on leave. They say he's written his memoirs, but nobody has read it or seen it. He's just seen out and about with Archie.'

'And the lost mind belongs to him?' Lucy said, putting the pieces together from this morning. 'He lost his mind that night, and the children he heard were his own, in his memory. Wait – let me show you.' She left Ben and fetched her journal. She opened it to the page she'd written about Bob. He read the word 'soullessness' underlined.

'D'you see, Ben, that's what I saw when he talked to me about my writing. His eyes were empty, but he said writing frees the mind. He's written it all down; he's not talked about it, but he's written it all down somewhere. In a journal, maybe even as poetry.'

'Yeah, I guess you're right. Come here.' He pulled her to him and hugged her. 'You'll talk to me, won't you? You won't lock things away?'

'I'll try,' she said and kissed him.

Chapter Twenty-Two

Saturday, 20th March

Lucy felt an arm pull her closer in. She shuffled closer to his and opened her eyes. She closed her eyes and smiled. She was happy in Ben's arms under the warmth of the duvet; she didn't want to wake or stir. His body was like a hot water bottle against hers. He kissed her head and stroked her hair.

'What's the time?' she said. Light from the window sneaked through a crack in the curtains.

'Ten o'clock,' he said, pulling her closer. 'Shall I make tea?'

'Hmm, that sounds nice,' she said, 'but come straight back.'

'Like I'm going anywhere else.' He smiled as he walked across the bedroom wearing just his boxer shorts.

Lucy lay in bed and listened to the kettle boiling. She had let Ben stay overnight and it felt right. She was beginning to let go of the past that had haunted her; now she had let the guy on the bike into her world, her life. He stood at the bedroom door, his bare chest toned and defined, the tattoos on his upper arm on show, two steaming mugs in his hand.

He climbed back under the duvet and kissed her forehead, then drew her into him.

'Sleep well, gorgeous?' he said as his hands mapped out the line of her body under the duvet.

'I did,' she said and let his fingers ripple over her stomach, lifting her T-shirt to feel her soft skin. She felt his body against hers. He propped himself above her and looked into her eyes.

'Lucy Carter,' he said and kissed her nose.

'What, Ben Lloyd?' she said and made a face at him.

'Man, you're deliciously gorgeous.'

She giggled and let him move onto her.

'Hmm, you're not so bad yourself.' He kissed her lips then wriggled down the bed and kissed her stomach. She writhed beneath his touch.

'Lucy Carter,' he said again. She whimpered as his hands moved down further. 'I'm falling for you big-time.'

'Ditto.' She felt him slowly and gently take her underwear off. It fell to the floor. He lifted her arms and slid her T-shirt off, then kissed her neck, caressing her breasts. As she moved her body in time with his, she felt him enter her slowly and deeply.

Afterwards, he rolled off her and pulled her to him. He held her and didn't let go.

A message pinged into her phone, which vibrated on the bedside table. Ben kissed her forehead gently and rolled away. She grabbed her phone and felt the touch of Ben's lips on the small of her back, gently caressing her.

Hey, I'm down for the weekend to see Matt. Let's do lunch. Love to Ben. Xx

'Who is it?' Ben asked. He always asked. One day that would stop, and she would just answer the phone or read the message without worrying.

'Jo,' she replied. 'Do you fancy meeting her for lunch? She's coming down to see Matt.'

'Sounds great,' Ben said and continued to caress her.

Lucy messaged back.

Sounds perfect. Is Simon about too?

Not sure – will message him. I'm on the 10.56 train. Matt's picking me up. Lunch at Samuel Pepys, maybe?

Absolutely. We're still in bed, need to get a shimmy on.

We're?? ☺

Ben stayed the night.

OMG!!! I'm soo happy for you. You've found him and you're safe with him. Love you, kiddo. See you at 1pm xx

Fab, love you too x

Lucy closed her phone, rolled back into Ben's arms, and let him feel his way once more.

Chapter Twenty-Three

Monday, 22nd June

Lucy sat on the beach. She'd spent the last eight months writing on her stone step. She'd come to love Harwich and the people she saw as she wrote. She'd been with Ben for almost six months. When they weren't together exploring her new home and its surrounds, she wrote. Today she was writing the twentieth chapter of her wartime love story. She had researched the war and how people had coped; she'd even managed to talk to a veteran in the village about how life had been in the 1940s, how much a letter from their sweetheart meant, and the constant fear of not coming home, of dying in a pit of cold, dank mud.

As she penned the next chapter, Archie came sniffing around her. She patted his neck. 'Hello boy.' She put down her notebook and pen to make a fuss of him. 'How are you today?'

'I see you're writing your book?' came a voice from behind her. She turned and looked at him kindly. 'I am,' she said. 'It's a wartime love story. I'm Lucy, by the way.'

'Lucy, that's a pretty name. I'm pleased to make your acquaintance.' He offered his hand. 'My name is Bob.'

'Bob, it's a pleasure to meet you. Would you like to share my flask of peppermint tea? I've enough for two?'

Bob put down his stick and sat next to Lucy. 'Peppermint tea sounds wonderful, now tell me about your writing.'

'Gosh, what do you want to know?' Lucy said as she poured the steaming tea into a cup and handed it to Bob.

'Well, we don't see many young writers down here, and you're a new face. I can see why you enjoy being here; it's a perfect spot. Are the children here today?'

'Children? I don't have any.' Lucy said. She understood why he asked and pressed no further. 'Would you like to read a little of what I have written?'

Bob took her notebook and read the chapter about how Jim yearned to be with his sweetheart instead of in a cold, dark, wet trench, where rats scurried among the bloodied mud.

'You write beautifully. Each line paints a picture for the reader. When did you begin to write? You have a gift.'

'Thank you. I've written since I was a little girl. I've always loved writing and I was lucky enough to follow my dream and make my writing my career. I've never looked back.'

'Your work is published then?' he asked as he handed back her notebook.

'Yes. I've written quite a few novels, and I even have a few bestsellers.' She smiled wistfully. 'One was dramatised for the BBC not so long ago. If I didn't write, I'd be lost.' She stared out to sea and watched the clouds gently sail across the palest of blue skies. 'Do you like to read?' she asked.

'I used to read a lot, and write too, when I was at sea, but I stopped,' he replied. Maybe he'd said too much.

'What did you write?' she asked.

'Poetry – and my memoir,' he replied. A tear stung his eye – or perhaps the wind had made them water.

'A memoir of your time at sea?' Lucy asked, captivated by this gentle man.

'Yes, of my time at sea. A section of my life. I write poems about the sea too,' he said wistfully.

'And now?' Lucy asked.

'And now the journey has ended and the angels fly high.'

'The angels?' Lucy said. Was he talking about his family?

'The angels. I lost my mind when they left me.'

'Who are your angels?' Lucy asked, wanting to hear the story from him.

'The angels are those you cherish, who walk by your side on the darkest of days, when you feel the world is caving in. Thank you for the tea. Archie – here, boy.' Bob stood up. 'Keep writing, Lucy – it frees your mind.'

'See you another day, Bob, for a peppermint tea,' she called.

Lucy watched as he left, waving his stick in the air as a farewell.

'I'd like that very much, young Lucy.' His words caught in the air as they reached her. He walked off down the beach with Archie trotting ahead, sniffing and cocking his leg at every spot of interest.

In the eight months she had lived in Wrabness, she had been touched by two people who had endured unimaginable lives: Bob and Peggy. Peggy, she had learned about from Jim's letters to her, and now Lucy was commemorating her life by writing about her, and Bob, who she was just beginning to learn about. Maybe one day he would tell her his story; maybe one day she would tell him hers. But for now, chance encounters with him and listening to his wise words about writing was just right for her. She wrote fast, the words pouring onto the page, inspired by where she was. Life was hers again.

Day after day, Lucy came to the beach and watched it change as the seasons moved on. Her life had also changed. The guy on the bike cycled past and wolf-whistled and winked at her now. She smiled back, knowing she'd be in his arms that night and the next night and the next. Each day Bob joined her for peppermint tea and read a little more of her writing, spurring her on. On this particular day, Bob sat by her side. It was a warm September day eleven months after her move to Wrabness. She offered him a tea and in exchange, he took from his pocket a black leather book, no bigger than a mobile phone. It had a gold edging around it and the corners were dog-eared. He handed it to her.

'What's this?' she asked as she took it in both hands: there seemed a preciousness about it.

'Read it.'

Lucy read the first few lines:

> Today I realised you were gone,
> The world I had known torn,
> The anger inside me raging,
> Knowing I have lost you all.
> The nights are endless,
> My time is lost,
> My mind is lost.
> Why me? I ask.
> Why me?
> Why leave me here?
> But who else, if not me?
> If I could turn back time
> I'd have you all near,
> My children, my love, my life, my dear,
> Yet it's not possible.
> It's gone,
> Stolen from me.
> Stolen, cruel world that you are, cruel.

Lucy read the poem. 'You wrote this, didn't you? You're the poet who lost his mind.' She closed the book and turned to him.

'You see, Lucy, over the months I have watched you grow. I have read your beautiful words and now I feel you need to see who I am.'

'Bob, you don't have to. I'm just a girl on the beach,' she said, clasping his hand.

'A girl on the beach who has shown me kindness, who has let me read her work. I know how precious words are and, when you share them, you share them with trust and appreciation. I've not always been like this, you see.' He paused. ' I was in the Navy, a young officer, with a life of promotions in front of me, graduating from Pangbourne Naval College. I met Olivia, my one and only love. Together we moved here and bought Artillery House. Living there made us so happy. When I was away at sea we could still talk. It wasn't like the 1940s that you write about; we had technology, the internet, phones, Skype even. We had two children in that house, my son and daughter, fair-haired and beautiful. They loved the sea and this beach.' He smiled and sighed as he remembered them. 'Little scamps they were. Robin and Lottie.' He stopped and looked out to sea, then took a handful of sand and let the grains slip through his fingers. 'Five and seven years old, that's all they were. They never passed those ages – like Peter Pan they stayed child-like forever.' He wiped a tear from his cheek, and Lucy held his hand. 'While I was away at sea, a fire tore through our house. Neighbours said Olivia's screams could be heard from the street. I hear her screams, yet I wasn't there. I see her battle the flames, yet I wasn't there. I hear my children's cries, yet I wasn't there. I wasn't there. I was safe. I hear the children still on the beach, calling my name – Daddy, Daddy. I hear Olivia laugh, and the sound of the waves.'

'But you weren't to know what would happen! You can't blame yourself. None of it was your fault,' Lucy said, looking kindly at his face: a face that had aged from loss, not from time.

'I blame myself for not being there, and for surviving. When I lost them, my life caved in. Archie, the puppy the children had been given for Christmas, kept me alive. I tried to save them. I was flown back when the fire was still raging. I stopped writing poetry, I stopped reading. I couldn't enjoy life knowing they had lost theirs. I left the Navy on compassionate grounds. My mind was lost, Lucy. But when I see you, I remember how it feels to write. I wanted to tell you my story because I sense you have a similar one, and perhaps one day you will let yours free too. Freeing your mind.' Bob tucked his black book into his pocket. 'Here, Archie, here boy. Until our next peppermint tea, young Lucy.'

Everything he said was right. His poem of anger and loss stayed in her thoughts that day until a message pinged into her phone:

I'm coming over in half an hour. I need a snuggle and pizza and you xox

She smiled as she read Ben's message. She was beginning to fall in love with him and she needed to tell him. She messaged him back.

I have something to tell you.

Don't tell me – you've pretended to like pepperoni for eight months.

Silly ☺

OK, so it's the olives you don't like?

You are so silly, you make me ☺

Be with you at 8pm, gorgeous. Love you xx

Er Ben? Did you see what you wrote?

Yep.

Umm, you said….

I love you! I'll tell you again tonight. You've got it in writing though now. xxooxx

Lucy raced home. He loves me, she said over and over again in her head. Ben said he loves me. Oh my God, he loves me back, oh my God.

Eight o'clock felt like ages away; she wanted him right then, right there.

She swung the front door open and took the stairs two at a time. In her bedroom, she stripped off and ran the shower, half an hour before Ben arrived. She wanted everything to be perfect. Lucy hummed as she washed the sea salt from her hair. As she grabbed a towel from the radiator, her phone rang.

'Jo, hi, how are you?' she said, drying her ear and the now wet screen of her phone.

'I'm good,' Jo said. 'I've got some news.'

'Good news, I hope,' Lucy said. 'Come on then, what is it? Don't keep me in suspense.'

'It's Matt – he's asked me to move in with him,' Jo said.

'Oh my God,' Lucy squealed. 'That's awesome, Jo – isn't it?'

The line went silent. 'I don't know, Luce,' Jo replied. 'Part of me wants it and the other part needs London.'

'Oh, you can still have London. You can afford to keep your flat too. Oh my God, I can't believe you're not sure. He wants you to live with him – that's a real commitment. When are you next down here? I mean, look at it this way, you spend so much time here anyway, surely it makes sense?'

'I know everything you're saying is right, but you know me – I'm a city girl at heart,' Jo said.

'Well, listen, I did it. OK, I moved here for different reasons, but I moved. I can still have London, and you'll be commuting there for work. I have really left. I rarely go back, unless it's for a book launch or something. My life now is here with Ben and my friends. Seriously, you're not losing London; you're gaining something. Say yes. The question is, do you want to be with Matt?'

'Yes.'

'Well, you have your answer. Join the rest of the north Essex commuters and move in with him! And I'll get to see even more of you,' she exclaimed.

'You're right. I'll call Matt now. Catch you later, love you. Big hugs.' The line went dead. Lucy rolled off the bed and dressed in record time. She dried her hair and raced down the stairs. Seven forty-nine. She drew the living room curtains. As she did, the curtains of number eight opened and then closed. Mrs Pope, she thought. Ever the watchful eye – and one she had to be thankful for. As she lit a scented candle, Ben pulled up outside. The gate squeaked when he opened it. Before he had a chance to knock, she'd flung the door open and pulled him in and kissed him tenderly.

'You'll never guess what,' she said as she handed him a beer and the pizza menu.

'What?' he said.

'Matt's asked Jo to move in with him – how exciting is that?' She grinned and scrunched her nose up as she poured herself a large glass of red wine.

'That's pretty exciting. I take it she said yes?' he said, pulling Lucy into his arms.

'She's telling him now. I guess that just leaves Simon to find himself a girl. Pepperoni or four seasons?' she asked.

'Pepperoni with extra olives. Anyway, what were you going to tell me?' Ben put the menu aside and took a swig from his bottle.

'I was on the beach writing today and Bob joined me again for our peppermint tea. I love it when he sits with me. Sometimes we say nothing, sometimes he reads my work and comments like an editor. But today was really special,' she said.

'How so?' Ben asked.

'He let me read his poem – the last one he wrote after he lost Olivia and his children. It was so poignant and sad. Then he told me his story, and then he told me to keep writing. He told me it would free my mind. He said he knew I had a past too, a past that haunted me.'

'Does it still haunt you?' Ben asked as he pulled Lucy in closer to him.

'I feel safe with you, Ben.' She looked into his eyes. 'I love you.'

Chapter Twenty-Four

Two Years Later

As dusk began to fall, Bob sat on the beach where he'd sat with Lucy and drank peppermint tea. He'd spent the best part of two and a half years sitting with young Lucy. He fondly called her the girl on the beach. He had read all her books. She had listened to his stories of the sea, of his sadness, of his loss, and she had brought meaning back to his life. She had managed to persuade him to read again, to free his own mind. She'd told him all about Ben and how Simon needed to find love and how her best friend Jo almost now lived here with Matt. But she had never told him her own harrowing story. She had left that behind her, thrown it into the sea like a pebble, letting the memory sink beneath the waves.

She seemed content. He looked up at the moon. Was the old, silver girl winking at him? Did she know something he didn't? Was she keeping a watchful eye on Lucy? What secrets did she hold, sailing in the silence of the black sky?

Getting up from the cold step and calling Archie, he slowly made his way back to his house. Tomorrow was New Year's Day. Another year had passed, but this time he felt hopeful. Perhaps the new year would mark a new beginning for him. At home, he stoked the fire and the embers jumped. He threw a log into the fire and watched as it caught. He picked up his notebook and eased his way in gently: he took up his pen and began to write. The first poem he had written in years. Lucy had given him back that: his creativity, hope, the gift of writing.

Archie sat by his feet and slept.

There was a hive of activity at number three as Matt and Jo piled through the front door armed with champagne. Ben was in the kitchen with Lucy.

'Simon!' Lucy squealed as she opened the door.

'I've brought someone. I hope you don't mind,' Simon said, ushering forward a pretty, petite, mousey-haired girl, bundled up in a scarf and duffel coat. 'Katie, meet Lucy, Lucy, meet Katie. She's working alongside me and Matt as a training officer for twelve months.'

'Lovely to meet you. Come in, come in, the more the merrier. You know Matt, then, obviously? He's here with his girlfriend Jo, and my boyfriend Ben is in the kitchen.' She closed the door behind her and pulled the curtain across.

Over the road Gladys Pope let the curtains drop back. 'Lucy looks like she's having a lovely night,' she said, nestling into her armchair next to Stan. 'She deserves it after the time she's had, poor girl.'

Stan looked up. Instead of grunting, he rested his hand on Gladys's arm. 'You did right, Mrs Pope, you did right.'

As the laughter and chatter continued through the evening, none of them were aware that in London, Charlie was preparing for his release date: the seventh February 2019. The three years she'd spent in Wrabness since Charlie had been sent down had been a happy time for Lucy. She'd found love and friendship while he had sat behind bars, counting the days until his release. Three years served, two years on licence.

***

Charlie packed his few belongings into a navy blue holdall. He lay on his iron bed and stared up at the lightbulb. An officer paced along the metal floor outside, locking each cell door for the night.

'Last night, Wainwright,' an inmate shouted.

'You'll be back,' another taunted.

Charlie stared at the ceiling. The yellow light blurred. His life had been a routine for three years, with only his dark thoughts to keep him company.

The seventh of February would give him back what Lucy had ripped from him. She had ruined his life, his career, his reputation.

He hadn't smelt fresh air for three years of his life – while she enjoyed living by the sea in her new home. She had taken his freedom from him – and she would pay. The night seemed endless. The dim light that came from the single bulb cast a meagre shadow on the wall. He must have fallen asleep, as he was abruptly woken by a banging on his door.

'Get up, Wainwright, release day,' said the prison officer.

Charlie sat on the edge of his bed and pushed his hands through his hair. Through the bars of his window, he could see the cold grey sky. He splashed his face with cold water and brushed his teeth. He threw the grey duvet over his bed. That would be the last time he'd sleep on a metal bed with a paper-thin mattress. The double bolts on his cell door were unlocked and his heavy door pushed open. This would be the last time he'd see this landing with its closed metal doors and steel grid floors.

'Out,' said the officer.

Charlie picked up his few belongings, with no help from the prison officer, who escorted him to the reception area.

'Leave your bag at the desk, Wainwright,' the officer said and led him to another room where three officers stood waiting.

'Strip,' one ordered. Charlie was strip-searched then placed in a holding cell.

Even on the day of his release he was still locked up, treated like a savage animal. Finally, the cell door opened and he was led to the reception desk. He put his holdall on the floor.

'Name?' said the officer behind the desk.

'Charlie Wainwright,' he replied.

'Address?'

'Two Mansion House, Waldermar Avenue, Fulham, SW6,' he replied.

'Can you sign this please?'

Charlie signed the release form and took his belongings from the tray that was placed on the desk: his Apple watch, mobile phone, house keys, car keys and wallet.

'You'll need to sign in at the probation office at the address on this form at 5pm every day until the seventh of February 2021. Any failure to do so will lead to immediate arrest. Do you understand?'

'Yes, I understand. Where's my car?' Charlie snarled, strapping his watch onto his wrist.

'At the pound in Chelsea. Here's the form to reclaim it. Your items of clothing are in the box at the end of the desk. Take them now and leave the box.'

Charlie stuffed his clothes into his holdall and pushed the box back across the counter.

The prison door was unlocked and opened. A beam of light flooded through. Charlie was back in the real world, a free man.

'Don't let us see you back here,' the officer said then closed the door behind Charlie. Charlie paused briefly then took a tentative step forward. Outside, the air was fresher and it seemed brighter. He hadn't noticed the change of seasons from inside – the seasons Lucy had seen for the last three years.

Wandsworth hadn't changed. It bustled with life. He flagged down a cab and gave the driver his address.

'Been away?' the cabbie asked.

'You could say that,' Charlie said, staring out of the window and watching London pass by.

'Anywhere nice? Somewhere hot would be nice, mate, it's pretty nippy,' the cabbie said as he headed over Battersea Bridge.

'Nowhere worth mentioning,' Charlie said. 'D'you mind if I smoke?'

'Out the window, pal, if you will,' the cabbie unlocked the window.

The cab driver took a left down Lots Road.

Charlie leant forward. 'Actually, can you pull up here at the car pound? Thanks.'

The black cab stopped at the gates of Chelsea Car Pound and drove away, leaving Charlie with his bag. He pushed the gates open and walked to the office.

'I'd like to get my car, please.'

'Where was it parked and lifted from? You'll need to pay the £150 penalty,' said the attendant behind the desk, pulling out a wad of files.

'It wasn't lifted or parked anywhere; it's been impounded for three years. A silver Jaguar.' Charlie handed over the forms from the police for the car's authorised collection.

'Right. OK, sign this, please. Your car is parked in lane K at number one hundred and seventy-five. I'll get one of the boys to check it over with you.'

Charlie threw his bag into the boot of his car and drove out of the pound, down Lots Road and on to Kings Road until he reached Waldemar Avenue. He pulled up outside the mansion block. He opened his apartment door. Everything looked as it had the last time he was there. Three years of post in a pile by the door, most of it junk. He added water to his Nespresso coffee machine and waited for the lights to illuminate. As the rich coffee poured out into the coffee cup below, he turned on his laptop. Lucy's smiling face beamed at him from his screensaver.

He touched his finger to her lips and shook his head.

Chapter Twenty-Five

Thursday, 20ᵗʰ February

When the alarm went off, Lucy rolled over in bed to turn it off. Ben pulled her back in. 'Five more minutes, babe,' he said, nuzzling into her neck.

'I'm meeting Bob,' Lucy said, rolling away from Ben. 'Five more minutes, and then I really have to go. But you're staying tonight, aren't you?'

She lay on top of him and kissed him, her hair falling over his face. She let go of his hands and pressed her hands against his face. He lifted her onto him and pushed her hard down onto him. She sat up, her back arched. He let his hands ripple over her body as she moved over him until they both came.

'Right – as much I love you and want you and enjoy you and everything else, I need to get a wiggle on and meet Bob.' Lucy climbed out of bed and turned on the shower. 'Are you coming in with me?'

Ben threw off the covers and followed Lucy into the bathroom.

When they left the house together, Lucy locked the front door behind her.

'See you after work. Make a sail for me.' She smiled. 'Love you.' She kissed him tenderly.

Ben wrapped his arms around her and squeezed her tightly. She didn't want him to let go but her time with Bob had become so special. She climbed into her Mini. The steering wheel was as cold as ice; the smoothness of it slipped through her even colder hands. She shivered, blowing warmth onto her hands as she drove. The flask of peppermint tea rolled backwards and forwards on the front seat. She loved spending time with Bob. It had become a ritual for them both.

She pulled up by the beach near the RNLI museum. She grabbed the flask and her satchel and made her way to her step. The sea lapped in onto the shore, each wave taking the pebbles back into the sea with scuttling sound. The cries of gulls broke the dulcet sounds of the waves' ebb and flow.

'Hello, boy.' Archie sniffed around Lucy's feet. She looked up and saw Bob, and thought how much like a father he was to her. He laid his stick down next to her.

'Peppermint tea, Bob?' she asked, then handed him a cup of hot tea. The aroma of peppermint floated under his nose.

'Here, read this chapter, tell me what you think. I want you to be brutally honest. I'm not really sure about the love side,' she said, handing him her notebook. He took it from her and read it.

'It's beautiful, Lucy, really. You've captured it all in a picture.'

'Really? You're not just saying that?' she asked.

'Not at all. I'm your number-one critic, Lucy, but I can't suggest any improvements. I want to read on. Here, I have something to show you.' He took out his black book and gave it to her. 'You see, knowing you has brought back part of my life I'd forgotten. I still have the heaviness of loss in my head and my heart, but now I can deal with it in a way I couldn't before, because I'm happier and more at peace. And that's down to you.'

She opened his book to a poem. As she read the words, she cried. 'Bob, this is so real.' She wiped tears from her cheeks.

'It could be about anybody. You know, I have a story and I have told you about it, but what about your story?' He looked at her face. Her eyes told him there was more to her than her novels. The way she wrote came from somewhere deep inside her.

'What are you thinking, Bob?' she asked.

'I'm wondering if you will ever tell me your story,' he said.

'You mean, why I moved here?' she said.

'Yes,' he replied.

Lucy looked out at the waves and closed her notebook. 'I owe you that, but talking about it is hard, harder than I thought. I didn't come here to be by the sea and write; I came here because I was running away.'

'Running from what?' he asked gently.

'I left a man. My boyfriend. He scared me, and he hurt me. I can't ever forget it; it lives with me, suppressed, but it's there.'

'But are you happy now?' Bob asked.

'Happier than I've ever been,' she replied.

'Then let the torment go.'

His words sat quietly in Lucy's head.

'He raped me, Bob,' she said quietly. She'd only ever told Ben, and now she sat on the beach in February with Bob, the cold wind biting at their faces, cupping their peppermint tea, and she told him her story.

'He was sentenced for five years but with two on licence. He's served three years; he was never charged with rape because I didn't tell the police about it. I've told nobody but Ben.' She looked away from him, out to sea.

Bob listened carefully to her story, occasionally glancing out to sea. A few flakes of snow began to fall.

'Do you think differently of me now?' she asked.

'No, Lucy. I just think you're brave.' He sat with her for a while, taking her hand in his, holding it tightly. 'You are brave, my dear Lucy. My leg is beginning to ache, though. Shall we meet tomorrow for tea?' He got up and picked up his stick.

'Yes Bob, tomorrow.' She stayed on the beach until the light began to fade, then she finally gave in to the cold and left the beach. It had a splattering of snowflakes that lay on the sand like a dusting of icing sugar.

She pulled up outside her house, parked, then went inside. She closed the door, shutting out the cold. A layer of snow had settled on the window ledges and her fingers tingled with cold. She turned the heating on then knelt down to clear the fire, when she heard the gate open.

Ben, she thought. She'd missed him that day and couldn't wait to be in his arms again. She looked at her watch. It was only five o'clock – that was too early for Ben. As she lit the fire, she heard the gate close again. She pushed the curtain aside and looked out of the window. The gate was closed. Maybe it hadn't been Ben. Maybe it hadn't been her gate she'd heard after all. When the fire caught, she threw on a log and watched the flames lick around the dried bark. Her phone rang. She went to answer it. No caller ID. After a few rings, it stopped. She looked at the screen, then her phone rang again.

'Hello?' she said, expecting to hear the voice of a cold caller, but the line went dead. She shrugged and left the phone on the coffee table.

The letter box rattled as she walked down the hall to the kitchen. She turned to look. A delivery curry menu jutted through. As she flicked the kettle on, her phone rang again. Exasperated, she ran to the sitting room and snatched it up.

'Hello?'

The line went dead.

She took the menu from the door. The letter box clanged shut and she jumped. Lucy left the menu on the table in the hall. As she pulled the curtain across, she heard the gate squeak again. She went back to the sitting room and looked out onto the street. The gate was closed. In the fire, the log fell down and embers darted onto the floor, losing their heat as they touched the rug. The lights at number eight were on and the curtains drawn. Her phone rang again. As soon as she answered it, the line went dead.

She pushed it hastily away, her hands shaking. The gate squeaked again. She looked out, but it was still closed. She went to the stairs to get her satchel and journal. The dark winter night was playing tricks on her; there was nothing there. Ben would be over soon.

Her satchel wasn't there. She went into the sitting room, it wasn't there either. Damn, she thought. She'd left it in the footwell of the car; she'd picked up her flask and forgotten her bag. The curry menu still on the table, it was Thursday, they delivered on Mondays. Her breath deepened. She opened the front door and shuddered at the cold. She took her keys from the hall table and went to the car. The gate was open, swinging. It had been closed minutes before. She looked up the street, nothing unfamiliar.

She unlocked the door of her Mini and leant over to grab her satchel from the passenger footwell. As she straightened up, she sensed somebody behind her.

'Ben,' she said, 'I'm glad you're—'

'Hello, Lucy.' He glared at her, his grey steely eyes piercing hers. He gripped her wrist and pushed her against the car.

'Charlie?' Her heart pounded. Her legs shook. She tried to call out, but his hand was over her mouth. What was the time? Ben would be here soon. If he arrived now, she'd be safe. Where was Ben? She needed him. Where was everybody? She twisted her face away from his hand, catching sight of number eight. Mrs Pope, please open your curtain. Open your curtains, open your curtains she said, over and over again. Charlie turned her face back to him, gripping her cheeks. His fingers smelt of stale cigarettes. He clutched her wrist harder, twisting the skin so it burnt. He licked her neck. She turned her head away. Thoughts of Ben flooded her mind. He would come soon. He had to. He would come and protect her. She loved him. He took her wrist again, the way he used to twist it in a bar when she spoke to another man. He'd put on a smile as he chatted, but he'd grip her wrist, hurt her, so subtly that nobody else saw. A reminder that she was his.

'You're hurting me – let go,' she said, trying desperately to push him off her. He let go of her hand. She held her satchel tightly and ran to the open front door. As she reached the gate a gust of wind blew the door shut. She ran to it, forcing the key into the lock. His footsteps were behind her. It wouldn't turn, it jammed. She'd never got it fixed.

'Damn it door, damn it, open,' her breathing uncontrolled, her hands shaking.

'It's too late, Lucy,' he said.

He took her hair and pulled it. Her keys fell to the ground. She knelt, trying to find them.

'Get up slowly,' he said, kneeling by her and whispered harshly into her ear. She felt his nicotine breath on her, and tried to feel in her pocket for her phone to press last dial, but she'd left it on the table inside.

'Get up,' he said again, twisting her hand behind her back. Inside, her phone rang.

'You're hurting me, let go,' she said. He pulled her to her feet and pushed her against the door. He was close behind her, almost on top of her. He moved closer to her and tried to kiss her. She turned her face away. Sickened by his touch.

The curtain of number eight opened. Mrs Pope watched them.

'Ah, they're kissing. Young love. I'm glad she's with that young man,' she said as she closed the curtain again.

He held her face hard, touching her hair, twisting a strand as he smelt it. Her heart raced and she froze at his touch. He took her wrist and dragged her to a black Audi. He opened the door and pushed her in. He tied her hands together behind her back with her white silk scarf and gagged her with masking tape. He pushed her down into the footwell, turned on the engine and pulled slowly out of Lambourne Terrace. He drove away from the village, towards the beach. Lucy tried to pay attention to the indicator, how many turns he was taking, where he was heading, but fear overwhelmed her. She tried to scream but nothing came out. She heard a motorbike roar past. Ben? When the car rounded a bend, Lucy's head hit the metal rails under the front seat. She felt blood trickle down her temple, then everything went black. She lay still in the car. Then the smooth sound of the road under the tyres changed to the crunching of gravel or stones. She stirred. Her head ached. The car stopped and the engine cut out. She writhed around in the footwell, trying to break free. The silk tightened on her wrists.

The car door opened. Charlie moved around to the passenger side of the car. His footsteps stopped. He opened the door and dragged her out. She tried to struggle, but he was much too strong.

The familiar smell of sea salt air hit Lucy's face and she gasped. She saw the cranes on the horizon. He'd brought her to the beach where she wrote. A place that gave her peace and serenity. A place that gave her sanity back. He was taking it again. It was deserted, not a soul about, as the light faded in the sky. A place where she'd sat so often and watched people: a man and his dog, a woman and her child. Tonight it was a raw, neglected space, familiar yet silent. It would soon be dark.

She wanted to scream but couldn't, due to the tape over her mouth. He grabbed her arm and pulled her to face him, then untied her hands and held her tightly. He pressed his lips all over her face and she scratched his cheek. He slapped her hard. She fell to the ground. She tried to scramble to her feet but he pushed her down again, rolling her over until she lay beneath him. He lay on top of her, pressing down onto her. Ripping the tape from her mouth, he went to kiss her again, wrapping the silk scarf around her neck, but she bit his lip and scratched his face again.

He wiped the blood from his lips.

'You bitch, you dirty bitch,' he said, covering her mouth with his hand, preventing her from screaming.

'Why, Charlie, why am I?' She'd found her voice with him, her courage.

'You tried to ruin me!' he shouted, his face red. 'You all did! If I can't have you, then nobody will have you. Do you hear me? Nobody will have you. Where do I go from here? What do I do? I've lost my job, my life – you have ruined my life. You have ruined everything I had.'

She scraped up a handful of sand and pebbles and threw it into his face.

'I didn't ruin your life, Charlie – you did!'

He covered his eyes, screaming as the sand momentarily blinded him. Taking advantage of his weakness, Lucy pushed his weight off her, scrambled to her feet and ran. He chased her and soon caught up. He grabbed her and hit her face again, so hard that her nose bled. He took her arms and held them, trying to kiss her again. She kicked his shin. He fell to the ground. She turned and ran towards the pier, away from him. He grabbed her again and she spat at him.

'You whore!' He hit her again. The force of the blow made her stumble. She fell, and her head struck a jagged rock that jutted out from the sand. She lay motionless.

He stood above her. The rock near her head had a splattering of blood on it. He stood still, his face pale and drawn. He kicked her leg. She didn't move. She was dead – he'd killed her. He dragged her body to the edge of the pier. She was silent, putting up no struggle. Her hair was matted and wet.

Alone, she lay on the beach.

He stared at her limp body. Then he ran, his feet sinking in the sand trying to hold his balance. He ran away from her until he reached the end of the beach. He climbed the wooden steps, breathless, and turned onto the close of the promenade. He crossed the road and made his way down a mews, until he was out of sight, still clutching the silk scarf, with her scent and now blood stained. He left her there, just like he'd left her in the locked room in the dark. Only now there was no room; there was just the sea to wash her away.

Chapter Twenty-Six

He licked her face and whimpered, then barked – an urgent bark. He ran back to his owner, then ran back to her and licked her face again, then sat and barked.

'What is it, boy?' Bob called, walking slowly across the beach. As he neared the pier, he saw Archie sitting on the beach – beside the figure of a girl. She lay cold in the sand, wearing one shoe, blood on her face. The gulls wheeled overhead, their cries piercing the sound of the tide washing in.

His face turned grey as he knelt down by her. Her head was cut and particles of sand stuck to her face.

'Stay here, boy.'

Archie lay down by her side. Bob ran from the beach, his lame leg dragging behind him.

'Help!' he shouted. 'Help! Call the police, an ambulance – help!'

The pain in his leg jagged through his body but he ignored it and ran until he reached the pavement. A familiar feeling of helplessness flooded him. He had to be able to save her this time. He had to. He'd lost his family, he had to save Lucy, the girl who'd brought life back to his broken heart.

A woman with a shopping basket stopped beside him. 'Are you all right?' she asked. 'Do you need help?'

'Please, do you have a phone? Call 999 – there's a girl on the beach. She needs an ambulance, the police. Hurry, please call.'

With shaking fingers the woman rummaged in her bag for her mobile phone, then dialled 999. After she had given all the details she could, she ran with Bob down to the beach. She gasped when she saw the girl.

Soon police cars had arrived, their blue lights flashing. Six policemen ran down the beach. Simon fell to his knees by the girl, his face ashen.

'Lucy...' He turned to Matt and shook his head. 'It's Lucy.'

An ambulance screamed along the main road, then paramedics raced down the beach and knelt by the figure. They laid out a stretcher and lifted her onto it. She was carried swiftly and carefully to the ambulance, her cold body motionless, like a porcelain doll. The sound of its siren broke the eerie silence. Bob stood with Archie as he watched the ambulance leave. The police cordoned off the beach with bright orange crime scene tape, which fluttered in the wind. Matt walked to the shore and called Jo.

'Hey you,' she said. 'What's up?'

'Jo, it's Lucy,' Matt said, his voice low, serious.

'Matt, what's happened? You're scaring me,' Jo said.

'She's been found on the beach...'

The line went dead.

'No!' Jo wailed.

Then Simon called Ben. 'Ben, it's Simon,' he said as he walked back to the squad car, trying to block out the abrasive sound of the sirens as they screamed through the streets of the quiet coastal town.

'Simon, I was going to call you. I'm not sure what I've done but Lucy is giving me the cold shoulder.'

'Where are you?' Simon asked.

'At the yard. Why? What's wrong?'

'I'm coming over now. Stay there,' Simon said, getting into the car and signalling to Matt to follow him.

'What the hell's going on? There are sirens everywhere. It's something bad, isn't it? I went round to see her last night, but there was nobody at home and she wasn't answering her phone. Is she with Jo? Where is she?' Ben asked urgently.

'Ben, I'm coming now.' Simon rang off and drove off fast, his blue lights on and siren blaring. Matt followed him. Ben was standing outside the yard when they arrived.

'What the fuck's going on? The place is crawling with police,' Ben said, clearly agitated.

'Ben, there's no other way of saying this, mate. I'm sorry. Lucy was found on the beach this morning. We don't know yet what happened to her or how she got there. She's been taken to hospital,' Simon said.

Ben stared at Simon in disbelief. His heart missed a beat. What had happened to Lucy? How badly injured was she?

'What d'you mean, she was found on the beach? I was with her yesterday morning. She was meeting Bob. What the fuck are you talking about?' he said, his voice trembling. 'Tell me you're lying.'

'I don't know any more than that, Ben. Bob found her this morning on the beach. I was one of the first officers on the scene. She has been taken to Colchester General. I can take you there to see her. Mate, I'm sorry.'

Epilogue

For Lucy's friends, time stood still. Ben, Jo, Matt, Simon and Bob sat on plastic seats in a hospital corridor outside a room that had a sign on it: 'Bereavement – in use'. In the room next door, the blinds were closed to shield the occupants from curious eyes. Lucy lay inside. Bob sat in the corridor with them, waiting for news. Simon and Matt had been here before. They knew all too well how these situations could go, but they were involved emotionally this time, trying to contain their own fear and sadness. In the end, they had been unable to protect her. She had lived in fear and now might die in fear.

Bob sat still, his face etched with sadness, thinking about the girl on the beach and the time they had spent together. She'd made him think differently about life. He couldn't bear to think that she might be gone. She had told him her story and now she was not here to finish it. What was this cruel world doing?

Ben had fallen in love with her the moment he saw her. He learned that she hated coffee but loved peppermint tea. He thought of the time they had spent together: the dates they'd had, the times they'd eaten jars of olives together, snuggled in front of the television. The girl he'd kissed the morning before and smelt her sweet dark hair.

The doctor came out of Lucy's room, his face grave. Stoic in professionalism.

'I'm Doctor Thiroux. Who is Lucy's next of kin?'

Jo stood up and looked at him. Her heart sank. 'She has no family, but her partner Ben is here.' Tears fell from her eyes as Ben stepped forward. She feared how this would go. It was real life, not a novel. There was no guaranteed happy ever after.

'She's gone, isn't she?' Ben said, his hands shaking and his eyes filled with tears.

The doctor looked at him. 'No. She had a faint pulse when she came in. She's a fighter.'

'Can I see her?' Tears streamed down his face.

Ben stood at her bedside, his hand on hers. The girl on the beach – the girl he loved – wasn't dead.

Then Lucy opened her eyes.

A policeman had stood at Lucy's door for the last couple of days.

The door opened slowly and a friendly, familiar face poked her head around.

'You got time for a visitor?' she said.

'Jo?' Lucy smiled and sat up in the hospital bed.

'I've brought you some grapes,' Jo said, perching on the edge of the bed. 'We thought we'd lost you, kiddo.'

'I thought I'd lost too. It was Charlie, Jo, the police questioned me this morning, said a black Audi had been found abandoned at Felixstowe Docks. He came to the house Jo. He bundled me into the car, gagged me, took me to the beach, then I can't remember anything else.' Her bruised face. Her eyes tired. Her arms grazed and bruised from his hold and struggle.

'I know, Lucy," Jo said rubbing her hand.

There was a knock on the door. Simon and Matt peered in. 'Room for two more?'

Lucy smiled. 'Come on in. Where's Ben?'

'I'm right here,' the face of the man she'd fallen in love with came into the room with a peppermint tea. He'd brought her peppermint tea daily, although those days for Lucy were a blur.

'Come on boys, lets grab a coffee,' Jo squeezed Lucy's hand and left Ben alone.

Ben sat looking at the girl he adored, he tucked her hair behind her ear and kissed her nose.

'I love you Lucy.' He pulled her gently up from her pillows and held her in his arms, his arms strong and where she wanted to be.

'He's still out there, Ben,' she said, 'the police have stood outside my room, a different one each day,' she was tired and frightened. The last few days a blur.

'I am here Lucy, I haven't left your side, nobody can get in, I've slept by your side in the chair,' Ben said stroking her hair with reassurance.

'Have you?' she said trying to remember.

'Yep, and Jo and the boys have been in and out, the doctors were talking of discharging you tomorrow, they're really happy with your progress. You've stunned them all,' he said as he laid her back into the pillows so she could have a small sip of her now tepid peppermint tea.

'The cottage, my car, the beach, he knows where I am, he knows though' she panicked, 'what if he comes back?'

'He will be found Lucy and then locked up and hopefully they'll throw away the key this time. I am right by your side. Now come here. I'm going nowhere.' He held her tighter than he could ever have held her. 'This is a new chapter in your life Lucy, we are going to ride this wave together. My girl on the beach, my beautiful girl on the beach.'

THE END